Nothing but the Truth

A crime thriller

Sam Flint

Published by Sam Flint
London
England

Sam Flint /Sam Flint Publishing
67 Castleton Road
Ruislip, London HA4 9QH, England
www.samflint.uk

Publisher's Note: This is a work of fiction. Names, characters, places, and incidents are a product of the author's imagination. Locales and public names are sometimes used for atmospheric purposes. Any resemblance to actual people, living or dead, or to businesses, companies, events, institutions, or locales is completely coincidental.

Ordering Information:
Print-on-demand copies are available from Amazon at http://www.amazon.co.uk/Nothing-but-Truth-Sam-Flint-ebook/dp/B00WIKSV06
E-book copies are available on all platforms
Title: Nothing but the Truth/ Author Name: Sam Flint -- 1st ed.ht © 2015 by Sam Flint.

Prologue.

Five years ago

The blue lights of the police car flashed in Aidan's mirror but there was no siren to accompany them. The patrol car just kept pace with him fifty yards behind as it had done for the last couple of minutes. They were both doing a stately thirty miles an hour through Cobham High Street at two pm on a Tuesday afternoon. What a very British car chase thought Aidan as first he and then the patrol car swerved around a double parked delivery lorry. No squealing tyres, no pile of empty boxes to side swipe. They knew where he was going and they would arrest him when he made it home; unless his pursuers were beaten to the punch by the officers already waiting at his house. Either way he did not care.

`Where are they now Rosetta?' Aidan barked into the dash microphone of his Mercedes SL 500.

`I don't know Senor Aidan. I am in the panic room like Senora Kristina showed me. The police show me a search warrant and tell me to sit down but I come upstairs and press the button. Now the door, she is locked and the police they bang outside. Can you hear them?'

Aidan smiled to himself and heard the futile threats from outside the panic room. He thought it was over the top when he had it installed and the builder could see him wavering. `The door of choice for nine out of ten meth amphetamine labs in the US' the guy boasted. Seeing Aidan's scepticism he showed him a YouTube video he'd downloaded onto his phone of a police raid on premises where they were making hard work of gaining entry. `I think your family and valuables will be safe behind that don't you?' he added, knowing Aidan would go for the deal. Now it was holding back the scumbags from the Asset Recovery Agency. Only the things the ARA were interested in were not in his safe.

`It's okay Rosetta' said Aidan not wanting to panic his housekeeper. ` What are they doing now?'

`I cannot see Senor Aidan.'

Off course she did not know about the hidden cameras. `Use the remote and switch on the TV on the wall Rosetta.'

`Senor Aidan so many cameras!' said Rosetta confirming everything was working. `The men in white overalls with hoods are taking things from your office. They take computers, hard drives and papers. They put everything in plastic bags. Now they take the big filing cabinet. They find a safe hidden in the bookcase.' She was surprised but now realised why Aidan didn't want her to dust the old volumes on the higher shelves.

Aidan swore to himself and put his foot down. The powerful sports car lurched forward doubling the gap from his pursuers. Aidan braked quickly throwing a left into Waitrose car park. His pursuers overshot and had to reverse but by the time they had entered he was exiting from the other side.

`Senor Aidan now they take paintings off the wall' said Rosetta keeping up the commentary.

Aidan could picture the scene. The bastards were raiding his home like he was some scumbag drug baron even though he had cooperated fully with the ARA investigation of Victor Garcia. What a bunch of slimy... A fat woman on a bicycle wobbled from a side turning into the main road without looking properly. Only Aidan's quick reactions prevented her from decorating his bonnet. He felt the bang as the wing mirror clipped her ample arse and sent her sprawling into the gutter, shocked but still alive. The police car had not caught up yet so perhaps that was criminal charge he would be spared from. A minute later he was at the main gate entrance to the St Jude's Estate. Aidan slowed just enough to allow the number plate reading camera to recognise his car as a resident and open the barrier automatically. Inside he stopped knowing that the barrier would not rise again until he moved off.

`I'll be there in a minute Rosetta' said Aidan cutting the call and trying his wife again. Still no answer, he hoped she had seen his voice mail to come home immediately.

Behind him the patrol car had arrived and the WPC in the passenger seat was in an altercation with the security guard to raise the barrier only to be told it would not raise until Aidan moved off. The police were clearly miffed that he had given them the slip after they had followed him in a civilised manner and now they wanted the pleasure of nicking him. The PC driving was threatening the rent-a-cop security guard with obstruction and to shut him up he raised the exit barrier. The PC reversed and headed for it ignoring the security guards' warning to wait. There was a loud bang and the sound of breaking glass and twisting metal as the patrol cars' front wheels found the ditch created by the slow moving moat mechanism which had not fully returned. Aidan opened his window and gave the security guard a cheery wave before driving off. The guard returned his wave before wandering over to the stricken police car with a smug smile on his face.

For the first time since he'd moved to the St Jude's Estate, Aidan did not begrudge the ridiculous annual management fee. The moat platform had been installed in the exit lane a couple of months before. A post facto upgrade to security following the theft of some hedge fund manager's wife's jewelry. The burglars had made their escape by just ramming the gatehouse exit barrier. Aidan took the six speed bumps along the private avenue leading towards his house at spine and suspension crunching speed. He had to leave his car with the engine still running outside the gates because his crescent shaped gravel drive was full of police vehicles. Two plain clothes cars, two squad cars, a Transit mini bus and a tall panel van into which his property was now being loaded. `Who the fuck do they think I am Al Capone?'

From behind him Aidan could hear his name being shouted. His heavily pregnant wife lumbered from her Audi and started to run towards him. She must have come in from one of the other estate entrances. For a moment Aidan was torn between running to the door and stopping the officials from ransacking his home and turning to support his wife who was teetering unsteadily. He caught her just as she lost her balance. She was breathless and crying.

`Oh Aidan what are they doing to our home? They are like the secret police at home, the KaPo'

`Don't worry Kristina, I'll sort this out' said Aidan trying to comfort his distraught wife. A WPC came over and took her arm and Aidan stormed towards his home. A figure he recognised emerged from the house wearing a high viz vest emblazoned ARA and carrying a clip board. Aidan exploded `You've got a fucking nerve Anderson. I cooperated fully with your investigation into Victor Garcia. I told you he was just an investor in a property company I put together. Just one member of the syndicate. I didn't know where his money came from. Now I get all this shit!'

Anderson was unfazed by Aidan's outburst. He handed Aiden a copy of the search warrant which gave him his powers. `Glad you could join us Mr. Wheelan and Mrs. Wheelan it can't be long now?' he said looking at the bullet like projection of Kristina's stomach. `Actually Mr. Wheelan it's you who have got the explaining to do. As soon as DI Cole emerges from your lovely home he will be arresting you on suspicion of offenses under the Serious Crime Act 2007 and associated offenses in contravention of the UK Money Laundering Regulations 2007. Ah, here is DI Cole now. I suggest you call your solicitor.'

Aidan was in shock and he did not realise his phone was ringing until it was screaming at full volume. He answered it absent mindedly.

`Aidan its Max, listen I don't have long to talk.'

`Max this is not a good time' said Aidan.

`You're telling me mate. Listen I've got to go away for a long time otherwise Siobhan and Annie are in danger. You won't be able to contact me, but I'll get a message to you when it is safe for everyone. Promise me you'll look in on Siobhan and Annie just to check they are okay. You're my oldest mate. There is no one else I can rely on.'

`Max what the fuck have you got yourself into this time?'

`I've got to go Aidan. Thanks man you're the best.'

Aidan stared at the phone. There were just too many things happening at once for his mind to make sense of.

`Mr. Wheelan do you remember me, DI Cole' said the tall thin policeman in a raincoat Aidan had thought was the used exclusively by flashers. 'I have to charge you now but before I do I was wondering if I could ask you a favour?' The sheepish look on the detectives face had Aidan bemused. `That wall paper in your living room. My wife has been on at me for that. Where did you get it?'

Six hours later Aidan and Kristina sat exhausted in the quiet saloon bar of the pub opposite the police station.

Their solicitor returned with their drinks. `A large Bushmills for you Aidan and an orange juice for you Kristina' said Henry Compton trying to inject a note of bonhomie to signify their immediate ordeal was over. With his button hole carnation and natural good humour the solicitor always reminded Aidan of a registrar of weddings.

`Thanks Henry' Aidan downed it in one. `I'm going to fucking sue. Five hours asking me the same questions they asked before. You know people in the Police Complaints Authority, don't you?'

`I would hold fire on that until we know more about what they have on you and why they have come after you again' his solicitor cautioned. `They don't need to show their hand at the beginning. Because of that I was able to get you bail without penalty, other than surrendering your passports.' Henry Compton squeezed into the pub chair. It fitted him as tightly as his trousers. Not yet in his forties, his love of food and drink meant the odds against him reaching retirement age were long. However his jolly fat man image did disguise a sharp mind as several opponents had discovered to their cost.

`Where am I going to run with a woman who is going to give birth next week?' said Aidan.

I know but these investigators have got a real hard on for you, if you'll pardon my French Kristina. They will keep digging until they find something' said the solicitor.

`But why Henry? They were after Victor Garcia. All he did was put a hundred grand into the property consortium I put together to buy that office building.'

`I know Aidan. But they've been unable to make a case against him directly for his drug dealing and money laundering. The Assets Recovery Agency has had no success under the Proceeds of Crime Act, that's why the government keeps changing the rules. The Serious Crime Act 2007 under which you have been charged recriminalises some of the offenses the ARA was established to fight through the civil courts. The word on the street is that the ARA is fighting for its life and is now going after the low hanging fruit just to get some runs on the board.'

`Fucking politicians. I'm not gangster number one' said Aidan running a worried hand through his hair. It felt thin and Aidan was sure he would be bald before all this was over.

`I know Aidan but any man who has had thirty-five first time buyer mortgages is not playing a completely straight bat' said the solicitor pleased to be able to complete his cricketing analogy.

Aidan was surprised. They really were going back. `That was years ago. The banks and building societies were throwing money at whoever wanted it and if you were good for the loan not many questions were asked. I've done nothing compared to what the bankers have got away with since, but none of them are facing jail.'

`I know Aidan, I know, I'm not sitting in moral judgment on you' placated the solicitor.

`What do you suggest I do Henry?'

`Sit tight for the moment until we know more about their case against you. They took all your computers and files didn't they?'

`For all the good it will do them' Aidan smiled for the first time that day.

`What do you mean Aidan?'

Just then Aidan's Blackberry beeped and he pulled it out and showed the screen to Henry.

`Intruder alert, have you had a break in Aidan?'

`In a way. Those PC's and laptops are location sensitive. After they switch on they search for a number of receivers that confirm where they are.'

`What do they do if they don't find them?'

`They assume they have been stolen and automatically start to delete the encrypted files on the hard drives. All that is left is gibberish.' Aidan could not help sounding smug at the thought of the so called forensic analysts finding nothing.

`Oh I see' said Henry not sharing Aidan's pleasure.

`What's the matter with that then?'

`Nothing except that they would argue that an innocent man would not need to go to such lengths. You may have just whetted their appetite more.'

`Well fuck'em Henry. Today can't get any worse. Another gin and tonic? What about you Kristina? You've been very quiet. You've not touched your orange juice. Can I get you something else?'

`Yes you can Aidan' said Kristina shifting uncomfortably on the seat of the wing backed chair. `You can get me an ambulance. My waters have just broken

.

1.

Today August 2007

At the back of St James's Park underground station stands an intimidating building that resembles a fortress of concrete and blackened out windows. It serves as the headquarters of the Assets Recovery Agency (ARA) and a number of other invisible government departments, although the reception desk gave no indication of its occupants. The only clues to its secretive nature were the In and Out glass airlocks that visitors had to pass through and the fact that all mobile phone signals died within its walls. The ARA was housed on the eighth floor.

`Acting Director your 10`o'clock appointment is in Reception' said the secretary in the outer office. Her faint

Edinburgh burr was still clear despite the poor sound quality of the new internet phone system. Stuart Logan wondered what was wrong with the old phones. They were only eighteen months old when they were replaced. It seemed that Whitehall were always willing to throw money at IT while real services suffered.

` Okay Moira can you tell them to send Mr Pendry up. Some coffee would be nice as well if you could manage it.'

`As you wish Acting Director' said Moira with studied courteousness.

Stuart sat back uneasily in the unfamiliar chair and looked around the office he had always seen from the other side of the desk. He could not blame Moira for being a bit standoffish. The events of the last couple of weeks had been a bit of a strain for all of them. Moira had worked for Stuart's boss, Gordon Sinclair for over ten years and was finding it particularly hard to deal with his abrupt absence on gardening leave following the catastrophic failure of the major investigation which in turn had triggered Sinclair's break down. Moira was loyal and Stuart suspected she partly blamed him for Gordon's ills. Hadn't Gordon hand picked him a fellow Glaswegian when he was asked to head up the newly formed Assets Recovery Agency? And weren't they close? Close enough to be known behind their backs as the `Two Jockies'. Stuarts first week deputising had flown by and he felt guilty he hadn't made time to take Moira aside and reassure her about things. He would act before he forgot again. Stuart phoned her back.

`Moira what was the name of that church we all went to ages ago. The one with the cafe in the basement?' said Stuart hunched over the speaker phone.

`You mean the one with the refectory in the crypt, St Savior's' Moira's posh Edinburgh vowels immediately made the place sound more up market.

`Aye Hen I was wonderin' if you would no' like to have your dinner there on Friday' said Stuart hamming up his Glaswegian. `I thought it would be good for us to get out of here and talk a bit about Gordon and all that has happened' he added more seriously.

There was a pause at the end of the line then Moira said `Yes, I'd like that.' The relief was clear in her voice. She knew it was unlikely that her boss would be coming back but she wanted to talk about it and not airbrush him from history as some in the Agency seemed to be doing. She was glad Stuart understood. `I'll book us a table for luncheon' she said humorously, unable to resist a final dig. Stuart could hear the ping of the lift arriving. `Mr Pendry is here, shall I show him in Director? `

Stuart smiled at the phone. It was always the little things that counted in the end. `Thank you Moira that would be good of you.'

Giles Pendry just about managed to stop himself from brushing imaginary dirt from the seat before taking the comfortable chair Stuart proffered. He eased up the knees of his trousers before sitting and crossing his long legs. He sipped his coffee almost disguising his wince at the quality of the drink. He missed the little refinements of the private sector. It was as if the public bodies he monitored were trying to outdo each other to provide the worst refreshments. Perhaps their heads thought it conveyed to visitors that they were running a lean ship. He doubted that they would drink the same filth privately, although a quick assessment of the man sitting opposite him pondering how he was going to start the conversation told Giles that anything better would be wasted here. One expensively tasselled loafer bouncing up and down betrayed his impatience to get on with business.

As Stuart poured his own coffee with deliberate slowness he surreptitiously observed Pendry. He could sense the irritation seeping through Pendry's act of calmness and realised the man was nervous and trying to hide it. Stuart had observed and conducted enough interviews of suspects to know the subconscious body language. He suddenly felt his own confidence increase. He let the silence play for a few moments longer. Giles Pendry like Stuart was in his early forties, but there the similarities ended. Giles was tall and slim. A long face and high forehead coupled with a mop of barely tamed brown curly hair gave him the donnish appearance typical of the policy wonks who operated in the Prime Ministers Policy Unit; an unelected inner cabinet who served as the PM's watchdogs over initiatives which had a lot of the PM's credibility resting on them. Having gone in his final term for an overtly presidential style of government the PM had needed his own corps to alert him to enemies from without and within. Those not in the know might have suggested Giles Pendry was the owner of a fancy South Kensington art gallery. The remains of a tan even now in early October suggested a man who did not let work get in the way of his pleasure. Yes thought Stuart, the perfect disguise for a Number 10 hatchet man with a brief to carry out preventative surgery on any policies that might leave a stain on the PM when the odour hit the fan. He wondered if Pendry knew his nickname amongst the political journo's was `The Cleaner', after the profession of the character played by Harvey Keitel in the film *Pulp Fiction.* Keitel gets called in to get rid of the evidence after John Travolta accidentally shoots a man inside the car they are travelling in. Stuart would not have put it past Pendry to have started the rumour himself. A visit from The Cleaner was never a happy occasion so Stuart thought attack was his best form of defence and he opened up as soon as they were both seated.

`I'm glad Number 10 could spare you to come and see us. I'd like to give you a preview of my plans to focus our resources on our most promising cases' said Stuart, ignoring the fact that he had been given no choice in accepting the meeting.

Giles Pendry smiled over tented fingers and paused before his spoke. Stuarts opening shots had missed their target. `Let's come to those in a minute. How are you dealing with what happened to Gordon Sinclair? I understand you and he are good friends' he said evenly.

The question had wrong footed Stuart and he did not know how Pendry was going to spring his trap. `It was a great... Gordon was under a lot of pressure' he stammered.

`So he did not confide in you or consult you on the progress of major investigations. You weren't part of his strategy?' Pendry continued smoothly.

Stuart felt torn between his loyalty to Gordon as his boss and mentor and the feeling that if only Gordon his confided in him more he could have helped avert disaster. `I was not as fully across the Michaels' case as I would have wanted to be' said Stuart diplomatically.

`Your loyalty is touching Acting Director Logan. But you have to admit your boss's decision to refuse the without prejudice offer of eight million pounds from Henry Michaels and instead pursue a failed prosecution has proved to be an unmitigated disaster for an agency that recovers less than one pound for every ten it spends.'

There they were, no niceties. The blow was swift and unexpected. Stuart could feel the heat rising in his face as he tried to control his anger. `Henry Michaels is an international criminal with known assets in excess of one billion pounds. The eight million he offered us does not even dent the interest from his loan sharking business. If the Crown Prosecution Service had more, how might you put it, "testicular fortitude", about them we could have got him to up the ante several times before making a deal.' Stuart could feel the sweat under the collar of his shirt. His tie felt like it was choking him and he had to fight the urge to unbutton his collar and take it off.

Both men knew Gordon would have consulted higher powers before he made his decision. Stuart suspected that the government knew that their case was weak and that they had deliberately encouraged Gordon to plough on knowing that failure would give them the excuse to shut the ARA down.

Pendry permitted himself a small smile at
Stuarts' attempt to slight him as an effete before replying. `But now you have nothing and no chance to have a second go at him.' He let the silence work for him before adding `So what would you have done differently? `

Stuart realised he was being asked for his elevator pitch for the future of the ARA. It might be a trap off course but he had to give it a go. `Mr Pendry the government's mistake with the Proceeds of Crime Act 2002 was to assume that changing the status of an offence from a criminal one to a civil one would allow the problems to be solved with civil methods. We have been going after sophisticated, organised criminals with forensic accountants and pen pushers when what is needed is proper investigative work. Only the careless or stupid ones leave themselves open to paper trail investigations and the cost of those investigations is uneconomic given the way we have to do them.'

`Are you saying the structure of the ARA is wrong?'

Stuart jumped over that bear trap `I'm saying that the emphasis has been misplaced. The legislation allows us to do more traditional investigation to provide robust evidence to support these analytical investigations. We need both. Instead we can't get the cooperation of other agencies who should be interested in catching these major criminals and our budget is spent on expensive forensic accountants from the management consultancies. We pay them per diem so they have little incentive to complete an investigation quickly.'

`Are you suggesting we make them sign up to no win no fee?' said Pendry.

`I'm sure that would be popular with the electorate but a more practical method might be to encourage them to compete for parcels of cases with lower day rates and bigger bonuses for success. I mean we're supposed to be an enterprise culture aren't we? ` Stuart finished slyly.

Pendry nodded as if to say touché. He leaned forward and Stuart felt like he had come to a conclusion. `Look, it's Stuart isn't it? Stuart the government has to come up with innovative solutions to long term problems. A radical government is one that is prepared to experiment with ways to meet these challenges. The ARA is an experiment that has not worked in spite of the sterling efforts of people like yourself and Gordon Sinclair. It is clear that changing the goal posts has not changed the behaviour of the players and as you yourself have said there needs to be more emphasis on traditional criminal investigation. I know from your work at the Benefits Agency you have an understanding of how criminals hide their assets that seems to elude many of your colleagues with a more book keeping mentality. The PM does not want to lose your expertise as we move ahead with the reorganisation.'

`You're reorganising the ARA? We answer to parliament not the government' said Stuart.

`Don't be naive Stuart. The ARA is a sinking ship and even the band has stopped playing. In half an hour I could have a dozen MP's willing to table a question "Does the Prime Minister think the government is getting value for money from the ARA in light of its costs and revenue to date?'

Stuart's shoulders sank. Only his second week at the helm and the Agency was going to sink on his watch.

Pendry delivered the coup de grace with surprising tenderness. `Stuart I'm sorry but time is not on your side. In less than a year the ARA will be run down and its functions subsumed into a new Serious Organised Crime Agency. The draft legislation is just waiting for the PM's nod. SOCA will rightly bring the activities of your clients back under police scrutiny.'

`Same shit, new shovel' said Stuart darkly.

`Innovative solutions to old problems my Scottish friend' said Pendry sympathetically. In spite of his reputation as a hatchet man, he was genuinely upset when a clean-up also took in people who were trying to do a good job. He felt instinctively that Logan was one of those. `A bit of personal advice if I may. Do not resign in a fit of moral outrage. Your wife Mona would not thank you, nor would Alice and Iona is going to need more help as things get more difficult.'

Stuart sat open mouthed at the extent of Pendry's knowledge of his family and his daughter Iona's MS.

Pendry continued. `In your position I would want to know who is heading up SOCA and have a chat with him off the record. Maybe take a dowry of interesting and winnable cases that will make the new management look good. Phone me on this number tomorrow and we can set it up.' He handed Stuart a crisp white business card that just said Giles Pendry, Whitehall and his phone number. Pendry stood and smoothed the imaginary creases from his trousers. `Good to see you Stuart. I'm sure we'll meet again. Don't worry I'll see myself out'.

Stuart looked around the office of the director of the ARA. A murder had just been committed but where was the evidence? The Cleaner had left the room spotless.

2.

From the other exit of St James's Park tube the entrance to New Scotland Yard is only a few metres away. Its iconic revolving sign is a natural draw for tourist photographs although the recent anti-terrorism barrier protecting the building from car bombers made a less cheery backdrop for their pictures. Stuart Logan wove through a Nippon crowd wielding Nikon's and showed his pass at the reception desk

In the end it had taken nearly two weeks for Stuart to get his appointment with the incoming head of SOCA; currently an Assistant Commissioner in the Met. The man full of his own pomp sat in dress uniform behind his large desk with a view of Big Ben while Stuart perched on a low chair on the other side. As Stuart outlined a small selection of his most promising cases where he thought the new agency could get some quick wins, he felt like an ageing courtesan trying to interest a new benefactor with morsels to temp his jaded palette. The new SOCA chief just about managed to prevent himself from yawning before telling Stuart that of the ten cases he had presented his people already had on-going investigations on six. When Stuart called his bluff and asked which ones the man bluntly said that he could not disclose any more for operational reasons. For Stuart any delusions that he could work for such a pompous arse ended there and then. On the hour the intercom buzzed from the man's secretary and Stuart took his cue to leave, gathering his files together. When asked if he could leave the files Stuart gave a false smile and said that he would get them sent over once he had tidied them up. Fuck SOCA he thought. He had tried to cooperate and they just shat on him like all the other police agencies who had resented the formation of the ARA in the first place.

On the walk back to his office Stuart remembered an old conversation with his older daughter. He was proud that she had discovered politics for herself at the age of fourteen and her left-wing leanings although predictable given her parents backgrounds were none the less pleasing. What he did not enjoy was her accusation that as a fraud investigator for the Benefits Agency he was working as an agent of the rich against the poor. He had tried to reason with her that the criminals he caught were not the real poor but con men who stole money meant for the poor. That seemed to placate her until one day he had to prosecute the parents of two of her school friends for multiple identity benefit fraud. When he took the job with the ARA Alice was finally happy that her dad was catching real crooks at last. From the way things had turned out in practice he was not so sure now.

Sitting alone in his office after everyone had left Stuart looked at his dowry again. He knew it was not a complete bluff that his list of suspects were on the radar of other agencies but they, like the ARA were making very little progress against these people, some of whom the public would consider to be amongst the good and the great. Stuart knew the government, any government would not have the stomach to take on these Champions League villains as one of his junior investigators had christened them. Instead Stuart turned his attention to the most up and coming ones. Those just outside the top echelon who had not yet managed to legitimise all their wealth making activities. He was still the head of an investigative agency for the next six months or however long the ARA had, and he was not prepared to just conduct the orchestra while the ship sank. He would focus resources on a handful of targets and before his time was up he would get one of them. For Alice, for Gordon but most of all for himself.

By 10 pm he had eliminated all but three of his possibles, of which one was a foreign national who represented everything that Stuart though was wrong with morals of Britain in the twenty first century. A man suspected of activities that brought death and misery to people in other parts of the world but who lived a privileged life here in England. From the profile they had Stuart could not believe such a man could be living in quiet retirement on the outskirts of London. But investigations had not turned up anything suspicious about his activities in the UK, most of which seemed to be altruistic. Nevertheless he was flagged as a person of interest by several agencies although the will to dig into the backgrounds of the newly arrived rich with money to spend seemed to have waned. The normal due diligence on money laundering appeared to have been suspended for the big influx of Eastern Europeans who were making London their home. Popular press stories of Polish builders on every street hid a much more significant trend; the colonisation of the stock broker belt by Russians and people from the other `Stan's that made up the former Soviet empire. The man in Stuart's sights was Ludovic Luchenko who arrived in the UK five years ago, just behind the first wave of football club owning oligarchs and ahead of the crowd who made their money in the new consumer boom in Russia.

Stuart put Ludovic Luchenko's name through a programme which trawled their case database for known associates but no hits came up. He was about to move on when he remembered the project he had set one of the IT trainees. He had seen the young man organise a night out by calling up a Google map with pins showing the work locations of all his friends. Clicking on a pin brought up the persons contact details for a call or message. Stuart had got him to plot the home locations of all their active cases. He now called up that map and added the post code for Luchenko. As he drilled into the map Stuart was surprised to see that Luchenko was a close neighbour of a man with who the ARA were having a long drawn out fight. Mr Aidan Wheelan had originally been investigated as an associate of a money launderer Victor Garcia and although that investigation confirmed that Wheelan did not have business dealings with Garcia beyond the fact that the latter was a member of the syndicate from whom Wheelan has raised capital to purchase an office building, subsequent investigation of Wheelan himself revealed the man had assets of which the tax man was unaware. It had been Wheelan's bad luck to be caught in a net meant for big fish. The Agency now desperate to get results from anywhere had gone after Mr Wheelan's property and after a protracted legal case Wheelan had settled. The settlement barely covered the costs of the expensive accountants and lawyers it had taken to get it. A year later when the Agency was preparing to sell Wheelan's properties in lieu of taxes owed the property market had dropped. Thinking that Wheelan would not have the stomach for another fight the Agency accountants went back after him for more and that's where they made their mistake. It seemed that pushed into a corner Wheelan was not going to go down without a fight and he had managed to get an appeal onto the Supreme Court timetable claiming that the Agencies' actions were disproportionate and illegal. Personally Stuart agreed with Wheelan's argument. A deal was a deal. He could not go back on it just because things had not turned out as anticipated, so why should the Agency be able to? By the time Wheelan had got his case onto the Supreme Court calendar the knives were already out for the ARA. Stuart could see the popular appeal of the plight of a man who had admitted wrong doing and ended up being more wronged by the state would play well with the media. If the case could have taken place earlier it might have shortened the life of the Agency considerably. Instead because of the court timetable it looked like the Agency would be dead by the time Wheelan got his day in court.

Stuart ran a Google search of Luchenko+Wheelan and found a surprising result, a captioned photograph showing Ludovic Luchenko presenting a trophy to Hannah Wheelan, captain of the girls under 18's polo team sponsored by Luchenko. So Aidan Quinn knew Ludovic Luchenko socially. Perhaps Wheelan could be persuaded to assist them in obtaining evidence that would allow a case to be brought against Luchenko, a real crook as his daughter would have said. But what inducement could Stuart offer Quinn in the twilight days of a dying Agency? Stuart noted that the appeal had delayed the sale of the property Whelan had already surrendered. Stuart smiled to himself. He knew what he could use to persuade Wheelan to cooperate. He could offer him his life back. But if this case was going to work Stuart would need help from outside the Agency. He scrambled in the office moving crate Moira was still nagging him to empty and found an old box for business cards and from it he pulled one for a man he had met at a conference on international fraud. The phone was answered on the second ring.

`Hello Harry Stanton, this is Stuart Logan we met at that International Fraud conference.'

`Yes I remember, hello Stuart. I take it this is not a social call at 11 pm. What can I do for you?' said the deep voice with the slight Wiltshire accent.

`Christ is that the time, sorry. Look I may be able to provide you with a contact who can supply information on a person of interest to you` said Stuart.

`That's kind of you Stuart. Who are we talking about? `

`Ludovic Luchenko. And before you ask it's because I want to do one case properly before I turn off the lights here.'

`I'm sorry things have turned out the way they have for your lot, but you weren't really given a fair chance. I take it that SOCA don't want to play ball? `Said Stanton.

`Christ Harry, have you got this place bugged as well?

Stanton laughed. 'Well we are the secret service but contrary to popular opinion we don't bug everyone as a matter of course. We will have to work with SOCA when their boss climbs off his ego so for the moment we are just keeping abreast of the situation to avoid any misunderstandings. Look Stuart if you really think you can give us an inroad to the person you mentioned we would be very interested. Lunch tomorrow?'

`Okay but not at your office. The state of the food in your canteen is no secret

3

Six weeks later Aidan Wheelan sat in a visitor's chair in an office he thought he would never see. The ARA office did onto encourage visitors. For five years his letters, emails and phone calls had got him no further than the old hag in the outer office. When they finally laid eyes on each other the look of disapproval was mutual. `The Director has asked me to show you into his office. He will be back shortly.' The Scottish crone left him with a look as if she did not trust him not to steal the paper clips. Aidan gave her his best false smile as she closed the door. He thought he would check his messages while he waited but his phone had no signal. Bored now he cast his eye over the desk. Empty and impersonal only a pad, pen, phone and lap top on an old blotter for stability. The screen saver showed a revolving and disappearing ARA logo spinning aimlessly around the screen. It seemed an apt metaphor for the Agency itself. Sheer mischief forced him to pick up the blotter to see if anything was written on the other side. A yellow post it note was stuck to it. Aidan smiled then he actually laughed when he read the pre-printed warning from the IT department against putting passwords in obvious places. Someone in the Agency had not had their sense of humour bypass. He just got it back in place when the door opened and a harassed looking man entered and shook his hand.

`Sorry to keep you waiting Mr Wheelan, I'm Stuart Logan Director of the ARA' said Stuart.

Aidan looked at the craggy Scotsman. He was surprised to be looking down at someone from his own lofty five foot seven. `Acting Director isn't it, until Mr Sinclair returns from gardening leave?' said Aidan.

Stuart bristled slightly at the implied rebuke until he realised that for the last five years the ARA had been this man's nemesis and he should not have been surprised that he had kept himself informed on its activities. The impending court case probably required regular communication between both sets of lawyers who doubtless had other connections between them. The Agency's woes were probably common knowledge amongst the legal profession.

`Quite so' said Stuart evenly. `Mr Wheelan I will not insult your intelligence. For five years you have been trying to get a face to face meeting with the Director of the ARA and you have been rebuffed. In that time we have seized control of £2.5 million worth of your undeclared assets whilst a case to prosecute you for tax evasion was planned. `

`A case you never intended to bring to court because that is not the way you want to work is it? You don't want any case law to restrict you activities. You just want to grind people down until they give in' Adrian spat. `If you had any real evidence you would bring a case within 90 days like they have to in criminal actions. Instead you hide behind your civil powers and just keep digging.'

`That's a very one sided view of our work Mr Wheelan' said Stuart, stung by the reality of how things had worked out in practice.

`Well that's the only one I know. I made a deal with your lot and where did that get me? Now you are coming after me for everything I've got left but you won't get me this time. In a year the ARA will be gone and I will still be standing' Aidan felt his face flush with anger. `You have no friends left in government Mr Logan. Why do you think I was given leave to take my case to the Supreme Court? The politicians need an excuse to close down a failed agency, one that does not make them look bad.'

Stuart paused before responding. This Wheelan might be a crook but he was no fool. `There's still a long time to go before the court date' he said.

`If this is an attempt to pressure me into dropping the action, I'll come after you and your boss for your pensions' Aidan threatened.

This was not going at all like Stuart was hoping it would. He had anticipated having the upper hand in negotiations with Wheelan but he was not sure it would work now. He might have to rely on Harry Stanton to swing the deal and that would colour the relationship going forward. He needed to diffuse Wheelan's anger. Stuart opened a small fridge next to his desk and pulled out two bottles of sparkling water handing one to Aidan.

`Mr Wheelan you assume the end game is in sight. That you will be able to slay Goliath in the next twelve months and then go back to your life. But what if that is not possible? `

`What do you mean?' said Aidan, nervous for the first time of the direction the meeting was going.

`What if we have to ask for a postponement in view of the hiatus of people leaving and your case ends up being transferred to SOCA so it outlives the demise of the ARA. Will you still be up for a fight in a year's time, or two or three?'

Aiden knew he was up for the fight but what about Kristina? His wife had stood by him when their troubles with the ARA had started. Not paying tax was a national sport in her native Estonia so she did not feel any shame when Aidan was caught. But he saw the strain grow on her as the case continued and they had to kowtow to the ARA over all their expenditure, even humiliatingly having to justify why their shopping bill was higher one month than the one before. One day he had found her crying silently in the kitchen. `I thought I'd escaped from a dictatorship when I came to England' she said. So he had thrown in his hand and settled for loosing most of what had taken a lifetime to build. To get them off his back. But just when he thought it was over they came back at him for more. This time Kristina's anger was equal to his and she told him to fight. How would she react if he had to go home and tell her they might still be fighting for years to come? Aidan realised that he had been alone with this thoughts for a while and Logan was still waiting for an answer.

`You bastards. Have you no humanity?'

`Mr Wheelan you are not an innocent in all this. You have obtained money by deception to fund the growth of your property empire. Your company accounts and tax records are extremely dubious. That was how we made the case against you in the first place. That and evidence from people you have upset along the way.'

Aidan glared at Stuart Logan. It was true he had upset a few people in business over the years and he could imagine a number of them queueing up to settle the score by informing on him. He could see his ex-wife Andria at the head of the queue.

`What do you want?' said Aidan, knowing he was going to regret asking.

`Mr Wheelan it was just your bad luck that you got caught in the net when we were looking at one of your associates Victor Garcia. Within these four walls while you are not he sort of criminal the ARA was set up to catch but our lack of success with bigger fish has made you a more attractive target. I want to offer you a way to end all of this. To wrap up your case and let you walk away with what you have now and possibly more before the ARA closes' said Stuart baiting the line.

`And what do I have to do for that then?' said Aidan.

`You have to cooperate with us and help us catch a bigger fish.'

Aidan paused in thought for a moment before making up his mind. `You mean do your job, the job you are not up to. Fuck off, I'll see you in court.' Aiden got up to leave.

`How much will all this cost you Mr Wheelan by the time it's all over? How much has it cost you already in money and stress? Do you know we have not disposed of any of your seized assets yet? As things stand now there is still the possibility of a settlement to redress the impact of our disproportionate actions.' Stuart played his last card. He knew that this was stretching the principle of self-funding from assets recovered, but if investing in a small crook could catch a bigger one that was okay in Stuart's book given the new realities the Agency was facing.

Aidan was still standing when he delivered his answer. `I made a deal with the devil once before and you went back on it. There's nothing to stop you doing it again. In fact there is all the more reason to back track if you are not going to be around to deal with the consequences.'

The other door into Stuart's office opened and in stepped a large man with a scar on his face. Aidan looked up to the six foot four bulk of Harry Stanton filling the door frame. `Where is he from, Henchmen R' Us?' said Aidan looking at Stuart.

Harry Stanton smiled` Mr Wheelan it is rare to meet a man whose life has been so motivated by the pursuit of money suddenly turn down the opportunity to get back what he feels was unjustly taken from him.'

`There are some deals that are not worth doing, especially with his lot' said Aidan looking at Stuart.

`That's what I said' Stanton joked as he sat in the other visitor's chair and pulled an envelope from his pocket. `I work for a government department. One that does not seek publicity. We protect the country from unsavoury individuals.'

`What you're going to try and deport me back to Ireland on some bogus charge? I thought those days were over' said Aidan.

`Indeed they are. That conflict is history' said Stanton rubbing the scar on his face. `This is different.'

In spite of himself Aidan was intrigued at this new development. `What's in the envelope then, blackmail pictures of me on the job with some old tart' Aidan joked until he remembered the celebration in the West End after he thought the case was over. He and his mate ended up spending the night at the flat of two girls they had pulled. With all they had weathered together Kristina would not pack her bags over a one night stand. Would she?

`No Mr Wheelan it looks like we missed that occasion but I'm sure you'll find these more interesting. Take a seat we won't keep you long will we Stuart?' said Stanton acknowledging him for the first time. It was clear Harry Stanton was in charge of the interview from here on in.

Aidan could not help being drawn to the envelope. `You remember the Bosnian war don't you Mr Wheelan? All those little countries that hatched when the Yugoslavian egg broke in the 1990's. Bosnian Muslims, Orthodox Serbs and Catholic Croats massacring each other like they were African tribes until the UN and NATO stepped in to kick their arses. Only it didn't always go to plan.'

Stanton pulled out a series of pictures showing the ambush of a NATO convoy of lightly armed vehicles. A Land Rover was thrown into the air when it hit a land mine and the other vehicles were hit by rocket propelled grenades. The final shots showed the overrun NATO solders being shot. The last one was of all the bodies piled together and three men posing with one foot on the pile and an AK-47 rifle in their hands. The looked like big game hunters. `You probably recognise the one in the middle as the war criminal Slobodan Milosevic. The one on his left is a unit commander and the one on the right is your neighbour. He supplied the arms for this little scene and these pictures are from a promotional video he uses to impress new customers. Do you like his tattoos? They tell the story of how he entered the criminal life. A confession in icons if you will.'

The third man was blond and shirtless. A couple of belts of machine gun bullets crossing his chest Rambo style. They obscured the big tattoos on his torso although the inked epaulettes on his shoulders and images on his arms were still visible. `What's that got to do with me? If you know where he is why don't you just go and arrests him?' said Aidan.

`It's not that easy Mr Wheelan. He's committed no crimes in this country, twelve years have gone by and Mr Luchenko is now a respectable and connected man.' Stanton slid over a picture of a group of people in evening wear at a charity dinner. `He's the one two down from the Prime Minister's wife' said Stanton. The same man was now smiling for the cameras his ink hidden by a dress shirt and dinner jacket.

`Look it's got nothing to do with me. If you people don't care who you let into the country as long as they have got money then that's what you can expect. You're wasting my time' said Aidan standing to leave again.

`Oh but that's where you are wrong. It very much has something to do with you. Look here is the same man awarding a prize. I believe that is your daughter he is handing it to' said Stanton.

Aidan grabbed the photo and studied it. Hannah was holding the trophy her under eighteens polo team had won. Hannah was Kristina's daughter from a previous relationship but Aidan and Hannah had hit it off right from the start of his relationship with her mother. Even after they married and had a second child of their own Eva, Aidan had always treated Hannah like his own. `So he sponsors the polo team where I live. So what, Lehman Brothers sponsor a tournament at the tennis club. There is a noble streak of patronage amongst rich crooks.'

`That's true Aidan but Lehman Brothers are not involved with your family' said Stanton trying to sound like a friend before he revealed his winning argument.

`What's that supposed to mean? ` Said Aidan suspiciously.

`You know who this is don't you Aidan?' said Stanton sliding another photo across the table.

`That's Hannah's boyfriend Simon Grayson' said Aidan, now alarmed at how personal it had become.

Stuart looked at Harry Stanton and realised why he had asked for some time before they brought Aidan Wheelan in. He had had the whole family under surveillance. He thought that was too intrusive but he hoped that whatever was coming was more persuasive than his offer which Wheelan had rejected.

`You may not be familiar with the term beard. It is used in the gay community. It is a joke on being macho. A gay man who has not come out may use a sympathetic female friend to act a disguise. Your daughter Hannah is Simon's beard' said Stanton.

Aidan studied the picture of Simon which seemed to have been taken in a club. He was part of a group of young men and he seemed very relaxed. Unlike when he came to the house to take Hannah out. Aidan had suspected that he was a virgin and that nervousness would go when the couple started shagging. Not that he wanted to hurry that along, being the protective father that he was. His own mother had been knocked up and abandoned when she was not much more than Hannah's age.

`There's something in it for Hannah as well. Simon keeps you off the trail of this man who is her real boyfriend' said Stanton.

The last picture showed Hannah in the arms of a young man of around her age. He had boy band good looks. Dark curly hair, dark eyes and pouting lips. Aidan could see the attraction for Hannah.

`I would be concerned for my daughter if she turned up with Tito on her arm' said Stanton at once sympathising and turning the knife on Aidan. `To end this little photo essay let me introduce his uncle'.

Aidan knew what was coming and the picture he turned over showed a much younger Tito on the knee of the man called Ludovic Luchenko at the boy's birthday party.

`Luchenko has no children and is grooming his nephew to become heir to his empire. Don't mistake this man for the financial crooks who made their fortune by swindling Russia out of its natural resources and bribing Putin for the pleasure. Luchenko is a *Vory*, a criminal from a long line of criminal nobility. He has served time at the hands of the people who now rule that country and he runs his empire in spite of them. An empire founded on drugs, arms, money laundering, prostitution and people smuggling. Help us Mr Wheelan and we can make him go away and take his nephew with him. Your daughter's broken heart will heal in time'. Harry Stanton finished his pitch and pushed the pile of photos towards Aidan.

`What I said about returning you assets still stands Aidan' Stuart reminded him.

Aidan sat shell shocked. An hour before he was looking forward to rubbing the nose of the man who had caused him so much grief in the mire. Yet now he was trapped even further in the clutches of these people. He looked at the surveillance picture of Hannah and Tito. They were coming out of a house and it was obvious what they had been doing. He knew there would be no reasoning with her. If it was true these people were offering him his life back and a way to get rid of an unpleasant intrusion on his family. If he was going to do this he would have to persuade Kristina to help him. ` I need to think about all this, I need to talk to my wife first.'

`It may not be as hard as you think Aidan, she knows Tito and she knows his mother Vera. Vera is Luchenko's sister but they don't really get on so Kristina has never met him' said Stanton.

Aidan was reeling that Kristina was in on this boyfriend subterfuge. He could see how Hannah would have confided in her mother and then the two of them would have kept it from him because he had enough to cope with in dealing with the court case and trying to keep his property business afloat. They would have thought they were doing him a favour by not letting him know. Aidan got up to leave. `Can I take those with me' he said pointing to the photos.

Harry Stanton took a couple of the gruesome ones out and gave the envelope to Aidan. `I think they will be enough to tell the story don't you Aidan? We'll be in touch in a couple of days'

Aidan Wheelan nodded and sleep walked out of Stuart Logan's office. Stuart looked at Harry Stanton. `Did we really have to dig into the man's life like that Harry?'

`Don't tell me you wouldn't have done it if you had the resources' Stanton admonished. `Besides the money was never going to be enough to motivate him even if he believed you. Now we've given him an all or nothing proposition he cannot resist. Cheer up Stuart isn't this what you wanted?' said Stanton.

`Yes is it's' said Stuart, only the taste in his mouth was not victory.

4

It was three days before Aidan could bring himself to tell Kristina about his agreement to work with the ARA and the secret service man. He festered about her deceit in keeping quiet about Hannah and Tito's relationship. He wanted to throw that in her face before confessing what he had committed them to. In the end it was their younger daughter Eva who was the cause of Aidan coming clean. He arrived home early from visiting an office building his company were refurbishing and saw Eva's schoolbag and coat in the hallway. It was only 2pm and school did not finish before 3.30 so Aidan knew something was up. This was confirmed by the tone of his wife's voice from the kitchen.

`Your father is home. Now you must be explaining to him why you hit that boy.' When it came to chastising the children Kristina seemed to channel her own mother in halting English even though her own was fine. When Aidan first challenged her on it Kristina denied it, then on reflection she admitted it was an automatic reflex when she was in angry mode and she was not even aware she was doing it. In the kitchen a stern faced Kristina stood over a sullen child who swung her legs in defiance under the table.

`What's all this about then Eva?' said Aidan, careful not to sound too sympathetic because Kristina was expecting him to back her up.

`I was called to school to take Eva home because she has been fighting with a boy in her class. Neither of them would say what it was about' said Kristina before Eva could reply.

`Maybe it was not Eva's fault' said Aidan taking the child's hand in an attempt to coax the answer out of her. The stern look he received from Kristina almost convinced him it was his fault.

`It was Bryan's fault. He started it' said Eva happy to have an ally now.

`Let's you and me make mum a cup of tea while she sits down' said Aidan. Kristina took the hint and left the kitchen but hovered outside the door. Eva slid off the chair and got the cups out of the cupboard while Aidan boiled the kettle.

`Dad have you done bad things?' asked Eva.

`What did the boy say?' replied Aidan avoiding the question.

The words tumbled out of the child. `We were playing shops and I was giving Bryan his change from the till...and I counted it on the table...and he took it away...but then he came back and said some was missing. I said he must have dropped it but he said I stole it when he was putting his things in the shopping bag. I said he was a liar...and he said I was a thief. Then he said you were a crook because his dad had read it in the papers. Then I hit him.' Tears rand down Eva's face. `It's not true, you're not a crook are you Dad?' She hugged her father around his waist as her shoulders moved up and down with her sobs. Aidan put his arms around Eva wishing he could take the hurt away from the six year old. Behind her Kristina stood in the doorway with silent tears rolling down her face and a look of resignation in her eyes.

After dinner and with Eva tucked up in bed for an early night their brave faces fell and Aidan and Kristina were on tender hooks each waiting for each other to start the conversation. Kristina broke first. `When all this started I said I would stand by you Aidan. I owe you everything so this is not difficult for me. But the children, that is another matter. They are innocent in all of this and I cannot stay here and let them be hurt. Hanna says nothing but I know people have also said unkind things to her about the case.' Aidan looked up surprised. `We know it's hard enough for you but we can't go on like this. Not all the time until the case is heard.'

Aidan felt exhausted. He could not face the rest of it on his own. `Kristina all I have ever wanted to do is make a better life for you and the girls. We don't have the connections or privilege so we had to do it by our wits. I swear I did not know it was drugs money Victor Garcia was investing in the project. I would have never of taken it, even if it meant losing the job.'

`I know Aidan. I believed you then and I believe you now. But when the ARA could not make the case against him and came looking for you instead, all the corners you have cut over the years have caught up with you.'

`Kristina I've done nothing worse than those bastards who live around us do every day. But they are bankers so it does not count as crime and they do not get their names dragged through the papers.'

`It's been five years Aidan and we've all suffered even though you have done your best to shield us from it. If you win this Supreme Court case will it really be over? Can we go back to our old lives again?

Aidan looked at Kristina's worried face. `Okay, here's the thing. When we made that deal with the ARA two years ago we thought that was the end of it. It cost us almost everything we had worked for but the alternative was to go cap in hand to their accountants every month for permission to spend our own money and then to keep pissing away what we had left on the legal fight. It would have been okay if they had just left it at that, but they couldn't could they? They had to come back for more. Final is not final as far as they were concerned. If we win in the Supreme Court all it will prove is that they were wrong to come back for a second bite.'

`So your daughter will still have to fight at school to defend your reputation?' Kristina said it without malice and that hurt all the more.

`What if there was a way we could come out of this so we did not have to fight anybody? A way to get them to give us back everything its cost us so far' said Aidan. Kristina looked at him disbelievingly so he continued. `We would have to do it before the court case is heard, because by then the ARA will be wrapped up and everything transferred to SOCA. It could even delay the case coming to court.'

`Oh Aidan will we never be free of this?'

`We will Kristina but we have to act while the people who run the ARA are in control. I need your help because what they want us to do is not straightforward.

`I don't like the sound of this Aidan. I don't want any more lies.'

`That's an interesting choice of words Kristina.' Aidan had his opening. `Would you say that Hannah and Simon are a happy couple?'

`What's that got to do with what we are talking about?' said Kristina, wrong footed by the change in direction. She knew Aidan was on to something but she did not want to give anything away.

`Would you day that Hannah and Simon were a normal couple?'

`I suppose so' said Kristina non-committedly.

`Or would you say their relationship was a lie. A camouflage to hide who she is really seeing because you know I would not be happy.'

Kristina broke. `Hannah and Tito are in love. They are besotted with each other. It's him she has relied on through all this trouble. I knew you would not approve but if you put your foot down I honestly think she would run off with him. Is that what you want, to do drive our daughter away?' Aidan could see that the subterfuge had not been easy for Kristina. `Hannah confided in me when I asked her if she was sure Simon was interested in girls. She admitted it was a mutual convenience to keep both dad's happy. He's not ready to come out as gay.'

`Christ, we are fathers not monsters.'

`If you could see how happy Hannah and Tito are you would understand.'

`I understand he is fucking a girl who is barely legal!'

`Don't be disgusting Aidan. Hannah is nearly eighteen, she is a young woman.'

`How old is he, he looks older?'

`What do you mean Aidan?'

Aidan took out the envelope he had hidden under the couch and showed the picture of the two of them coming hand in hand out of a house having obviously been engaged in a romantic tryst.

`That's his mother's house. For Christ sake Aidan are you having him followed?'

`No but someone else is. Someone who wants us to do their bidding so we can finish this whole business with the ARA.' Kristina looked puzzled. `What do you know about this Tito Kristina?'

`He's Russian from St Petersburg. He's twenty-one and studying music at Guildhall. That's where Hannah met him when he showed her around on her interview day.'

`What about his family?'

`He lives with his mother in Chiswick. His father died in a car accident when Tito was four.'

`His uncle is a neighbour of ours. This is what he does for a living.' Aidan pulled out the war photographs and presented them to Kristina one by one. `Here he is demonstrating his stock on a NATO armored personnel carrier in the Balkans. That's one of him sharing trophies with another war criminal after they mopped up the survivors. Kristina picked up the picture of the gun totting men holding a handful of dog tags and studied their faces. She gasped and dropped the picture back onto the table. He knew the bloodshed would shock her. `Here is something different, a family scene' said Aidan showing her the picture of the smiling blond man with cold grey eyes. It was a face you could not easily forget and one she thought she would never see again. `Tito's uncle is a man called Ludovic `Lucky' Luchenko. He is an arms dealer, drug runner, money launderer and many other things. He is the man the security services and the ARA want our help to gather evidence against in exchange for making the whole business with the ARA go away. That's our deal Kristina.'

She looked at Aidan and fled from the room.

Kristina knew Aiden was watching her from the windows of the orangery while she fed their little clutch of chickens and ducks in the pen at the end of the garden. Aidan had scolded her that they were the most expensive eggs in the world once you'd factored in the cost of feed and everything else it had cost building the chicken coop, duck house and the little paddling pool for them. But he knew they comforted her as they reminded her of her childhood in Estonia and the farm they had before her father left and she had to move with her mother to Tallinn. But it was not to those happy childhood memories where Kristina's mind returned now. The picture of the man balancing a young Tito on his knee brought up memories she thought she had suppressed forever. She recalled the night she and her mum had been sat in Uncle Maanus' house when he got the call to come back to work at the docks as they were a man down because one of the crane drivers wives had finally gone into labour. Maanus Koppel had not worked nights in a long time and his wife thought it was because he wanted to spend more time with the family now that Kristina and her mum had joined them. Years later she found out that as a shop steward of the crane drivers, Maanus had been vocal in objecting to the illegal cargo's that were unloaded at night. He had said a little too loudly for some people that `if Russian gangsters wanted these things they should take them straight to St Petersburg and not pollute Tallinn with their weapons and drugs and stolen cars.' The other crane drivers who were happy to take their kickbacks kept him out of the way after that.

On the night in question Uncle Maanus came home just after midnight. It was not even halfway through his shift. Kristina and her cousin Petor sat at the top of the stairs listening to his mother and father and Kristina's mother talking loudly in the kitchen. There had been an accident while a ship was being unloaded. One of the crane drivers had been drunk and had not stacked a container properly before releasing it. It slipped and injured three men, trapping them in the aisle between stacks. The crane could not retrieve the container so Uncle Maanus had jumped into a big fork lift truck and managed to lever the container off the injured men. He did not have a good grip on it and it slipped backwards smashing on the edge of the dock before falling into the water. The sound of breaking glass and the smell of whiskey covered the whole dock. The men waiting with a container lorry and two cars to take the illegal alcohol were angry. One climbed the crane ladder to deal with the driver while two others came after Maanus Koppel. The other dockers held them off as he got away but the sound of gunfire ended their resistance.

Kristina's mother was telling Uncle Maanus he had to get away before the gangsters came for him. Her Auntie Irene said when they had calmed down the crooks would see that by saving the men he had avoided an official investigation which would have been more trouble for them. Maanus said he could not risk what they might do to his family. He had to get away until it was safe to come back. When his father said he would go her cousin Petor started crying and so did Kristina. His parents came out of the kitchen and told the kids to come down stairs. Uncle Maanus told them they had to be brave and look after their mothers while he went away for a little while. He kissed them all and then with final look that betrayed the fear in his face he slipped out of the back door. It was the last time they would see him alive.

Two hours later there was a banging at the door and three men pushed their way in demanding in Russian to know where Maanus Koppel was. When her aunt said `You gangsters can go to hell', the youngest one struck her across the face with the back of his hand. An arc of blood spurted from her split lip as she fell to the floor. The man leaned over and kicked her in the stomach and Kristina screamed. The man looked up. He was no more than a boy close up. His blonde hair made him look like a choir boy but the gleam in his cold grey eyes betrayed something more sinister. He grabbed Kristina by the jaw. `Perhaps you can tell me where he is little girl?' Kristina was terrified but held his stare determinedly. One of the other gangsters grabbed his arm and said Maanus had been spotted on the other side of town and they needed to go before the police came. The grey eyed man released her and then did a most unexpected thing. He smiled and kissed her gently on the lips before he left. Four days later the body of Maanus Koppel was found, the apparent victim of a hit and run.

The quacking ducks brought Kristina out of her memories. She was touching her lips as if Ludovic Luchenko had just finished kissing her even though it happened over thirty years ago. She wondered what had disturbed the birds then she heard Aidan's feet on the stepping stones. Fate had given her a chance to avenge Uncle Manaus's death. He had been more of a father to her than her own and he deserved her help. Prison would not hold a man like Lucky Luchenko. His sort would never do time again. There would have to be a more permanent solution. Her cousin would help, it was really Petor's score to settle. They had kept in touch until he had left home at sixteen, lying about his age to join the army early. Petor had been around guns and violence, he would know how to do it although it might take her time to contact him. She felt Aidan's hand on her shoulder. She could not confess her true purpose to him but she would go along with his plan for now. She owed him that.

`I'm sorry I tried to involve you in this Kristina. I'll phone them to tomorrow and tell them the deal is off and we will take out chances with the Court of Appeal.'

Kristina turned around, smiled at Aidan and hugged him. `No Aidan, you tried to do the best for us and we should go through with it. But I want to meet the people we are dealing with before we do anything. We need to make sure they can't get out of their side of the bargain this time. And we have to save Tito, for Hannah's sake.'

Aidan kissed his wife. He was amazed at her change of heart and the determination he now felt radiating from her. `We can do this, you and me. We can get justice' he said hugging her.

Kristina smiled. `Yes we can Aidan. We can get justice.

5

The engine of the old van stalled as Max Quinn waited for the barrier to lift. Last time he visited Aidan the barrier at the gatehouse entrance to St Jude's Estate was a simple striped wooden pole, raised manually by pushing down the counterweight. Now it was a solid metal affair like a level crossing gate and there was even a moat like trench in the road beyond which came up before the barrier was raised. These defences would not have looked out of place outside the Falls Road police station. But it wasn't political ideology that was being protected here. Max thought he could almost smell the money in the air and after five years living without much of it the aroma was more acute than ever. Diesel smoke belched as the van kicked back into life. The security guard waived the air and gave a loud comedy cough. As Max drove up the tree-lined avenue he notice how many of the familiar landmarks had changed in the last six years. In what looked on the face of it to be a conurbation of traditional country squire homes on the outskirts of London a subtle but clear transformation was taking place. True at only an acre or so a piece the 400 odd homes did not have enough land to go shooting grouse, but that was not the point of St Jude's. It was country living without the chores of country life and all within an hour of Knightsbridge, where the Range Rovers parked on every second drive would be used to mount nothing higher than the curb outside a fancy restaurant. Max stopped outside the gates of what had always been his fantasy dream home if his numbers ever came up on the lottery. He was disappointed that the pretty country cottage had been razed to the ground and replaced by a yellow London brick neo-Georgian creation. It was the size of a small hotel. A smaller building housing a triple garage with accommodation on top was bigger than the original house. A barrel chested man in a dark suit and no tie came out of the second building and started walking towards the gates. Max had seen enough pub bouncers in his time to know this man was not the owner. With a cheery wave and a shout of hello he drove on and did not catch the reply muttered in a foreign language.

As Max breasted the hill a tall black man in a neon track-suit came into view. His gentle jog seemed to be in time with the beat of the music leaking out from a monster pair of headphones. Max wound down his window and shouted `Run faster Etienne I've got a hundred quid on you to score a hat-trick on Saturday'. The black man looked up at first puzzled and then he smiled at Max. `I will try' he said as he jogged past. Max watched him go in his mirror, noting that the man had not fully recovered from the thigh strain injury in his last match. He smiled to himself. He hated Chelsea and if their star striker was below par maybe his team would stand a chance this year. At the gates of Aidan's house Max got out and pressed the intercom. He was nervous at seeing his friend after all this time. They had been inseparable as kids and teenagers but married life had limited their meetings and events of the last six years had kept them apart completely. `Is it yourself Max?' came the disembodied voice of Aiden from the intercom.

`Aye that it is' said Max.

`Well you'd better come in then you fecker' said Aidan good-naturedly.

Max knew they would be all right. He drove through the electronic gates and up to the door. He was always amazed that he knew someone who lived in such a posh house. The two storey six bedroomed home was wider than it was long but it was the four white classical columns supporting the pitched lintel at roof level that gave the house its imposing appearance. It always reminded him of trips to the British Museum or a tour of the White House.

The van spluttered to a halt as Aidan opened the front door. `You could do with an engine in that thing' he teased.

`I'm thinking of getting one of those stickers that says my other car is a bike' said Aidan.

They embraced in a hug before stepping back to examine each other. Recent events had taken their toll on both men and now they looked like they were in their late thirties. Their once youthful faces now carried worried foreheads and lines around the eyes. Max's manual lifestyle had kept him quite trim whilst Aidan's waistline was suffering under the assault of Kristina's delicious home cooking.

`I see we use the same barber' said Aidan touching the grey on his own side burns.

`We look like our dads now' said Max.

`How would we know?' said Aidan. Both men laughed. They had each come from single-parent families. Their mothers were neighbours in adjoining flats of a grotty council block in Cricklewood. `Come in man and take a load off. Whiskey good for you?'

`It's 9.30 in the morning Aidan' said Max.

`Sorry, I didn't know you missed your dad and went straight to your grandma!' said Aidan.

`You cheeky cont' said Max giving Aidan a playful hit on the arm. Both men had missed their banter. Kristina had forbidden swearing in the house now that Eva mimicked everything she heard so even Irish swearing where you just changed the vowels was out of bounds. But this morning they had the place to themselves as Kristina and Eva were on the school run and Hannah was sleeping off a late night having come back in the early hours from a party to celebrate the end of her A level exams.

`I'm sorry I couldn't be there for you when you had to all that trouble with the taxman. I would have if I could have' said Max hoping that his friend had forgiven him for his abrupt departure.

`I know Max. It's all sorted now, well after a fashion. What about you. How much do you still owe Lester Connolly?'

`Not too much. I paid him back thirty grand already and got his okay to come back to England to work off the rest.'

`Why did you do it Max?'

`I know it was crazy. I was into him so deep, but there was always just one more bet, cards, horses, dogs. It didn't matter. Then we got into that Stock Market nonsense and it all went mad. Huge wins and huge losses. I had a big win and could have paid him back, but instead I gave the money to

Siobhan and said that she and Annie should have a proper life instead of being stuck with a liability like me. I gave her the money when I went to visit them back home in Ireland and then I got away.'

`You know she's seeing someone else now Max? It's been a couple of years.'

`I know Aidan thanks for keeping an eye on her to make sure she was okay.'

`Does she know you're back?'

`I don't think so, but I don't want to see her until I'm out of the woods with Lester. I'm going to clear my debts first and then see if she'll take me back.

`Is that such a good idea Max?'

`I still love her and I think she still loves me. You know I speak to her Christmas, Annie's birthday, her birthday. For the first time she phoned me on my birthday. She asked me if I was with anyone special in Boston and I said no. I asked if she was calling to ask for a divorce and she said no not at all. I asked her what the chances were of her taking back a man who had not gambled for five years. She said, the chances were between slim and none. I said I'd take those odds. So here I am.'

Aidan looked at Max. He didn't know if Max could really have got it out of his system. The betting fever had really taken him in the last couple of years before his hasty departure to America. But that was over six years ago and it was possible that Max now had it under control. He could not broach the subject there and then. `Are you hungry Max I could get the housekeeper to do you some breakfast?'

`Are you having any yourself?' asked Aidan.

`No I'll give it a miss this morning, I had a dodgy meal out last night that's taking its revenge.'

`What poisoned in your own restaurant?' said Max

`No I was sussing out the new competition, an Arab place on the High Street.'

`Do you remember that Middle Eastern place in Kensington we took our mam's to that time?' said Max

`Yes. First week's pay packets and I'd washed the Escort.'

`We even had suits on.'

`What was it your mam said Max when we pulled up outside?'

`Are you boys not coming in with us to eat?' said Max

`When you mam asked why, my mam said because it's one of those restaurants' said Aidan.

`And then your mam looked at the sign and said no Mary it's a Lebanese restaurant not a lesbian restaurant!' said Max laughing.

`And then your mam said Jesus Eileen it's these new feckin' glasses. I can't see a thing' said Aidan.

`And then you mam said Mary you aren't wearing any!
Both men broke into belly laughs the like of which they had not experienced for years. Each time they stopped one would look at the other and they would break out again.

`For feck's sake Max stop it. My ribs are aching and I'm about to piss myself.'
They eventually recovered and sat there in the easy calm. It had been too long.

`So how are you going to pay that money back and earn a living' said Aidan bringing them back the real world?

`With something I've got in the van and a favour to ask you' said Max finishing his tea and getting up.

`I'm not sure I'm going to like this Max' said Aidan.

`Aidan I bet you bloody love it. Come on let me show you.'

Max opened the back of his van and took out a box containing half metre long black poles, electric motors and circuit boards. Aidan looked puzzled as Max began to assemble the pieces. `Remember that idea I had back in 2000 for an on line diary for travellers.'

`Yes walk something wasn't it?' Said Aidan.

`That's right, Walkabout-Talkabout a website, well actually what they call a blog now. You could upload pictures and comments and your friends could follow you and keep in touch with messages everyone on the site could read'.

`I remember now, that wasn't a bad idea.'

`It was a feckin' brilliant idea but I didn't see that people would want to post messages about their everyday lives and that fecker who started Facebook did and now he's worth billions. He offered his idea to people free, while I made the mistake of trying to sell branded versions to holiday companies.'

`Well that's the way it goes sometimes mate' said Aidan.

`Yes but not this time. What do you think this is?' Said Max

Aidan was looking at a circular hub with six spokes but no rim.

`If you've just invented the wheel I can see a design fault with it' Aidan joked.

`Ha, Ha. Stand back and prepare to be amazed' said Max. He attached motors and propellers to each spoke and fitted the printed circuits inside the hub. `When I was in Boston I hung out with some guys at MIT. They were working on unmanned aerial vehicles, drones in the popular parlance. They've come up with a design which has become the standard for these things. He attached the battery to a central hub and switched it on and indicator lights flashed on some of the spokes. He took out a conventional looking radio control unit, that sort of thing people use to control cars and planes. It had a long aerial and two joysticks. Max hung it round his neck with a strap. `The problem with conventional helicopters is stability. The rotor on the back is to stop the fuselage from spinning in the opposite direction to the top rotor. But these are different, a pattern of contra rotating blades makes this design incredibly stable...look.' The spider-like craft rose into the air with an angry buzz and hovered perfectly still just above their heads.

`How high will it go Max?'

`How high would you like it to go ten feet, fifty feet, seventy-two point five feet?' The craft rose and fell and for the first time Aidan noticed the pad in Max's other hand. `These things are computer-controlled now.'

`I still don't see it Max?' said Aidan.

`You will' said Max excitedly. He landed the craft and attached a small harness to the central hub into which he slotted a tiny box with an aerial. Then he opened up a laptop and started a program. The screen came to life showing a display similar to that of a flight simulator overlaid on a picture of their feet. The craft rose again and the screen showed the ground falling away and then the two of them were in the picture, then Aidan's house and a house of his neighbours. Aidan knew how long it would take to walk between the two properties. He looked up and the helicopter was hardly a speck in the sky and almost completely silent.

`That's amazing Max a proper robot heliocopter' Aidan said laying on the Irish brogue of his mother. Max flew the helicopter out of sight. `Aren't you afraid you'll lose it?'

`Its Wi-Fi controlled up to a kilometre. Wi-Fi also sends the pictures back. And if it loses the signal...watch.' Max switched of the remote control unit and the screen went blank. They could not hear the helicopter anywhere. A minute later, the machine was back and hovering ten feet above Max's head. `The GPS system knows where home is if you tell it' said Max knowing Aidan was impressed.

`It's a feckin' boomerang mate' Adrian joked.

`You had some repairs done on the roof?'

`How do you know Max?'

Max wound back the footage which had been recording on his hard drive. `Want to see what sort of job they did?'

Max launched the craft again and this time hovered inches from the roof. Aidan looked the picture of his roof on the computer screen. Aidan could see where the builders had skimped and not fixed the lead flashing properly after their repair. `The cheeky bastards have not done it properly, I'm getting them back in' said Aidan.

`I'll send you an extract of the film so you can show them exactly what the problem is' said Max.

The light went on in Aidan's head. `You know what Max. I think you've got a real business idea here. Building inspections, marketing materials for estate agents.'

`Golf course flyovers, sports event filming' added Max.

`Where can you buy one of these Aidan?'

`That's just it, there is no commercial supplier moment. These are made from kits by research students and model aircraft enthusiasts. But that market will be here in a couple of years.'

`And the thing to do is to get in and out before the crowd' said Aidan.

`Exactly. That's what I was hoping you can help me with. Look at this neighbourhood. How many of these people would like to have an aerial photograph of their homes. Then there's the tennis club up the road. In the States they use UAV's in sports coaching. It's early days yet but the motors will get more powerful, the cameras better and the batteries longer lasting.'

`Alright, you've convinced me.' Aidan hoped that Max was serious about making a go of this business as a way to get Siobhan back. He would not tell Max that he spoke to her quite often and could confirm that she still had feelings for him. `We've got an 18th birthday party for Hannah at the weekend. Big marquee, roast boar and all that. Why not come along to that and take some aerial shots of the festivities. Quite a few of her friends' parents will be here at some time during the day and I'm sure word-of-mouth will spread.'

`Thanks mate, I really appreciate it. Hannah's eighteenth already, how time flies. Is it okay if I practice a bit before I pack up I want it all to run smartly on Saturday?'

`Sure, why not. I've got to go in and make some calls but come back in before you go' said Aidan and he turned back to the house.

Max changed the battery. It was going to be a roasting day. It was not yet past 10.30 and the temperature was already in the high 20's. Max went into the garden and thought he would take film and stills of the back of the house. He would ask Aidan if it would be okay to have a show reel running while he worked at the party. The estate agent idea was a good one. He flew the helicopter over the wide lawn towards the back of the garden where a hedge hid a small patio. He remembered he had Aidan being banished there by Kristina when they wanted to smoke cigars. How many years ago was that? Max heard a scream. He looked up and could not see anything, then he looked at the screen and saw an attractive young girl on the sun bed wearing just sun glasses. She sat up and tried to cover her ample charms but fell back on the sun bed her head knocking the backrest down and her legs flying up spread-eagled. She could not have been more exposed if she had posed deliberately. The next moment she was up and pulling a see-through cheesecloth sun shirt around her. She grabbed her bikini and headed to the door of the orangery. `Bloody peeping Tom' she shouted from a distance.

Max packed up his things and went back to the house to apologise to Aidan for disturbing his guest. `Aidan I didn't realise there was a young woman sunbathing in your garden. I do apologise.'

`Come in' said Aidan laughing behind the desk of his home office. `You remember Hannah don't you Uncle Max?'

The young woman was now back in her bikini not that it covered much. `Little Hannah?' said Max not believing the shapely young woman in front of him was a grown-up version of the 12-year-old with braces he remembered.

`Not so little anymore and don't keep pointing those things at Max you're embarrassing him' said Aidan.

Hannah blushed and hugged her arms around her shoulders only succeeding in making her ample cleavage more pronounced. `It is me Uncle Max' said Hannah pleased with his discomfort of wanting to look her body but not being able to because she was the daughter of his best friend. She'd had a bit of a crush on Uncle Max when she was a kid and she was sad when he went away unexpectedly. `Dad says are going to take some aerial pictures of my party. Everybody will be so jealous.'

`Well I hope they are good. I'd better be going now. Sorry again Hannah. See you on Saturday Aidan.'

`I'll walk you out Uncle Max' said Hannah. She went on ahead of him and Max could not help looking at her shapely arse. He turned to Aidan in despair. `I'll have a word with her' said Aidan in mock sympathy. At the front door Hannah whispered `Uncle Max there are no pictures of me on your camera are there?'

`No I ran out of film before I got to you.'

`That's a relief' said Hannah.

Max leaned in conspiratorially. `But if you really must have a Hollywood you might want to put a higher factor sun lotion on it. That place is not used to seeing the sun, you know.'

Hannah went red with embarrassment. `Oh my god, you saw my ... I mean, I fell back and you saw everything.'

`So can I put you down for a set of eight by ten prints then?' Max added maliciously.

`Shut up' she said sulkily.

`Bye, Bye then not so little Hannah' Max said as he laughed all the way to his van.

6

The front of Aidan's house was festooned with balloons and banners wishing Hannah a happy birthday and welcoming guests. In the back garden a marquee housed the food tables and a drinks bar from which formally dressed waiting staff departed with trays of glasses. Classical music was playing softly over the PA system while the DJ dozed in a garden chair catching up on his sleep. His skills would not be needed before sunset.

Max refused a second glass of Bucks Fizz with regret. It was really nice champagne but it was going down too easily and he was here working after all. It had been a good turnout for the birthday party. Hannah was a popular girl and had many friends. The marquee on Aidan's lawn where the waiting staff were serving drinks and floating round with trays of canapés was filled with the noisy giggle of teenage voices. Max was glad Aidan had persuaded the waiters to wear the chest cameras he'd provided. It took an extra twenty quid in their pockets, but they seemed happy to ask everyone they served to say a few words and make a toast to Hannah. When Max edited it all together it would look good. The cameras were unobtrusive and the guests would look more natural when they spoke. Younger people had no problem with the idea as most of them were taking pictures of themselves with camera phones anyway. Some of the older people were quite quaint in their disbelief that such a small device could be a proper camera. They were invited to go over to the table where Max had put on a small display with a couple of laptops. One contained greetings filmed earlier. The other was of stuff he filmed in the States and his aerial survey of Aidan's home set to a classical music soundtrack. Hannah had watched the first showing along with Aidan and Kristina who was disappointed that she had been out on the school run when Max had filmed it. She said it would have been nice to get the whole family in it. Max agreed to do something towards the end of the party.

As Aidan and Kristina looked at their repaired roof Max leaned over to Hannah and whispered. `Don't worry, your performance has been saved for the director's cut.'

She blushed and said, `You said you'd run out of film before then.'

`Maybe I did, or maybe I didn't?' said Max enigmatically.

`Mum and Dad, Uncle Max is a pig' said Hannah sulkily.

`Hannah that's not nice' said Kristina.

`But true' said Aidan.

`Now I definitely won't let you have a go, it's for grown-ups only' said Max, hoping he'd given a plausible explanation for what caused her comment.

`I'm eighteen thank you very much and I don't want your stinky old helicopter anyway' pouted Hannah sounding all four years old. She walked off towards the crowd and the three of them watched her leave. In her cream-coloured shift dress and flat shoes she looked more stylish and grown-up than her contemporaries. Tito emerged from the group of guys and kissed her before picking up round the waist and spinning her around. The boy looked back nervously to Aidan. His relationship with Hannah had only been out in the open for a few months and Tito knew that as far as Aidan was concerned he was still on probation.

`She could be married soon' said Kristina wistfully.

`Don't say that' said Aidan. `We all got married young the first time, and that didn't work out too great, did it?' They were all lost their thoughts for a few moments before Kristina changed the subject.

`Anyway Max, I see you've got a lot of interest in your aerial photography idea.' She nodded at the pad and a small pile of business cards next to it.

`Yes quite a few are from boys who want me to build them one if their dad's will give them the money. But there are also some serious requests from adults. I didn't think there would be that many parents here' said Max.

`That's Kristina's fault' said Aidan, suggesting it had been a bone of contention between them. `When our trouble with the ARA started people we thought of as friends dropped us like flies ... bunch of scumbags. Not exactly Mr Clean themselves half of them' said Aidan bitterly.

`That's my point darling' said Kristina hugging his arm. `They came after Aidan from an investigation of someone else. That's how they work. People were scared that they might be next.'

`They were afraid you would grass them up?' said Max.

`That's why they kept clear. Would we have done anything different?' said Kristina.

`I kept schtum in spite of what I know about many of these so-called respectable businessmen' said Aidan sourly.

`Now they want to say sorry and thank you for not making it difficult for them,' said Kristina brightly. `It's five years on and they have not been investigated and it looks like we will do okay in the Supreme Court.'

`I started to get calls from people who had gone to ground. It's Hannah's 18th birthday, isn't it? Can we pop over with a card it would be so nice to see you again' said Aidan in a smarmy voice.

`Maybe it's time to forgive even if you don't forget' said Max earning a smile from Kristina, glad have an ally.

`Well here comes someone who's been straight with us' said Aidan pointing at a man striding confidently across the lawn with an entourage of heavies behind him.

The man wore a cream coloured suit and Ray Ban aviator sunglasses. He had that `please don't notice me' false modesty that celebrities affected when paparazzi were around. Although tall he was physically dwarfed by the two man mountain minders who trailed in his wake, but his air of authority made it clear who was in charge.

`Max let me introduce you to Ludovic Luchenko, sponsor of Hannah's polo team and Tito's uncle. He'll be interested in your box of tricks' said Aidan.

Max extended his hand and Luchenko paused to remove his sun glasses before accepting it. In these few moments Max had the opportunity to study him more carefully. Close up Max could see that he was older than he first thought. He now put Luchenko in his mid-fifties. His still blond hair was starting to grey at his temples and sideburns. There were lines on his forehead and around his eyes but Max thought he detected a hint of subtle plastic surgery around his mouth and jaw. The dimple in Luchenko's chin made Max recall an actor from an old gladiator film Max had seen as a kid, but also from something more recent. In the States he had seen a film about Russian gangsters, Viggo someone was the lead and he had a dimple in his chin. Has this man copied that to look more like that caricature? His thoughts were interrupted by the pressure of Luchenko's firm handshake and Max focused on the clear grey eyes appraising him. They conveyed a coldness that the man's smile could not thaw. The phrase cruelly attractive could have been invented for him.

Luchenko held Max's gaze before taking Kristina's hands and kissing her on the cheeks formally while muttering something in Russian that she understood. Max noticed Kristina stiffened slightly at Luchenko's embrace.

`Max is my oldest friend' said Aidan.

`Pleased to meet you Max. Please call me Lucky, everyone does.' Lucky's English was heavily accented but

Max suspected some of that was put on to conform to some stereotype. He also recognised Lucky's crocodile smile from many poker games in which he'd almost lost an arm and a leg.

The waiter appeared with a tray of drinks and Max notice the red warning light winking on his chest camera. `I'll take that from you now it needs charging.' He hoped that the one already plugged into a socket on the kitchen table was ready.

`We are under surveillance?' said Lucky. The two minders cast heads around in Pavlovian reaction to the word.

`Relax Lucky, only friendly surveillance from Max here. He's just back from the States with the latest innovations in aerial photography' said Aidan providing a natural segue for Max to point to his laptops and their display.

Lucky stared with interest at the aerial photographs of Aidan's house. `You fly helicopter in here Max? CAA tell me I can't have one. It's true, isn't it?' He looked at one of his minders for confirmation.

`Is true, not even big bribe can change minds' said one of the minders matter-of-factly.

`Not a real helicopter one of these' said Max pointing to the collage of footage on his other laptop. `These machines are home made at the moment but soon there will be a business, to film where the CAA won't let you fly and cheaper too' Max added hoping he was not overselling his pitch. The two minders watched with professional interest as the collage went to a group of free runners leaping across rooftops and a paintball fight filmed from tree top level. Max could only guess what their Russian comments were.

`Very interesting Max. You make these helicopters and cameras?'

`I buy the cameras Lucky.'

`Show me what is on this one?' Said Lucky.

Max put the memory card from the camera he retrieved from the waiter into a slot in his own PC. Soon they were watching his footage of the crown from a first person perspective. Various people were coming up and raising their glasses to the lens to toast Hannah. `After a while people forget the camera is there Lucky'.

`How many cameras you got Max' said Lucky?

`Only three at the moment, I'm still building up the business and I'll invest in more when I get some income' said Max fearing that Lucky's interest would wane because he was a one-man band. But Lucky seemed to be making a decision.

`You a gambling man Max? I have proposition for you.'

`I used to be' said Max defensively.

`I give you a loan to get more cameras. You come to polo team training session, film girls wearing cameras on horses. You speak to the trainer, convince her they are good idea. If she agree then you film rest of the matches for free and we forget about the money. The season is nearly over anyway.'

`What if the trainer does not like my idea?' said Max.

`Then you owe me a favour until you pay me back the money. Is good bet no?' The crocodile smile was back on Lucky's face and Max could already feel his arm hurting but he had no option. If dealing with Lucky gave him the investment to take on more work and pay off his bookies bill then it was a risk worth taking.

`Okay, you have a deal Lucky' said Max, shaking his hand.

`How much you need Max?'

Max tried to stay calm as Lucky told one of the minders to give him two grand from a huge wad in his jacket pocket.

`Now I speak to some people, come to training session next Thursday. Hannah knows where it will be.' With that Lucky turned and headed towards the crowd with the two minders in his wake.

Aidan reappeared and Max realised he had not seen him go. `Thought I'd give you some privacy to clinch the deal. How did it go with Lucky?'

`Fine thanks he's just subbed me two grand to do some filming of the polo team.'

`That's great Max.'

`I suppose so but I feel like I just got myself a business partner for life.'

Aidan looked at his friend's worried face and was sorry that he dragged him into the whirlpool that was Lucky Luchenko.

`Anderson said your place was much nicer than the photographs he took and he was right.'

Aidan turned around was surprised to see Stuart Logan standing there. `What are you doing here? I told you never to come here' Aidan whispered as he drew Stuart to one side.

`Relax Aidan I'm telling people I'm one of your investors if they ask. I suppose that's true in one sense. I've come to reassure you and Kristina, that we are doing everything possible to bring matters to a speedy conclusion.'

`But you could have done that on the phone' said Aidan.

`You have been very elusive Aidan. You don't answer my calls and you have missed our last three debriefs.'

`Isn't it obvious why I've not been in contact? I've not made any progress, there is nothing to tell.'

`Aidan this investigation is about more than just your efforts. Occasionally we may have things to tell you, things that will help you to know what to look for. We could make your job easier.'

`Such as?' said Aidan sceptically.

`Our friend with the scar thinks the target is preparing to shift all his business to the UK. It seems that now he has taxed all the oligarchs, Putin is putting the squeeze on the criminals. Not to put them out of business though, just to make sure he gets his share.'

`Perhaps you should send him your CV for your next job Mr Logan. You have a lot of experience to offer' said Aidan.

`Okay I suppose I deserved that one' Logan conceded. ` Luchenko will need fronts for his illegal activities, businesses that can serve a dual purpose. You could ask him if he's looking for premises for anything because you have a number of potential commercial refurbishments in mind but you would like to secure a tenant before committing to them.'

Aidan thought for a moment. It was a good opening. A legitimate way to engage with Lucky about his business interests. `Okay Stuart I hear what you say. What sort of premises should I be looking to let?'

`Cash businesses would be good. Restaurants, bars, hire companies. Places with high volumes of low value anonymous transactions. Sales where it is difficult to trace the buyers. These are the places he will try to launder his dirty money.'

`Okay I'll have a conversation with him next week. As it happens I do have a couple of mothballed projects that would make the interest plausible.'

`Just don't count on him being able to come through on them Aidan. Remember the outcome we are all working towards.'

`Okay are we done now' said Aidan keen to get Stuart Logan out of his home.

`Almost. I wanted to observe the man in the flesh. And this might be the only opportunity before a court appearance'

`What you think of him then?' asked Aidan.

`The thing that gets me about his type is their arrogance. They don't really hide who they are or what they do. They challenge you to prove it and for the most part they get away with it; but not this time.'

Aidan looked at the way Logan was standing. The way he never took his eyes off Luchenko all the time he spoke. He saw a man obsessed with catching his big fish before they called time on his outfit. `Have you read Moby Dick, Mr Logan? Captain Ahab went after a big fish and look what happened to him.'

`I won't make that mistake' said Stuart Logan finally breaking his stare. `I'll just find your wife and pay my respects and then I'll leave you to enjoy your party.'

He found Kristina in the kitchen alone. She looked surprised to see him and then turned her head quickly. He noticed her red eyes. Stuart looked around to make sure they were not overheard then he said softly. `I know this is all a big strain on you, but we're doing everything we can to end this quickly. You will have your life is back soon I promise.'

Kristina turned to face him. She could see the honesty in his eyes. `Make it soon Mr Logan, that man unsettles me.'

`What has Luchenko done Kristina?' said Stuart unable to control his genuine feeling of sympathy for her.

`Nothing I haven't seen before. He's like the Russian men I thought I left behind in Estonia'.

Stuart knew from Stanton's files that Kristina had fallen pregnant and had been abandoned by a married Russian man during her youth back in Tallinn. `You know, you can talk to me, if you feel it's just too much to share with Aidan.'

`Thank you, Mr Logan but we will cope. We have done since this all started.'

Stuart did not think he would ever feel sympathy for one of the criminals he prosecuted. But he did now. `Mrs Wheelan you have a beautiful daughter go and enjoy her birthday. I will see myself out.'

Kristina could see Logan was a decent man but she was not ready to confide to him or anyone else about her recent experience. Lucky Luchenko had all but sexually assaulted her in her own kitchen. She had seen it coming and had deluded herself and Aidan that she could control the man. But the truth was that men like Lucky always took what they wanted no matter what other people thought. He had come into the kitchen all smiles as then he dismissed his minders when he saw she was on her own. He started complimenting her about the garden and asked who did it for her. Kristina was proud of her green fingers, but she knew if she said it was all her work it would result in an invitation to do his garden, which meant being in his company more often. So she lied and said she had a man who did most of it and that she would give him his details. That settled, Lucky did not mince his words. She not been spoken to like that in so many years.

`You know the women I could have? What they would do for me if I just asked? But it is you that you my balls ache for Kristina. You know this. I could give you everything you deserve.'

Before she could answer Lucky had her trapped against the counter top his hands on her hips holding her thighs against his obvious erection.

`Please don't' she said, turning from him but not making any attempt to push him away in spite of her revulsion. She knew she had to keep him interested in her if she was going to get her revenge.

`You know you want it' Lucky said pushing his hand crudely between her thighs.

`Stop Lucky, not here in my own home, please' she pleaded.

`Then you will come to me Kristina and soon' he demanded. It was only the sound of someone coming into the kitchen that caused Lucky to release Kristina. Suddenly he was all smiles again, greeting the woman who was a mutual acquaintance and carrying on a conversation with her as if nothing had happened.

Hannah appeared in the kitchen. `Dad's looking for you mum' she said. Kristina knew Aidan had sent Hannah on a mission as the minders were outside and there was no sign of Lucky.

`Hannah on Thursday we have a surprise for training. Tell Max where to come. Kristina don't forget to give me the name of your gardener and we must attend to that other matter soon.' Then Lucky was gone.

Kristina felt her pulse starting to return to normal. She did not know how she could keep Lucky off. His strength as he trapped her against the counter was terrifying. She knew now she would not have the strength to take him unawares except in one place. And if she did that would Aidan really be prepared to forgive her and understand it was just about revenge? The one consolation about the whole encounter was that Lucky had given her an opportunity. She would find him a gardener a man she could trust completely to help her do what had to be done. A man who would beg her for the opportunity to deal with Lucky himself.

The finale of the formal part of the party after which parents would be expected to take the hint and leave the young ones to it, was the presentation of Hannah's birthday cake and the fly past of Max's helicopter to capture the crowd rendition of happy birthday. A TV set was connected to Max's laptop and people were amazed to see themselves live on pictures taken from the sky. Someone asked how high up it could go and Max flew the drone higher until even Lucky's house was visible a mile away. They could even see the two minders loading a black bag into the boot of the Range Rover that had bought him to the party. Hannah was by now more than a little tipsy and insisted that now she was officially an adult Uncle Max had to let her have a go. `That's right isn't it?' she said whipping up the crowd.

`Give her a go, give her a go' they chanted and Max realised he would look like a dick if he refused. Reluctantly he put the strap of the remote control around her neck and held her hands from behind to guide the joysticks. She backed into him suggestively earning a few oohs from the crowd and a scowl from Tito who did not appreciate the drunk Hannah. `Are you sure you know what you're doing Hannah. You got to have a subtle touch' said Max.

`Honestly Uncle Max, I'm going to a conservatoire to play the violin. You can't do that without a subtle touch, can you?' said Hannah. She seemed to have control of the helicopter and started to move it left and right and people cheered. `This is easy' she boasted. Then suddenly a gust of wind took it and she lost control. It disappeared over the trees and the TV went blank. `I'm sorry Uncle Max. I didn't mean to break it. Dad you will pay for a new one, won't you?' she pleaded.

`Well, you're an adult now Hannah as you keep telling me and adults pay for their own mistakes. You remember that trip to America you were planning to go on' said Aidan unsympathetically.

`Oh dad! I wish I never touched the thing 'said Hannah ruefully.

`Well your wish looks like it's going to be granted' said Aidan.

They all looked up as the helicopter appeared over the trees and came to hover above Hannah's head.

`What did you do Uncle Max?' said Hannah, relieved that her holiday was still on track.

`It's got GPS built-in. If it loses the signal from the controller it flies back to where you told it home is' said Max.

`You knew it would come back but you let me think I'd broken it! You are a pig Uncle Max.' Hannah slapped him on the arm and then hugged him. `I'm sorry' she said contritely.

Max gave two pig like grunts in response and everybody laughed.

The following day Max reviewed the footage for an edited highlights film he was going to present Hannah as his own birthday present. He thought the day had been a success. He picked up some real business opportunities from people wanting him to build them helicopters and others wanting aerial films of their homes. One prospect was the owner of an estate agents who was talking about a retainer for Max to film all the prestige homes on his books. Max thought his luck had finally changed but then a few things brought clouds into his sunny day.

The first was that even though it was from far away and it only for a few seconds, he could not help thinking that there was something moving in the black bag the minders had loaded into the back of Lucky's Range Rover. Perhaps the fact that he was a Russian wide boy with minders that made Max see things that were not really there. He would not have suspected it of anyone else but the more times he watched the clip the more uneasy he got. He vowed to keep any business arrangement with Lucky at arm's length because it would not do him any good to know too much about his dealings.

The second thing that disturbed Max was his quip about friendly surveillance turned out to be a lie. The returning helicopter had caught a top-down view of the Victorian street light on the corner that led to Aidan's home. All traffic to the house would have to pass by it.

Max noticed a non-traditional feature that was missing from the other lamp posts. A small lid on the top of the light. He was sure it contained recording equipment allowing others to remotely monitor those who came and went from his friend's home.

The final thing was the most disturbing. The camera he had put on Aidan's kitchen table to recharge had switched itself on once the power was sufficient. Aidan thought the lens was broken because of the distorted image it recorded but then he realised that he was looking at what was reflected in the chrome surface of the kettle. It showed two people in a clinch and when they separated Max recognised it was Lucky and Kristina. He could not make out what they were saying that well but as Kristina moved away from Lucky and towards the camera he clearly heard her say `Stop Lucky, not here in my own home please'. He played it over and over to try and work out the meaning. Was Kristina trying to rebuff Lucky's unwanted advances, or were they already lovers and Lucky had just chanced his arm for the thrill of trying it on with Kristina in her own home with her husband only yards away?

Max sighed. His friend was still under some sort of investigation and he had just committed to work for an active gangster who might be screwing his wife. It looked like his luck hadn't changed at all.

7

It had been good to see Max at the party and it was nice to think he would be part of Aidan's life once more. They had been inseparable as kids and even as teenagers Aidan and Max saw a lot of each other, often going on double dates and arguing whose turn it was to take the ugly one. It was on one of those double dates that they that they met the girls they would marry. In Aidan's case he and Andria soon discovered they were incompatible. The horizontal time had been fine and Andria had proved to be an enthusiastic and adventurous lover. What 20-year-old man wouldn't want to marry that? Unfortunately her airs and graces which had been amusing to begin with became a source of annoyance to Aidan as Andria grew more patronising. They soured the couple's relationships with Max and Siobhan who had gone from being best man and maid of honor at their wedding to acquaintances with whom a visit became a clock watching exercise after an hour. When he and Andria divorced it had cost Aidan everything but the shirt on his back and he swore that he would not get caught like that again. That was until he met Kristina.

Aidan knew what was bothering him. He had been so pleased that Max had hit it off with Lucky and he had prospects of earning some real money to get himself out from under the heel of the bookie Lester Connolly. He knew Max would not ask him for money and in any case until the ARA had been put to bed he was not exactly flush with cash himself. In contrast his own efforts to get information out of Lucky Luchenko in the three months since he met with Stuart Logan and the MI5 man had been unremarkable. It also peeved him that Lucky was making little effort to hide his attraction to Kristina. Now with Max involved as well it looked like his whole family and friends were falling into the clutches of a Russian gangster.

He and Kristina had discussed Lucky's interest in her when it first became apparent. Aidan had been keen to break off the deal with Logan as Kristina was at risk but she said she could handle it and it would make it easier to get evidence on Lucky. She seemed even more determined to nail Lucky than he was. But something had happened at the party, something Kristina was hiding from him. Aidan wondered about taking Max into his confidence about Lucky but Max was such a loose cannon, he would probably put them all at risk.

Aidan's glum mood was not improved by a call he received from a letting agent, telling him that a tenant had been in touch about a broken boiler. Aidan had dispensed with the property management services offered by the agents a while ago and it seemed a good economy measure. But now he had to get all the way to the Midlands to fix the problem or pay the agency's extortionate rate for a one-off job. So he had to find a builder he could trust who operated it in the Midlands. After a couple of fruitless enquiries among his contacts Aidan chanced upon the call which would change the whole outlook of the day and probably the rest of his life.

`Tommy Boyle, its Aidan Wheelan. How's life been treating you?'

`Aidan Whelan long time no speak. I read about your trouble with the taxman ...ouch.'

`Yes is not great, but it's over now. Listen, I need a favour. You still operate out Bromsgrove Way?'

`We do, got a refurb job not far from there at the moment as it happens' said Tommy.

`Don't suppose one of your guys would like to earn a bit of overtime cash in hand by fixing a boiler for me? A hundred quid in their hands plus parts if they don't stiff me. `

`Make it one-fifty and you're on Aidan.'

`Bloody hell Tommy I thought all the pirates were in Somalia these days! Okay then.'

`Give me the address and I'll get my bloke to look into it this evening.'

Aidan gave him the details. `Thanks Tommy I'm up your way on Monday. Okay if we settle up then?'

`No problem Aidan. Oh before you go, I just remembered something I wanted to tell you. Saw your daughter in the paper a couple weeks ago, some sports team. They were all lookers. I don't envy you, I've got boys myself.'

`You don't know the half of it Tommy. It was her polo team.'

`That's right, some Russian bloke with them.'

`Ludovic Luchenko, `Lucky Luchenko' most people call him' said Aidan.

`Anyway, whatever his name is, he owns a hotel out this way except he don't seem to want no customers.'

`What you mean Tommy?'

`We got an emergency call out to fix a leak in the kitchen of this place right. My bloke gets there and there's half a dozen taxis outside. It's about a mile and a half from main roads down this gravel track. So he goes inside and the place is empty. Just a few people who don't seem to be like proper hotel staff. Anyway my bloke fixes the leak and asks when they are going to open because it seemed a nice place to take his missus.' Aidan knew what was coming, but he tried to keep his voice normal as he made grunts to keep the story going. `They could not give him an opening date could they? Said they was still trying to get the staff. So my mate tries to put a word in for his daughter; she's been working for Burger King but its three year since she qualified from catering college. But the hotel manager is lukewarm which is strange if they need staff isn't it?'

`It's a mystery mate but what has this got to do with Luchenko?' said Aidan keen for Tommy to get to the point.

`I'm coming to that. My mate leaves and finds out later he's left an adjustable spanner there and thinks no problem I'll go round and collect it after my last job. When he gets back there the kitchen lights are off and the taxis are still standing empty. It's seven o'clock on a Friday night and people are going out into town.'

`It does sound as unusual' said Aidan casually, hoping that he was succeeding in discouraging Tommy while at the same time trying to keep his heart from beating faster.

`Anyway, my man is in the kitchen now and finds his spanner. No lights on in reception but there is someone in the back office on the phone taking bookings.'

`So what it's a hotel' said Aidan just managing to stop himself from telling Tommy to get to the fucking point.

`Yes but they were booking in the past, from six months ago. Who did we have staying with us in February Mr Luchenko said the guy in the hotel. It's got to be the same man, I mean it's not a common name.'

`I don't know Tommy it could be their Smith' said Aidan trying to sound casual and feeling anything but. `What is the name of this place?'

`It's the St Peter's House Hotel. It's near Ashby de la Zouch.'

Aidan could not stop a little chuckle, St Peter's House. Luchenko came from St Petersburg and in Aidan's mind Ashby de la Zouch had always sounded like the name of an English gentleman spy from the 1930s. `Well nice story Tommy. I got to go. When I see Mr Luchenko next I'll ask about the hotel, see if we can get your mate's girl in. Best not to say anything to anyone else yet. Maybe he wants to keep the place hush-hush. These rich Russians made a lot of enemies when they made their money.'

`I suppose you're right, Aidan. Anyway we'll settle next week when we meet' said Tommy glad he had secured the favour he was angling for. After all one good turn deserves another.

Aidan pondered for a few moments before calling Stuart Logan. This was break he had been praying for and with no way for Lucky to link it to him once it all came out. That had been his main concern about approaching Lucky directly as Logan has suggested at the party. Stuart answered and Aidan did not give his name as they had agreed. `Thought you might be interested to hear our friend is running a ghost hotel in the Midlands.'

`That's interesting, tell me more' said Stuart. Aidan gave him the details from his earlier call, including how he found out. `Nothing for weeks and then you get this. Must be some truth in that saying about the luck of the Irish.

`Something like that. It had to turn sometime. Listen you will find his books in good order. There will be transactions showing payments from foreign travel companies for rooms booked by his bogus guests. There'll be receipts for taxi fares and payments to caterers and cleaners. But there is one type of bill he can't forge' said Aidan.

`What's that?' said Stuart making a mental note to check if a hotel was among the assets they had seized from Aidan.

`He can't forge his energy bills. Get the meter readers to check the gas and electricity use. With luck they will have forgotten to light and heat the place as if it was occupied.'

`Very good' said Stuart. `Would you like a job with the good guys when this is over?'

`With what you pay in tax, no thanks. Listen Logan when this pans out I want out of all this quickly. We know he's a dangerous man. I want my family safe long before his he suspects anything.

`Of course, you have my word we will keep them out of harm's way. I'll be in touch Aidan. Good work.'

Despite initially being happy to use Aidan Wheelan to get his hands on a major criminal, Stuart Logan became more concerned during the course of a deeper briefing from Harry Stanton when he discovered the full extent of Lucky Luchenko's criminal enterprises. The drugs business in this country had proved too lucrative for Luchenko to ignore when other Russian criminal gangs started up distribution in the UK. Luchenko could see that his organisation would be left behind if he didn't take a stake in it as well. Stuart had not told Aidan about this thinking that he would be safer if he just thought that Luchenko was a money-launderer and arms dealer. Now he realised how ridiculous that sounded. He phoned Harry Stanton. `We have a lead on our friend, a ghost hotel and taxi business. Certainly money-laundering but who knows what else.'

`That's good news Stuart. I think it time to bring this operation over to our place. We can give a couple of your trusted people special passes and keep tabs while they follow the money trail.' Stuart did not like it but he realised that he had no option as the Agency was haemorrhaging staff as the deadline to transfer them to SOCA loomed.

`Okay Harry, you make the arrangements but this is still our investigation remember' said Stuart.

`Don't worry we won't spoil your finale' said Harry. In spite of his words Stuart did not feel reassured.

8

Stewart arrived at his office at 8 AM as usual. He liked that first hour of the working day when he could think and make real progress in what he was employed to do, rather than get involved in firefighting and wondering who was going to jump ship today. The loyalty bonus they had offered staff as an inducement to stay to the bitter end had only tempted the deadwood. People Stuart would sooner be rid of. The better people were getting out of Dodge quickly. One ray of hope that kept him going as he wrestled to hand over a going concern to SOCA was that they'd had their first real break in their investigation of Lucky Luchenko. Aidan Wheelan's chance discovery of the ghost hotel would need more work to prove the laundered funds went to Luchenko in the end, but it was a solid start. The trail would uncover a whole raft of bogus companies and businesses that formed his network. Stuart had agreed with Harry Stanton's suggestion that the investigation should now be based on MI5 premises and only trusted staff should be involved. Stuart has seconded two of his people part-time to help with the financial analysis. He was impressed with the way they were suitably shaken by Harry Stanton's insistence that they signed the Official Secrets Act again. They were shocked and impressed when Harry told that they'd all been positively vetted before they'd been offered the job. When he went on to reveal personal information about each of them only their nearest and dearest were privy to Stuart's people were confident of their new colleagues abilities to investigate.

Stuart felt sure that there would be no leaks from their side of the investigation, but when he saw the unexpected visitor waiting in his office that morning, alarm bells started ringing.

`Good morning, Director I wanted a catch you before the events of the day got ahead of both of us' said Giles Pendry rising from the visitor's chair to shake Stuart by the hand.

`How did you get in here? I mean good morning' said Stuart remembering his manners. He cast his eye around his desk for once grateful for his clear desk paranoia.

There was nothing on display that could interest the casual snooper.

`Forgive me Stuart. My Whitehall past got me through the reception desk and I thought it might be better to wait in here until you arrive. I'm afraid tongues do wag' said Pendry, sounding not entirely displeased that his profile as a government adviser had made him recognisable as the deliverer of several news sound bites.

`I did not expect to see you here... again' said Stuart letting the man know his displeasure. He had said his piece the last time and there was nothing to be gained by soft-pedalling now.

`Indeed so, neither did I, but it seems that our paths are set to cross again Stuart.'

`Why is that?' said Stuart his radar now on full alert.

Pendry was not going to be rushed. `I understand you took my advice and went over to see our friends at SOCA.'

`I'm sure you know how well that went Giles' said Stuart mocking Pendry's attempt at helpfulness. He now suspected that Pendry had briefed the SOCA man to give him the bum's rush.

`Yes I did hear something. That was a disappointment' said Pendry diplomatically. `I know you're a man of action Stuart. `Not likely to sit on your hands waiting for the end. Been working on anything interesting recently? Any new lines of enquiry?'

`I'm spending all my time firefighting here trying to shore up our sinking ship, as I believe you put it Giles. Where could I get the time for new initiatives' said Stuart?

`Quite so Stuart, quite so. It would be wrong for you to be distracted from important work by others who may not have the best interests of government at heart.' The lure hung from Pendry's line and he watched Stuart wrestle with whether to bite.

`We are not affiliated with the Labour Party I can reassure you' Stuart joked.

Pendry changed tack. `The peace dividend of the last decade has not created prosperity for everyone. The fall of the Berlin Wall and the Good Friday Agreement has left some parts of government facing the new millennium uncertain of their role and purpose.' Stuart could see the lecturing style that had carried Pendry through several Whitehall campaigns. He continued, `There are agencies and I'm sure we both know who they are who have been left seeking a new mission, unclear where they should be focusing their attention. The old Cold War warriors just won't leave things alone. They still fear Reds under every bed.' Stuart felt his stomach lurch. How had Pendry got a whiff of his agreement with Harry Stanton? Where had the leak come from? `Fortunately not everyone in these dinosaur organizations are so backward looking. Some can see the big picture' Pendry added thus answering Stuart's silent question.

`What big picture is that Mr Pendry?' said Stewart admitting to nothing.

`A financial crisis is coming Stuart. Every country is going to be swept up in it. People will be sitting on their money and not lending.'

` I take it at some point you will explain what this has to do with me?' said Stuart tiring of Pendry's lecture.

`We can't afford to scare foreign capital away, especially at this time' said Pendry finally come to the point.

`We're not looking at the oligarchs and you know that' said Stuart. `Besides I thought all their business was legitimate now. At least what they do over here.'

`Indeed they are, the more famous names everyone knows about. But that's not the case with the newer arrivals. If we were to go after these people for their financial wrong doing it might spook the rest of them. Herd mentality and all that.'

`So you're telling me this agency should not go after the crooks we were set up to catch because it might scare off the bigger crooks the government is relying on to bail them out of a financial crisis' said Stuart

`Well I would not put it like that Stuart' said Pendry offended at both the bluntness and accuracy of Stuart's statement

`Off course you wouldn't Giles. But tell me where would they go with their laundry bags full of dirty cash? If America is going to be the epicenter of this crisis as everyone says it is they are not going to move there. They won't want to go back to Russia and the Chinese government is worse than the one they escaped from. The truth is that going to stay here and weather the storm. If one or two of the smaller fish get caught as you clean up your act then the others will be relieved that no one is looking too deeply into their affairs.'

`I had hoped you would have been more corporative as I took you into my confidence Stuart' said Pendry sounding disappointed.

`You confided nothing in me and you know it. You're here because you got wind that one of the patrons of a charity dear to the heart of the PM's wife is not as clean as you would want him to be. You are hoping to stop any potential embarrassment of an investigation which brought his activities to light. You should be so Lucky.' Stewart added the name obliquely so they were both sure who they were talking about.

`Pendry stood up to leave. `I hope you enjoyed your career in Government Stuart. Career prospects for martyrs are not that good.'

`Giles someone made a judgement on him and someone else signed off that he was kind of person who you could deal with in spite of what was suspected, but not proven at that time. It's that person, you should be turning the thumbscrews on'. Stuart looked at the shocked expression on Pendry's face and realised why he couldn't do it. Because the person who had made the critical error of judgement was Pendry's himself.

Stuart waited until he saw Giles Pendry exit the building. The Jaguar pulled out of the disabled parking bay and Pendry got into the back. Stuart knew what its next destination was. Would the PM really risk meddling in a criminal investigation, to prevent the political embarrassment of having one of his wife's major charitable contributors exposed as a crook or worse? Stuart could seek Pendry advising that the situation was too unstable for the PM to get involved in. He'd advise him to quietly sever links with Luchenko. Number 10 would not meddle as long as he did not play up the personal connection during their investigation. Stuart could even see the Pendry spinning his line back to the PM. `It would be good for the big fish to see the little one's caught now and again. Remind them that they were not above the law'.

Stuart picked up the phone and called Harry Stanton. Before Harry could answer Stuart said he'd had a visit from a mutual acquaintance. `You have a leak over there.'

There were a couple of seconds pause, while the man on the other end pondered. `Thank you for the information. I think we will have to proceed with Moscow rules from now on. I will explain when I see you. Give me two hours.'

Stuart looked at the handset buzzing with the disconnected tone. Moscow rules, Stanton was too much. Was all this cloak and dagger stuff really necessary? He could not deny that the excitement of it was making his heart beat a little faster and even the prospect of a morning full of annual appraisals could not dampen it.

9

Max pulled into the car park at the address Hannah had given him, a tennis club in Kingston upon Thames. He found a spot next to a couple of similar vehicles, grateful that he did not have to leave his battered old Transit amongst vehicles that had all come from this century. The complex was busy with the majority of the outdoor courts occupied as matches and coaching sessions took place under floodlights. `Hello Uncle Max' came a voice from a white BMW convertible which had pulled up behind him. `I'm sorry, do I know you?' said Max to the stunning looking Chinese girl. Giggling came from inside the car and then a head loomed over from the driver's seat. Her hair was in sensible blonde plats and she would have looked fourteen were it not for the make-up which gave the impression of a twenty-four year-old trying to look fourteen. Max felt uncomfortable about the unsavoury images of Hannah that sped across his mind.

`They let us use these courts' said Hannah pointing to her left. Her car headed in that direction and Max reversed his van and followed them rather than lug all his equipment over. The girls in the back of the car pouted and blew kisses at him in the most distracting way. He had to brake sharply to avoid hitting a car that had backed out without looking. He could hear giggling coming from the car at the distraction their antics had caused. This is not going to be as easy as I thought Max cautioned himself as the girls got out. Two of them had street clothes on but Hannah and the driver already wearing what he assumed was the appropriate polo uniform, figure hugging white jodhpurs, brown riding boots with some sort of knee protectors and white polo shirts. The tight outfits were eye-catching and drew wolf whistles from a group of boys standing with the rest of the team. Everyone was young and healthy and in spite of the boys attempts to look cool in their skateboarder outfits of hoodies and baggy jeans the good manners of everyone there stood out as soon as they spoke. A crowd of youths like this on the corner of where Max was living would be menacing. But this lot were just having a good time. Hugs and exaggerated Hollywood air kisses were exchanged among the group and Max wished he was twenty years younger so he did not feel so out of place.

`This is my Uncle Max. He's here to film us' Hannah announced to the crowd provoking jeers and wolf whistles from the boys. ` I asked to film you and you said no Katie' one of the boys joked.

`It's not that sort of filming you pervert', said the pretty Chinese girl back at him.

`Mr Luchenko thought it might help to have some in play video of the team for coaching points. I've got body cameras for the girls to wear' Max explained.

`It is that sort of video' said the said the same boy and the laughter started again.

`You can go home, if you're not going to behave' said Hannah, adopting a school mistress tone. `We don't need supporters for a training session.'

`But we're more than supporters, we're cheerleaders' said the black boy. `Show the man your moves guys'. Six of the guys got into a hasty formation and went through their boy band routine to whistles from the girls. When it was over he asked what Max thought.

`Well the running man and the robot were good but the kicking needs more work' said Max.

The spokesman's face formed a frown. `I told you' he said to the others.

`My Uncle Max is down with the kids' said Hannah taking his arm proudly. Another van pulled up next to

Max's and beeped. `Ah, here are the horses' said Hannah. Max could not see any horse boxes. A heavyset man got out of the driver's seat and a middle-aged lady emerged from the passenger side. A third person got out and Hannah shrieked and ran over to him. It was a moment before Max recognised it was Tito. They walked back to the group hand-in-hand. They were very much the alpha couple of the gathering and Max could sense that most of the group would have been happy to swap for one or other role.

`Hello Tito, you practising tonight?'

`No Max, it's the girl's team practice tonight. I've come along to make sure that this lot do not stare at Hannah's arse all night.' Tito earned himself a playful slap from Hannah and good-natured cheer from the other guys who obviously friends of his.

`This is Mrs Matthews our coach' said Hannah, introducing an intense looking middle-aged woman with a long face. Max was reminded of that saying that people grew to look like their dogs. He thought it applied to horses as well.

`Please to meet you' said Max, offering his hand. She often her hand in return and gave a look that suggested she was anything but pleased with the idea of meeting him.

`I hope this is not going to get in the way of my coaching?' She said, establishing quickly that she was in charge.

`Not that all' said Max giving her his most charming smile. `It is for afterwards to give you the evidence to help reinforce good technique and iron out problems. Enlightened coaches in many sports in America are using the body cameras.' Max's deferent tone and flattery hit the right note and Mrs Matthews was mollified.

`I suppose it won't hurt to give it a try' she conceded. `I just don't want Mr Luchenko wasting his money, that's all' she said.

`This does not replace the need for qualified coach and besides, I'm not charging him for this session' said Max.

`In that case we'd better get to work'. Mrs Matthews was relieved Max's role with the team was not a done deal. `Right let's go, same teams as last time' she said. The girls all now in uniform ran past Max and he saw them standing behind a line of folding bicycles. `We come here for shooting practice and bicycle polo is a good way to improve technique without getting the ponies out at night' said Mrs Matthews. Max nodded in understanding. `Right girls, are you ready?' The girls stood behind the folding bikes. Mrs Matthews blew her whistle and the girls went at the bikes. There was obviously a technique to opening a Brompton. Hannah made it look like she just flipped her wrist and had it assembled in about ten seconds. The slowest took almost a minute to chorus of disparaging remarks from the others.

Max fixed chest harnesses and action cameras to Hannah's team drawing unsolicited advice from the boys until Mrs Matthews's stern look, shut them up. He set them all recording and Mrs Matthews started the training session. The girls peddled the small wheeled bikes furiously, charging after the fluorescent ball, swinging their mallets to shoot or hook the attacking player. It was a full-blooded competition with thrills and spills. High fives for goals and harsh words and cold looks for mistakes. There was also something vaguely erotic about these young woman straining in exercise. The way their faces were excited and flushed as if they were in a heavy bout of lovemaking. The occasional sighs and shrieks also added a soundtrack. Max looked at the rapt attention the boys were paying to their actions. It had little to do with their appreciation of the sport. Max nudged the heavyset Russian in the shoulder. `I wonder what they are really fans off?' said Max pointing to the boys.

The Russian looked at the boys, and then back at the girls. `Makes you want to fuck them all one after the other' he said giving voice to his thoughts.

During a break Max swapped cameras onto the girls who had not had a go yet and he mounted two more static cameras on the chain link fence. While everyone else was concentrating on the action he went back to his van and launched his drone with the camera underneath. He'd been filming a bird's eye view of the session for about ten minutes before one of the boys noticed. After that he had a crowd around him obscuring his view of the monitor and begging him to have a go at flying. They were only placated by his promise to film their band antics from the air at the end if they gave him some peace. When the training was over, Max collected the cameras and pre-viewed some of the footage captured on the SD cards by plugging them into his laptop. Everyone crowded around the back of his van to get a proper look at the screen without the glare of the floodlights. Mrs Matthews conceded the quality of the footage was good and it did give her a unique teaching perspective. Max showed her some of the bird's eye view footage where she could study passing and team play and she was convinced.

`So you won't object if I suggest to Mr Luchenko that we use the cameras for a match' said Max, knowing her support was make or break if he was to earn something from all this effort.

`Of course I won't. What enlightened coach wouldn't want this information' she said smiling.

It was almost 11 o'clock by the time they had watched the boy band footage twice. It was only Max's promise to put it on the web tomorrow that made them leave. He had gained instant hero status. Every one of the boys asked

him how much it would cost him to build them one of those helicopters and Max came up with a price that gave himself a healthy margin. Even so none of them batted an eyelid at it and one even said for that money he wouldn't even need to ask his mum to work on his dad. As he packed his stuff away Max felt heartened that his idea was not just a pipe dream and that he could actually earn a living from this and get himself out of the hole he had dug six years ago. Preoccupied with thoughts on how it was going to manage his business he did not hear the big Russian come up to him quietly from behind. His footsteps were silent as if he practised approaching people unnoticed. `I am
Timor', he said holding out his hand.

`Hello Timor' said Max feeling slightly strange having spent the last two hours with the nameless heavy. `Do you work for Mr Luchenko as well?'

`Yes, import-export business' said Timor offering no further explanation. `You buy this or you make this?' he said pointing to the parts of the helicopter.

`Make it but soon there will be kits, probably from China. That's where all these parts came from' said Max

`How much for make one to carry one kilogramme?' asked Timor.

Max doing mental calculations of power and weight. `Maybe even eight rotors instead of six. Would cost about five thousand American.'

`You can make underneath like this?' Timor asked making claw like motions between thumb and fingers.

`It's possible' said Max his mind whirling with all sorts of applications.

`Good, we speak again' said Timor. He turned to leave and then turned back toward Max with a smile on his face girls. 'Those girls hey? Bet like me you want to fuck them all?'

Max gave him a weak smile and made a mental note to tell Hannah never to accept a lift from Timor.

10

Max pulled up at the gatehouse and recognised the same security guard from his visit a couple of weeks before. `Didn't think that heap would make it back here' said the guard, casting an eye over Max's van. `You back at the Wheelan place then?' Either the guard had a good memory or they did keep a record of where every visitor went since the robbery Aidan had told him about. `Probably later, but I'm here for the match. Which way is the polo field? 'Said Max.

`Take the third on the left, it's signposted. I didn't have you pegged as a fan of the sport of kings.'

`I'm just here to film it. Will there be much of a crowd?' said Max.

`It's more popular than you'd think. They play County Polo, shorter matches so they need fewer horses. The equivalent of five aside football if you like.'

`What you mean fewer horses?'

`Each player needs at least two and they change them after each chukka, about seven minutes play so they don't get knackered. The match is usually about four chukkas so it's over pretty quickly. You'll probably see two or three games today.'

`I see, I had no idea' said Max, wishing he'd prepared a bit more. `So is it just rich toffs today then?'

`You'd be surprised. Like I said you can get away with two ponies so some people own them and others rent them from a syndicate.

`Like a hire car?'

`More or less like that. There are a lot of newly rich people who want to get into the sport for the status and a lot of the young posho's prefer the more open, youthful atmosphere of the County Game. You get a different crowd here than say at Hurlingham.'

Max looked properly at the security guard for the first time. He was only in his mid-20s and obviously took an interest in his job and the people he met. `Why do you do this job?' Max asked.

`It's the peace and quiet I like. I'm studying with the Open University for a psychology degree.'

`So this is just ethnographic research then?' said Max.

The security guard smiled back. He recognised the intelligence Max usually kept hidden. `Sort of. I'd better get back to it, here come more spectators.'

Max looked in his mirror as a Saab estate pulled up to the barrier. Its occupants a couple in their thirties wearing matching green waxed jackets and pastel cashmere jumpers. The man had a Paddington bear scarf and the woman had something round her neck that looked to Max's untrained eye as if it were a genuine Hermes. He noted the look of expectation on their faces as the barrier rose. It said `one day we'll live here.' Their car overtook Max's van which struggled with the hill and in the back two boys were pulling faces at him and giving him V-signs until their mother noticed and leaned back to slap them both on the back of their legs. `What have I bleedin' told you before' said their mother in an accent that was more Romford than Rodean. To add insult to their injury Max could not resist pointing his finger at them and mouthing a silent ha ha as he overtook them where the queue diverged for spectators and staff.

Max parked behind the beer tent which seemed to be doing a roaring trade selling Pimms by the bucket to those who were determined to enjoy the English country life experience. More conservative patrons sipped their gin and tonics and real ales with olde worlde names. Max stood for a minute taking it all in. England in the first decade of the new millennium was a much more cosmopolitan place than the Kentish Town of his youth where the Jamaicans and Pakistanis were the only foreigners. Here there was a good smattering of Middle Eastern types to go along with Chinese and Eastern Europeans. Of this last group the men were dressed expensively but conservatively in their country casuals wanting to fit in with the people they saw inside the pages of glossy magazines. But they seemed unable to restrain their wives and girlfriends who could not resist the opportunity to put on expensive but inappropriate dresses and all of their jewelry. Max looked at them remembering the old saying that money did not buy class. A voice behind him said `I don't fancy yours much'. He turned to see Aidan wearing a pair of cream-coloured chinos and a Ralph Lauren polo shirt with Ray Ban sunglasses hanging from a buttonhole. He shook Max's hand warmly.

`What do you think then mate?' said Aidan sweeping his hand across the crowd before him.

`It looks like the Irish are not the foreigners anymore' said Max. They both laughed.

`Here let me show you around' said Aidan. They passed the food marquee selling burgers and roast boar and then came across a small set of Portakabins. `Here's the temporary changing rooms and showers for the players. The new clubhouse should be finished by the end of the year' he said pointing to the foundations of building works across the field.

`This must have cost a fair bit Aidan?' said Max.

`It's not a pocket money sport but it's reasonable for us, about the cost of a couple of expensive golf club subscriptions and I hate that game. Besides Lucky Luchenko sponsors the team and people pay what they can afford. You've met Hannah's friend the Chinese girl?' said Aidan.

`Katie isn't she?' said Max.

`Yes, Katie's a girl you don't forget. Anyway her dad is a postman and her mum works in Marks and Sparks. There's no way they could afford it on what they earn. Lucky was even good to us last year when the ARA were counting every penny I spent. Hannah would have been heartbroken if she had to give up playing but Lucky helped by subbing me. I'll pay him back of course' said Aidan.

Max had wrestled with saying anything to Aidan about the secret footage of Lucky and Kristina he'd collected. He could see there would be consequences for the whole family if he said anything to Aidan that forced him to act. `What's in it for Lucky then? He does not seem the type to throw his money around. And I don't think he was born with a silver spoon in his mouth' said Max not wanting to dwell on his fears.

`No you're right. I don't think he made it all by the honest sweat of his brow either, but he's probably no worse than the oligarchs who came here couple of years before him. I think he does this to impress those guys. He's pretty shrewd' said Aidan.

`What you mean?' said Max.

`The other rich oligarchs brought football clubs, taking a working class sport, investing a lot of money in it and pricing it out of the hands of ordinary people. The oligarchs are despised by many football fans. In contrast Ludovic Luchenko has taken a posh sport and made polo more accessible to ordinary people. The old money likes him because he's made one of their privileged past times more acceptable in the modern age. The government likes it because his sponsorship of the team sends an aspirational message. The team is a charitable trust. I think he even gets some sort of Lottery grant. He also got planning permission for the clubhouse where every other planning applications for new building on the estate has been turned down for the last 20 years. He certainly got some influence.'

Max mulled it all over. Luchenko might be a dubious character, but it was obviously well-connected and not someone it would be sensible to fall out with.

The sound of cheering and applause interrupted his thoughts. `They've arrived' said Aidan pointing to the place where a fleet of Land Rovers were towing horse trailers. Two smart people carriers drew up and disgorged their occupants wearing team uniforms. Max recognised Hannah and Katie and some of the other girls from the training session. Their uniforms now sported tight fitting T-shirts in the red white and blue of the Russian flag. The other teams seemed to be dressed more traditionally.

`Those outfits are a bit skimpy' said Max.

`You mean sexy' said Aidan. It was the girls idea they designed themselves. They can all play of course but it's no handicap that they are all lookers as well. They get a fair bit of press coverage and the website gets a lot of hits every time new pictures go up.'

`Speaking of pictures I'd better get my gear ready for the girls. I was going to put up a couple of standing cameras as well. Where's the pitch.'

`You mean the field, you're standing on it' said Aidan.

`What, all this is the playing area?' said Max suddenly realising why they might need more than one horse for a match. It was about twice the width of a football pitch and two and a half times as long. His static cameras would be useless. Besides there were many spectators with video cameras to capture the ground level shots like you could see on TV. He was hoping that his view from the saddle with the chest cameras and the bird's eye view of the action from the helicopter would provide something new that would guarantee more business from Lucky and possibly an entree into other sports.

`I'll leave you to set up, see you later' said Aidan heading towards the players.

By the time Max returned with his kit all the horses had been removed from their boxes and were being saddled up by the players and their helpers. Max notice that the horse trailers all carried a discreet logo announcing Lucky enterprises as the sponsor. They were certainly more plush than a simple affairs that Max remembered from visits to county fairs in Ireland. He stood inside one and felt the warmth on his feet and looked down.

`The floor is heated. It's good for the horses. It's Mr Luchenko's own design.'

Max turned to see who it was who was. `Katie you're looking well.'

In response the girl arched her back subtly attracting Max's eyes to her chest as she had intended. `You remembered me Uncle Max?' she said in a voice that promised so much. `Hannah is over there with Tito' said Katie.

`He is on duty again' said Max. `To stop the boys looking at her bum' he added, reminding her of Tito's comments at the training session.

`Yes of course, but who's going to guard mine?' Katie said turning her back to him and pouting over her shoulder.

Katie was half his age but his body was not considering that. `Jesus, young girls. Why weren't they like this when I was your age? You'd better go before I do something I won't regret.'

`If you're sure Uncle Max' said Katie pleased that she had made him lose his cool. `Let me know if you change your mind.' She walked away with that exaggerated one foot in front of the other gate models used on the catwalk knowing that Max's eyes were following her all the way. The voice of reason finally cut into his thoughts. `You're supposed to be doing this job so you can pay off your debts get back with Siobhan. Dicking young girls is not the way to go about it'. The tannoy announced that the match would start in fifteen minutes and Max thought he'd better get his skates on and get girls harnessed up.

The match was a spirited affair. Perched on top of his van to get a better visibility of the helicopter, Max could

see the strategy of the game. Hannah played number three, the sort of midfield general launching attacks for Katie who was number four and an out and out striker. The tall West Indian girl at number two seemed to be the centre half and the other blonde girl at number one was a rush goalie. It was three all at half-time, or the end of the second chukka as he now knew it was called. Max was just about to bring the helicopter back when he noticed the crowd mounting a pitch invasion. Then he recognised it was something different; a tradition of getting spectators to stamp the divots back into the ground before play resumed for the second half. Armed with glasses of champagne and tubs of strawberries and cream the crowd milled about the field, which became a sort of huge garden party as people bumped into old friends and broke into conversation. Max thought it would make nice background footage for a voice-over to promote his aerial photography business so he decided to continue recording the scene. There must have been two hundred people strolling around the field, but in the middle of it he caught sight of Lucky Luchenko in conversation with some of the Russians he had noticed before. Every now and then Timor would lean over his shoulder and say something. Eventually the group split up and the Russians drifted over to speak to other men. It looked to Max like Lucky was conducting business here under cover of the half-time social niceties. This was confirmed when Lucky, who by this time, was glad handing it with another group of people, was summoned discreetly by Timor. The pair of them headed over to where Timor had come from and Max could see two of the Russians escorting an Indian looking guy away from the field. One of the Russians stood close behind the Indian giving him no choice but to follow his colleague. Max thought he could move the helicopter over to see where they were taking him, then he saw that the battery indicator was flashing red warning that he was dangerously low on power. Max just managed to steer the craft back towards him before the power cuts completely and the helicopter fell the last ten feet to the ground, narrowly missing a group of women who were in such animated conversation they did not even notice.

In the second half Max wanted to save some battery to see what was going on with the horse trailers which had all been parked neatly on the edge of the field. While the crowd's attention was focused on the match which was now drawn five all with only a couple of minutes to go, Max noticed a series of discrete comings and goings from the group of trailers. He would have thought nothing of it but for the fact that the men reappeared from the back of the horse boxes carrying non-descript bags. Sometimes a carrier bag or an ordinary shopping bag. Something that would not draw attention. It came to him that Lucky was using the cover of the polo match as an opportunity to distribute something. God knows what the packages were. It could be drugs, money and guns, whatever. It was perfect. The smell of horses would disguise the odour of anything hidden in the heater panel of the horse trailers. The matches provided an opportunity for exchanges to take place on private ground where the chances of observation were reduced and the spectators gave the perfect opportunity for the couriers to come and go without drawing attention to themselves. Some might come to every match and others only occasionally. Just like supporters of any other team.

A loud cheer and screams brought his attention back to the game and Max swung the helicopter back to cover the action at the other end of the field, where a rider from Hannah's team had scrambled out of a close scrum of horses. The girls sped towards the goal at his end of the field, pursued by an opponent who Max had recognised earlier as the best player on the field. The attacker was slowing down, trying to keep control of the path of the ball while swinging her mallet. This allowed her pursuer to close the gap between them to a couple of feet. Max could see the attacker was Hannah. Her brow frowned in concentration as she fought to keep herself on the line of the ball which bobbled quite badly on the churned turf. She miss hit and the ball skidded left. The other girl saw her chance and gave Hannah a shoulder charge although it was probably called something else in the game. Hannah was no match for the weight and momentum of the other girl so she pulled her horse up quickly and the other girl went charging past. The other riders were galloping up the field to join them, but it would be these two who would settled it. Hannah and the other girl turned almost at the same time, but Hannah got to the ball first and the other girl positioned herself to stop Hannah from turning right, which was a natural way to take a shot. The chasing pack were almost upon them and Max thought the moment was lost, but then Hannah did something extraordinary. She swung her mallet forward and did what Max could only describe as a backhand. The ball flew behind her and between the legs of the defending horse and into the goal. The players screamed and the crowd cheered and Max nearly fell out of the garden chair perched on the roof of his van. He managed to get the helicopter to hover over Hannah and her team mates who are holding their mallets up to the camera in triumph. He did not care what sport people followed they would love those scenes.

At the end of the day Max was packing up his things as Lucky approached with Timor at his shoulder. He was all smiles. `You win the bet with Mrs Matthews, she like you. Now it cost me money' he joked smiling.

`Lucky you took a chance on me and I am grateful. I'll do this match and the next one free of charge then we can talk about a price for any others.'

`Very good Max' said Lucky. Timor whispered in Lucky's ear. `You see everything you want to see today Max?'

Max did not know what Lucky was alluding to so he played a straight bat. `I took some film of the crowd at half-time. All that strawberries and cream and treading down the divots. Very traditional, good social occasion. I'm sure it will help the team to become more popular when we put the video on their website.'

Lucky thought for a moment. `Okay Max, good idea. You show me all the footage before you edit anything.'

Max knew it was not a request. `Sure, no problem. Just give me a couple of days to put it together.'

`How about tomorrow afternoon, it does not need to be fancy' Lucky insisted. `You can come to the house, Aidan too, we can have a drink to celebrate victory of the team. Yes?' Lucky and Timor turned to leave.

`Sure, that would be nice Lucky.' Max knew would be up most of the night editing the film and doctoring the time code to hide what he'd seen. He had to be subtle and leave some footage of Lucky in it otherwise he would become suspicious. If Lucky really suspected Max had something incriminating he was sure he would have instructed Timor to take the memory cards there and then. It had been a close call but Max could see Lucky was a careful man who did not leave much to chance. He could not afford to underestimate his new benefactor.

11

Max balanced his parcels in one arm as he fished his jacket pocket for the door keys. Despite his misgivings about working with Lucky and his worries about what Aidan was involved in, things had gone well for Max in the two weeks since the polo match. He had posted highlights of the match on YouTube and that proved popular, especially the closing scene with all the girls on horseback raising their mallets up in victory towards the hovering camera. The clip generated dozens of enquiries about how it had been shot and Max directed people to his website where he answered them and explained how he built and flew his helicopters. Aidan had looked at the site and said that Max had given away his trade secrets and the chance to make any money from it.

Max said that he had borrowed the ideas from other people in the first place and they were just all one big community anyway. `Well enjoy being a poor hippy' chided Aidan, but when Max showed him he had taken deposits on his first ten machines and the orders would keep Max busy for the next six months, Aidan had to concede that Max's way of doing business was both cheap and effective. He even offered Max rent-free use of shop premises he was about to refurbish so Max would have more room to work in than his tiny flat offered. It was on the doorstep of the shop where Max heard the voice behind him as he finally found the right key for the lock.

`I thought you'd be out looking for work to pay off your debts, rather than spending money Mr Quinn.'

Max turned to look at the pockmarked young man in his mid-twenties with black greasy hair. He wore a black leather three-quarter length coat and a stance that said wannabe gangster.

`I am working, not that it's any business of yours. Just deliver your message and piss off so I can get back to it' said Max.

The young man tried to shrug off the fact that Max had him rightly pegged as a messenger but it stung.

`Mr Connolly would like a word...now!' That voice had come from the other half of the double act who had been standing around the corner from the shop. He was an equally young man but he was built like a mountain. He must have been at least six foot four with a head and arms that sprouted out at right-angles from his over the developed body. His Adidas tracksuit had probably fitted him once but now it looked like he was testing props for a remake of the Hulk. His flat square face had a natural air of menace.

`Now that's what intimidation should look like' said Max to Blackcoat while pointing his thumb as his mate. `Let me put these things down first.' He put his parcels of helicopter parts on the counter of the old cafe and then locked up. The two men frog marched Max to the passenger seat of an old black BMW three series, then they set off from Shepherd's Bush to Lester Connolly's bookmakers in Kilburn.

Max looked behind him while they were stuck in traffic on the Harrow Road. He thought the big man had taken a back seat to guard over him. But he could see the man sat with his head in his hands.

`Headaches getting worse are they big fella?' said Max.

`What's it to you?' the man snarled.

`Too many 'roids will do that to you. You're trying to put on weight too quickly' said Max.

`Shut the fuck up!' said the man.

`See I fucking told you Finn. If it's obvious to him it's obvious to the police. I swear to God you's better not be carrying any of those pills now. We don't want you drawing attention to yourself.'

`You're not my mother Pat, just drive the fucking car' said Finn.

`What's this all about Pat?' asked Max. `I saw Mr Connolly, when I came back from America. It's all sorted.'

`There's been some developments Mr Quinn' said Patrick smugly and he would not be drawn to say any more for the rest of the journey. Lester Connolly's book makers on Kilburn High Road was where Max had his first real job which was also the start of his ill-fated affair with gambling. His mum had worked there as a cashier and on Saturday Max had a job sweeping up betting slips, emptying ashtrays and making the tea. The shop windows looked like they'd been dressed as a funeral parlour but inside the sober image changed. On Saturday the place was packed and an atmosphere of stale cigarettes and desperation hung in the air as men bet the remains of their week's pay. Those wives who had not been canny enough to tax their husbands pay the night before would have missed out on the meagre allowance they needed to keep their families clothed and fed. Once their men returned from a day in Connolly's and a night in The Black Lion there would be nothing left.

Max did not think deeply about the morality of being a bookmaker in those days. As a kid he was too addicted to the adrenaline of the big win. Old man Connolly had two daughters who their religious mother had forbidden from entering the betting shop. She was a horrendous woman and Max suspected that there was something going on between Mr Connolly and his mother but he didn't care as they both seemed happy with it. Connolly took Max under his wing and explained the workings of the betting business, as if he were passing on the knowledge to the son he would never have. That proved to be the beginning of Max's downfall. He finished university and just when the world seemed to be his oyster his girlfriend fell pregnant and Max needed to raise money quickly. The City was awash with money and in those days banking and gambling had become twin brothers. It was a case of the wrong man at the right time and Max persuaded Lester Connolly to stake him in betting on the stock market. Max explained all the bets on options and futures and more exotic financial products to Lester, returning the old man's favour for schooling him about dogs and horses. For a couple of years they all made good money and Max provided a good home for Siobhan and Annie, who returned to Ireland while Max worked in London during the week. But without a wife and family to keep him grounded Max went off the rails. Drink, drugs and tarts were not a good diet for an occupation where success depended on a clean head. Max then had a bad run and took on more and more risky bets without having enough money to lay off some of the risks. In the inevitable crash Max lost all his money and a big chunk of Lester Connolly's stake. The house in Ireland was in Siobhan's name thank god, but Max felt guilty for Lester's losses. Lester's brother Kieron a silent partner in the bookmaking business was all for breaking Max's legs as a sign to other debtors and it was only Lester's friendship with Max's mother that had prevented him from agreeing. Although their relationship had been soured by Max's stupidity.

Max did a bunk to America without repaying Lester and in the six years he'd been away he scrimped and saved and paid back thirty grand and asked Lester if he could come back home to work off his debt off. He was the first person Max saw when he returned to England. Lester was an old man now and not in the best of health but he greeted Max warmly and listened with interest when he explained his ideas for the aerial photography business, even though he didn't fully understand it. When Max gave him his first grand from his work for Lucky and swore it did not come from gambling, the old man was as pleased as punch. What could have happened in the last ten days to turn things round so dramatically?

`We're here now' said Patrick bringing Max out of his memories. Max did not recognise the front of the betting shop now boasting full-length, brightly lit windows with posters of girls in too tight sports uniforms, offering the latest odds on football, racing and even evictions from reality TV shows.

`A bit different from my day' said Max. Patrick grunted something unintelligible to prove he was not impressed by Max's experience. The inside of the betting shop had undergone its own transformation with bright lights, clean carpets and comfortable chairs set around multiple televisions. An espresso maker shushing in the corner as a young girl served a punter was the only noise. It was now the sort of place Mrs Connolly could allow their daughters to enter, but the clean-up had changed the atmosphere. Not just the absence of stale booze and cigarette smoke. The corporate makeover had taken the soul out of place and Max wondered if the fourteen year old version of himself would still have been tempted by what the place was today.

`They're in the back' said Finn, giving Max a gentle but insistent push on the shoulder. They went through the side door next to the cashier's position where his mum sat all those years ago and then down the familiar corridor that seemed to have been spared the makeover. Max opened the office door and expected to see old Lester behind the desk with his Racing Post and pile of betting slips. Instead the desk was clear and behind it sat a man of around Max's age in an expensive looking dark suit and open neck shirt. He looked familiar to Max and then he realised that it must be Patrick's older brother.

But fully grown into the look the younger sibling was still trying to cultivate. `I'm James Connolly, Keron's son. I'm running the business now' He said without preamble.

`What happened to Lester?' said Max with genuine concern.

James nodded towards the corner and Max saw the old man in a wheelchair with a blanket over his knees. Lester looked awful; shrunken head and scrawny neck. He'd aged twenty years in little more than a week. He had an oxygen tank attached to the chair and a clear plastic line fed air into his nostrils. Although that did not seem to be helping his
laboured breathing.

`My uncles' had a stroke and our father asked me to take over the business until he recovers.' The phrase said all Max needed to know about Lester's prospects.

`I'm sorry someone should have told me. I'd have come straight away' said Max taking the old man's cold hand in his.

`I said that, but they wouldn't let me' said Lester in a weak voice. His glance at James showed Max he was clearly at the mercy of his nephews. `This is not my idea Max'. The effort of talking led him to break into a fit of coughing.

`Patrick take Uncle Lester home' said Jimmy, earning himself a scowl from his younger brother to indicate that he did not like being treated like an errand boy in front of strangers. Patrick turned the chair.

`I'll come and see you when you're better Lester' said Max.

`I'd like that' the old man replied with a weak smile before Patrick wheeled him through the door. Both men knew they would not be seeing each other again in this world.

After a pause to ensure they were out of earshot James Connolly said `I did that as a courtesy to old Lester, but I want you to understand that things have changed. This business has to shape up or we'll bin it. Old Lester was too sentimental. He's let run a number of debts that should have been settled in full ...a long time ago' he added looking up at Max.

`But I've got an agreement with Lester and I'm doing that' said Max.

`No Quinn, you've got an agreement with me and it's this. You'll pay up the forty grand you still owe by the end of this month or there will be consequences.' James's threat was real.

`What good would it do you to kick the shit out of me?' said Max.

`It won't be you Quinn. We'll be taking a little trip to Wicklow to pay that wife and daughter of yours a visit.'

`Leave her out of this' said Max launching towards the desk before his progress was halted by Finn's vice like grip on his arms.

`Looks like you'll be doing a lot of overtime in the next three weeks doesn't it?' said James. `Finn will show you to the bus stop.'

Max trudged the Kilburn High Road to the tube. Forty grand in three weeks was impossible. Perhaps if he had started six months ago he might have had a chance. But even if he had some other shit would have happened. His life was just like that. He was in a bind; working for a crook to pay off another crook. He would have to find a way to cut out the middleman. On the tube home a plan started to form in his mind. He was desperate and it was dangerous for him and probably for Aidan as well. But was that any worse than whatever Aiden had already got himself into? Max realised he would have to find a way to raise the subject with Aidan and find out where he stood. He knew he was betting once again. The safety of his family against Aidan's. Why were the odds always so bad?

12

The next home match at St Jude's polo ground was a sell-out, thanks almost entirely to word-of-mouth supported by Max's YouTube footage. As Max was checking the girls camera harnesses an ebullient Lucky Luchenko came up and hugged him warmly. `Max look at this crowd. My girls are beautiful of course but you've made them superstars!' The girls traipsed into the tent behind him and Max did a double take as he noticed how beautifully made up they all were.

`Wow its Charlie's Angels' said Max. They all giggled.

`It was Mr Luchenko's idea' said Hannah. `Good sports woman does not need to look like lesbian' she said in a heavy mock Russian accent.

`You think I really sound like that girls?' said Lucky sounding injured.

`Don't be sad Lucky' said Katie hugging him and soon he was the meat in a sandwich of teenage girls.

`You think Abramovich get this from his Chelski?' said Lucky to Max. `Go and speak to the fans girls I have some business to talk about with Max'. The girls shuffled off and Lucky turned to Max. `We need more cameras next time and two helicopters. You need help as well, we must invest in our partnership' said Lucky.

Max just about stopped himself from flinching at the mention of a partnership but he knew that Luck's money could solve his problems. `Actually Lucky I was hoping to talk to you about investment'.

`How much you need, another two grand, five, ten' said Lucky?

Max realised he could not ask Lucky for the whole forty grand without providing some explanation and he did not want Lucky to know anything about his dealings with Lester Connolly. `I'll do some calculations and come and see you on Monday' said Max.

`Good. Now I go and meet VIP guest. Lucky looked theatrically around the empty tent. `I'm not supposed to tell anyone, Prime Minister's wife come to match today. I am on her charity and she is on this one. Even Stephen as you say'. Lucky was proud of his mastery of English sayings.

`Yes Lucky, Even Stephen' Max smiled to acknowledge Lucky's quip.

If this were true then there would be extra security today, which might curtail Lucky's activities. Max had to hope not. Off course there would be a discreet police presence, a close protection squad with all eyes on her safety. But they would not be able to cover the whole area. As Lucky departed Max watched for a few moments before exiting the tent himself. He would have to be quick. He went over to the half built clubhouse where a ground floor was in place and the foundations of a first-floor had started. On this upper level he had earlier stretched a tarpaulin between the scaffolding poles. It would allow him to see the monitor screen properly and keep him dry if it rained. From up here he had a grand-stand view of the match and could control his helicopter without fearing for his safety perched on the roof of his van. The other advantage of the clubhouse was that the back of the building would allow Max sight of the rear of the horse trailers from which he could monitor comings and goings via a small camera hidden in the rough brick-work of a window recess.

On the field, the girls mounted up to give the horses a warm up before the match and Max spotted Aidan giving last-minute best wishes to Hannah. Max whistled and called him over.

`In the director's box already' said Aidan looking up at Max on his first-floor perch.

`Care to join me mate?' said Max. He threw down the key that would give Aidan access to the boarded-up building site and Max was soon beside him.

`Your films have brought the crowd out today Max' said Aidan, looking out on a sea of heads from their advantage point. `There must be five or six hundred people milling about.'

`Lucky says the Prime Minister's wife is visiting today' said Max in a stage whisper, although no one was in earshot.

`Is she? That man has a finger in every pie.' The bitterness in the way Aidan said it had Max looking at him.

` Aidan are you in some kind of trouble? Is it Lucky, I know he can be very forceful?'

`You don't know the half of it Max'.

`Then tell me'.

`I can't Max.'

`Do you know your home is under surveillance?' Aidan looked shocked. `There is a camera on a lamppost that photographs everyone who comes and goes from your drive' said Max.

Aidan's shoulders seem to drop with the news.

`I can help you mate. Just tell me what they are after you for' said Max.

`It's the tax people Max. I will never get rid of them.'

`I thought it was all settled Aidan?'

`So did I mate, so did I. Look I've just seen someone I wasn't expecting to turn up. I'll talk to you later Max'. Aidan climbed down the ladder and Max saw him merge into a group of people near the beer tent and then he lost him. Max picked up a small pair of field glasses he used to keep track of the helicopter and through these he found Aidan again. His friend was in animated conversation with a tall man with a scar on his face. The man seemed to be trying to placate Aidan but he was having none of it. They finally moved off behind beer tent when their conversation began to draw stares.

`What the hell are you doing here?' said Aidan.

`The name is Anthony Sharp' said Harry Stanton with a smile as he pulled out an official looking security pass. `I'm here as a member of the close protection squad for a VIP, fully accredited. Chummy has got some important friends, hasn't he? I wanted to get eyes on him.'

`Christ, first Logan and now you' said Aidan.

`Actually I was planning to come to your daughter's eighteenth birthday party but I found out that Logan was there. I thought it might be a bit much for you' said Stanton.

` And how did you find him? Was it through the surveillance camera in the lamp post?' said Aidan.

The smile dropped from Stanton's face. `How do you know about that?' he asked.

In answer Aidan pointed to Max's helicopter that was doing a lap of the field taking some crowd shots.

`Christ by the time we get approval from the top to evaluate those things they will already be in the shops' said Stanton automatically turning his back towards the drone.

`Why am I still under surveillance?' demanded Aidan.

`It's not you we're interested in its him. You know he comes to your house while you're not there' said Stanton.

`Off course I know that' said Aidan but the shock of the news caused him to pause for a moment too long before snapping back and Stanton saw it.

`You know he is interested in your wife?' said Stanton.

`And she's not spurring him completely because we are trying to get the information from him that will get you people of our fucking backs' said Aidan.

`Look I know this is difficult for both of you' Stanton sympathised. You're not trained for fieldwork but you are doing a great job, better than we could have ever expected. We are following up on the hotel lead you discovered and very soon will be able to take our friend off your hands. Just hang in there a bit longer Aidan'. Aidan wondered if this was a standard pep talk for reassuring jittery agents. `That camera is for your protection and

Kristina's' said Stanton. Aidan looked at his face and realised he could not tell if the man was being honest or lying which was probably a good asset in his line of work. `Speaking of protection I have to go and check on the VIP and make sure that he's not pinching her arse' said Stanton trying to lighten the mood.

Aidan watched Stanton stride off and he felt trapped in his nightmare scenario which he'd made worse by letting slip to Max with a careless comment. The longer this went on the more likely it was he would make a serious mistake.

Max noticed the police handler with his sniffer dog doing the rounds of the perimeter of the polo field. It stopped in several places including the well-used portaloos with queues outside. The moment of truth came when the dog made its way to the line of horse trailers, some of which still contained ponies who would be swapped for the second chukka. It must be going mad with the smell of horse shit and the noise of the crowd Max thought and then he realised what perfect cover it was for whatever was being shifted around using the horse trailers. The dog did not react when it sniffed at the heater units, telling Max that whatever was hidden in them was well sealed. The stream of visitors to the back of the horse trailers at the last match did not materialise this time but Max was still sure a transfer was going to take place. His hunch was confirmed when he noticed that during the half-time ritual of treading down the divots a whole new fleet of vehicles had arrived to take the horse trailers away at the end. They would unload the contents of the secret compartments once they had safely reached their destinations. This was no good for Max. He needed evidence of the transfer taking place if his plan was going to work. He came down from his perch to check the girls' cameras as they changed over their mounts. Whilst no one was looking. He let down the right tyre of the very first horse trailer and the spare as well. It was worth taking the chance as he had nothing to lose. He just had time to reposition his hidden camera so it framed the first horse trailer completely and then it was time to get ready for the second half of the match. The match ended in a four - three win for Hannah's team and a delighted looking Lucky persuaded the Prime Minister's wife to hand out a commemorative medal to all the players. For the first time Max noticed a couple of the football oligarchs in the presentation group. Lucky took great delight in in presenting them to his VIP guest. You could see the look on his face which said `In this country I'm as good all of you'

Max packed up slowly and was amongst the last people preparing to leave. He saw a small crowd arguing in Russian around the horse trailer with the flat tyre. `What's going on over there?' He asked the steward.

`Flat tyre. Some idiot forgot to check the spare. None of them have got a pump between them. Not that clever these Russians are they? Anyway I finish in ten minutes so they'll be waiting on their own if help does not come soon' said the bored official.

`Well I'm sure they'll remember next time' said Max as he pulled away. He hoped that the empty field would reassure them that was no need to go to any great subterfuge and that they could conduct their business out here well away from prying eyes.

The next morning Max retrieved his camera from the building site and he was not disappointed with the results. He set it up to take a picture every ten seconds and after an hour it showed clear pictures of another vehicle and horse trailer arriving. The horses were put in it and driven away but then the remaining men entered the broken box and moments later appeared with hands full of packages, which they deposited in the boot of one of the cars. Max counted at least a dozen items about the size of a gold bar. There was a conversation between the car driver and the remaining men and he produced an electric pump which he gave to the last two for them to pump up the tyres and take the empty trailer away. Max sat back satisfied that his hunch had paid off. He wondered what he would do with his information. There must be well over forty grand's worth of drugs in the back of horse trailer. But what about Aidan's predicament? Was his friend part of this? He had to know where Aidan stood before he acted. He picked up his phone.

`Sorry to bother you on a Sunday night mate.'

`No problem Max. It was a good match yesterday, wasn't it?' Look what I said about the tax people, just ignore it.'

`Sure no problem Aidan. Listen do you have a horse trailer like Lucky's?'

`No but I'm thinking about it as Hannah is really keen'.

`Good because tomorrow we're going horse trailer shopping. I'll explain when I see you.'

13

Okay Max we're here now. Will you tell me what this is all about?' said Aidan.

`Just bear with me Aidan. I need to see something and then I'll explain everything then we can decide what to do.'

`You're talking in riddles Max.'

`Come on Aidan before he has the chance to make a call. Just tell him you want to buy a horse trailer for Hannah. It's the truth anyway' said Max getting out of the car.

`Okay Max we'll play your way' said Aidan knowing that his friend would not be more forthcoming until after their visit. They were dropping in unannounced on a light industrial workshop on a small trading estate near Sevenoaks. Barton coachbuilders had been a big company in the 1930's, building trailers and lorry conversions for agricultural use. The bread-and-butter work disappeared with the decline of the British commercial vehicle industry in the 1960s. Manufacturers fighting for survival started offering the conversions Barton did straight from the factory instead. Then when foreign vehicle manufacturers started supplying the same thing at even cheaper prices, it looked dire for the company. Barton's limped through the 1970s and 80s sustained only by their equestrian business which provided a living for the third-generation of Barton's and a few old retainers prepared to stick it out because they did not have any other option. Fortunes revived in the 1990s as the newly rich sought to ape the mannerisms of toffs and their country pursuits. Revived interest in eventing, riding more generally and latterly polo had led to a boom in orders for horse trailers and horse boxes. Barton became a heritage brand, like Barbour and a Barton horse box was the one to be seen pulling behind your Range Rover. All the horse trailers for Lucky's polo team were supplied by Barton.

`Can I help you gentlemen?' said a middle-aged man appearing from the door of an industrial unit. Arthur Barton was in his early sixties and had the ruddy complexion of a farmer and the stained and scarred hands of an engineer used to working with metal in the traditional way. He wore an old fashioned brown storekeepers coat over his cardigan, shirt and tie.

`You must be Arthur Barton, pleased to meet you. I'm Aidan Wheelan and this is my friend Max Quinn. We're sorry to drop in on you unannounced but we were just in the area.' Arthur Barton shook both of their hands with a quizzical expression on his face. `My daughter Hannah is a member of the polo team, sponsored by Lucky Luchenko' said Aidan.

`Off course, I thought I recognised the name. I saw a picture of all the girls in the paper' said Barton, now smiling.

`This is the man who took it using an unmanned helicopter' said Aidan pointing to Max.

`Unmanned helicopter really? What they can't do today' said Barton.

`I was hoping to talk to you about an order for a horse trailer' said Aidan. `Hannah is very keen on polo, and we hope she can keep her training up while she's away at university. We'll have to get our own horse box. We can't rely on Mr Luchenko's generosity forever.'

`He's a very good man. Truth be told, he's been the saviour of our company' said Arthur Barton.

`How's that?' said Max.

`Mr Luchenko has been investing in our company for many years now. He helped us out when the banks would not look at us. If it had not been for his export orders a few years ago we would have gone under.'

`Really?' said Aidan knowing there was something more in this.

`Oh yes, we supply trailers for his transport business in Eastern Europe. Well, just the livestock part of it anyway' said Barton.

`I didn't know that. I've been around Eastern Europe quite a lot and I can't remember seeing your name on trailers' Max lied.

`No we don't brand them. Mr Luchenko insisted we keep the name for the prestige products, horse boxes and trailers and it seems to be working. What some people will do for status you know? My lads sometimes joke that they think that some of the customers don't even have horses. They just want to show off to their friends'. Barton laughed.

`You know, I've seen a few of those types at the polo matches. They go there just because it's the place to be seen at. Still, its all money isn't it?' Said Max.

`That's true. We're doing okay, but success brings its own problems'.

`What's that?' said Aidan.

`We're a hand built business and this boom has taken us a bit by surprise. All my men are involved in the horse box fabrication business and we've got an order book eighteen months long.'

`So how do you cope with the rest of it? Said Aidan.

`Well you can't get the skills in this country, but we've been fortunate. Mr Luchenko has a manufacturing business back in Russia that had to close. New health and safety rules or some other nonsense made it uneconomical to keep it going. But their loss is our gain. The men Mr Luchenko brings over are hard workers and after a year they go home again with enough money to feed their families.'

`And they've all turned out to be good?' said Max sceptically.

`We get the odd one who is not up to it, but I have a quiet word with Mr Luchenko and he moves them on' said Barton.

Max and Aidan looked at each other. `I guess Lucky Luchenko has been lucky for all of us' said Aidan.

`Well certainly for me. Like I said it's an eighteen month wait for a new horse trailer' said Barton.

`That's a shame. I was hoping you could help me out by the end of the summer.' said Aidan. He looked at Max uncertain of how they were going to get inside the building.

`I don't suppose you've ever thought of getting a video done of your craftsman at work? People love to see traditional skills. You can put on your website' said Max.

`One of the apprentices keeps banging on at me to do something like that but I can't be dealing with cameras and lights all over the place' said Barton.

`It's not like that anymore Arthur' said Max. `I could fly the helicopter in here and your men would not even know it was there.' Barton looked incredulous. It's only three feet wide' said Max.

`Oh I see' said Barton finally getting that it was not a full sized machine. `How do you control it?' he asked warming to the idea.

`That's easy' said Max `pygmy leprechaun pilots. Let's see what we can do'. They all laughed at the joke and Max took the opportunity to steer Mr Barton towards the entrance of the workshop. He started engaging the owner in questions about how they fabricated the shapes. It never occurred to Barton not to invite the two of them into his business. `I guess it's easier if I show you' said Arthur Barton as they stepped through the entrance. Max turned to Aidan and gave him a wink.

`Gift of the gab' said Aidan under his breath. For once pleased there was something in the Irish stereotype.

The workshop had probably changed little since the 1930's save for the new CNC lathe that sat in the corner surrounded by more traditional drills, jigs and presses for forming the sheet metal into the panels for the horse boxes. Two men were fitting box steel bars into a jig in preparation for welding to fabricate a trailer chassis. A row of six chassis stood down the centre of the workshop in various stages of completion. The steady pop of compressed air powered rivet guns as men joined panels together was giving Aidan a headache. He was surprised that none of the workers were wearing ear defenders. The older ones must be quite deaf he thought.

`So this is the model we produce for Mr Luchenko' said Barton coming to the end of their impromptu tour which had taken almost an hour. His throat was a little dry after having had to raise his voice to make himself heard above the noise of panel beating, rivet guns and grinding. They were looking at a trailer chassis about three meters long and two metres wide. The end where the doors would go were square while the other end tapered like the bow of the boat except, it was squared off rather than coming to a point.

`It's pointier than other trailers' said Max.

`There's a reason for it, as well is giving us a trademark image. It's more streamlined in the wind and it also allows a tighter turning circle when maneuvering. It was my grandfather's invention' said Barton proudly.

Max nodded in appreciation. `What's that recess in the floor for?' he asked, knowing the answer.

`That's Mr Luchenko's invention. It's where we put the heaters' said Barton. They were looking at a metre square recess in the floor panel of the horse trailer into which a number of wires led. We assemble the underfloor heating mesh a bit like you'd have under a domestic floor and the wires connect to the electric motor in there.

That powers the elements that heat the horse boxes. While they are moving, it's driven by the axle.

What happens when the vehicle is stationary?' asked Aidan.

`There is also space in there for two storage batteries that are charged while the trailer is in motion. There is enough power in them to heat for at least three hours. Long enough for most events' said Barton.

`Ingenious' said Max. `But what happens if it breaks down?'

`There's a failsafe. The two batteries work independently. You could take one out and there would still be enough heat' said Barton. Max caught Aidan's eye and he could see he shared his thoughts. `Look here's the finished article, this one got damaged so we use it as a demo model.' They were looking at a completed horse trailer, which had been cut in half lengthwise. The floor hatch had been removed showing the axle connected to the electric motor and one of the storage batteries. The battery was about a foot wide and eighteen inches long. The edge of the recess was lined with a thick rubber gasket.

`What's this all about?' said Max feeling the hard rubber sponge.

`Its marine quality and watertight' said Barton proudly. You can't have the electrics exposed roadside so that's sealed, they have to go in from the top. I don't know about you, but I've yet to come across horses that don't shit and piss when they are nervous. Most horses are not good passengers. But when accidents happen it doesn't matter, we've got everything safe with a water-tight seal.

`So does it really work Arthur?' said Aidan sceptical of any therapeutic benefit.

`Well the side panels are also insulated with a thin lightweight membrane so it's nice and cozy in here for the horses. That means they're less stressed and there's less likelihood of them injuring themselves in the warm up because their muscles are already relaxed. And if they do get a strain during the match the heat helps to reduce any inflammation as they cool down' said Arthur Barton confident in his own sales pitch.

Max stood behind Mr Barton and made a head movement indicating that Aidan should try and get him out of the way. `Thank you Arthur. We've taken a lot of your time. I don't suppose I could use your loo before we go?' said Aidan. He headed towards the office at the back allowing Max the opportunity to photograph the electric motor assembly on his phone before catching up.

`Doesn't seem to be any fully completed traitors here?' said Max while Aidan busied himself in the loo.

`No we just do the coach building, the final fit out of the electronics and testing is done on our other site. That's where the Russian lads are' said Barton. Aidan was coming down the corridor making similar signs for Max to occupy Barton while he poked around the main office.

`So can I come over on Tuesday and give you a demo of how we could film. No obligation. Only take ten minutes and we could do something like this' said Max outlining a mini blockbuster which captured Mr Barton's attention until Aidan had returned.

`I must layoff rich food' said Aidan rubbing his stomach. `Thanks once again for your time Mr Barton and do let me know if you get any order cancellations as I'd be happy to fill the slot. Here take my card so you know how to contact me.'

As they drove out of the car park they did not notice the driver of a low loader which had come to collect the next batch of horse trailers for electrical fit up. If they did, it would have taken a few moments to recognise the man in the overalls was the normally sharp suited Timor.

Aidan and Max sat in a country pub nursing their whiskeys and lost in their own thoughts. Max broke first. `You know what's going on in there don't you? He's using those horse trailers to smuggle drugs around the country.'

`You don't know its drugs' said Aidan.

`Who cares? Its drugs or money or guns or any fucking illegal thing. You know he's a crook, why are you defending him?' said Max suddenly wary that Aidan was more involved with Lucky that he had assumed.

`It's not straightforward Max' said Aidan. He feared his friend would go straight to the police and Aidan would lose a cast-iron opportunity to nail Lucky with evidence that would get Stuart Logan out of his life for good. He had to stop Max from doing something rash and the only way to do that was to tell him the truth. `Max you know when I said that stuff with the ARA was all over. Well it's not strictly true. I'm involved in the deal with them. A deal to do with Lucky.' Max sat in wonder as Aidan explained the bind he was in to provide evidence the authorities could act on.

`You believe they'll come through this time and not just kick you into touch when this SOCA lot takeover' said Max.

`The case will not got go to SOCA, someone else involved ... MI5'.

`Jesus Christ Aidan!' Max's loud remark drew enquiring looks from two couples, pensioners enjoying the lunchtime special for the over sixties.

`It will be okay mate honest' said Aidan and then put his arm on a nervous looking Max's shoulder to calm him down. The old couples looked away as they continued their conversation. One woman turned to the other and said something quietly that the other one did not hear properly. She repeated it in a voice that carried more clearly than she would have wanted. `I think they're just a couple of gays having a lover's tiff.'

Max and Aidan looked up in surprise and started laughing. `He's forgotten our anniversary' said Max.

`Typical man' said the old woman who was hard of hearing and everyone laughed. The old couples got up to leave and the other woman came over and grasped their hands. `I'm sure you'll work it out' she said with a smile.

They watched the old folks leave. `Jesus Max that's where went wrong, marrying women. I know Kristina will be glad when this is all over. Having to pretend she likes Lucky is taking its toll.'

Max was relieved that his friend's wife was just playing a part. He would hate to believe that Lucky's interest in her was being reciprocated. Although he suspected Aidan was not aware of how insistent Lucky had become.

Having shared his burden Aidan looked more relaxed. `Do you have a problem if I take what we learnt today to Logan?' said Aidan.

`Actually I do have a problem Aidan. Forty thousand problems to be exact. Aidan looked puzzled and Max explained his deal with old man Connolly which let him come back. He wound up recounting his conversation with the two nephews a couple of days before ending with their demand for £40,000 by the end of the month or they would be with visiting Siobhan and Annie.

`Bloody hell what is it with you mate?' said Aidan.

`Same shit, different shovel' said Max ruefully. `I'll get some more drinks'.

By the time he'd come back from the bar Aidan had the beginnings of a plan. `The only solution to this is to get them all off our backs at the same time.'

`How do we do that then?' said Max.

`If what you say about the young Connolly's is true, they are in a hurry to make money and would probably go for a deal where they could do it by ripping off someone else. We'll set them both up, the Connolly's and Lucky. Next week is the last polo match of the season. You tell the Connolly's there is a load to be had if they rip off Lucky. We also tip off Logan's lot that there is a deal going down and they can come in nick both groups.'

`Can it really be that easy Aidan?'

`Why do we have to make it difficult? We just have to convince Logan and the Connolly's that the opportunity is real and their greed will do the rest. If only we had some evidence of actual dealing.'

`What like this you mean?' said Max showing Aidan his phone onto which he'd transferred some stills from his secret filming at the polo match.

`Brilliant and when were you going to tell me about these?' said Aidan.

`If you were not going to be honest with me about your relationship with Lucky, I figured these would tip things one way or another' said Max.

Aidan looked at the pictures and tried to imagine himself making excuses for being in league with a major drug dealer. `Well thanks for trusting me mate. You could have just looked after yourself.'

`That's not what we are about though, is it?'

`No, you're right Max, It's not.'

14

It had been an hour since Aidan Whelan had left and Stuart Logan still could not control his grin. He and Harry Stanton had gone through all the evidence twice and they could not come to a different interpretation.

`They've done it! A couple of Irish chancers with a bit of luck on their side have succeeded where the combined efforts of our two agencies have failed' said Stuart `They delivered us evidence of a ghost hotel and taxi business for money-laundering and a transport system for moving drugs around the UK and abroad in trailers and horse boxes. Not to mention the illegals Luchenko is smuggling into this country under the guise of being an additional workforce for Barton's company. This will be a kick in the balls for our friend at SOCA' he added gleefully.

`Yes Stuart we have hit the jackpot' said Harry Stanton in more measured tones. The high value of their windfall had exceeded his most optimistic expectations and with that came a problem which he knew Stuart would never understand or accept. Lucky Luchenko was now too valuable an intelligence asset for them to burn as an epitaph to the head of a failed agency. He was even too big to be waived in the face of SOCA in the inevitable turf wars that would each ensue as MI5 moved more firmly into criminal intelligence. He would have to play their hand with finesse. Harry humoured Stuart for another half hour, ostensibly making plans for a joint MI5-ARA raid on the final St Jude's polo match that would net them both Lucky's senior dealers; and a new bunch of Irish hooligans looking to make a name for themselves in England. When Stuart had left Harry pondered for a while before phoning his boss the Assistant Director. `Sir there have been some developments with our Russian friend. The Irish boys have come up trumps... Yes sir it is the luck of the Irish. We need to have a chat about how we proceed from here given that there are others dimensions to this case... Very good Sir I'll come up in fifteen minutes.'

Giles Pendry sat looking at the view of Lambeth Bridge from the office in Thames House. He always thought that the MI5 HQ has more class than the Tetris shaped building of its sister organisation across the river. His team had not yet been asked to cast their eyes over the activities of the domestic spooks but the increasing cost of the war on terror meant that it was inevitable that they would come into his sights at some point. He assumed this meeting was some pre-emptive attempt by the spooks to get some points on the board. He'd seen it before in other departments where they'd been forced to undertake dramatic surgery.

The door opened and in walked two men. The first he recognised, the second a tall obviously ex-military man with a scar on his face would have looked more relaxed carrying a gun instead of the manila folder he was holding. He held out his hand to the other man `Assistant Director good to see you again. The PM sends his regards' said Pendry seizing the initiative. It did no harm to remind these cloak and dagger types who the top team were.

`Please give him my best wishes by return. I don't believe you've met my colleague Harry Stanton but you share a mutual interest' said the AD, smoothly putting Pendry on the back foot.

`Really?' said Pendry, his antennae sensing this was not the meeting he was anticipating.

`Yes Mr Pendry, Ludovic Luchenko. I believe you have an interest in our interest in him' said Stanton.

`Interest is perhaps too strong a word' said Pendry, instinct telling him to backpedal until he could see where this was going.

`I believe you told an Agency charged with the recovery of criminal assets that he was off limits' Stanton continued bluntly.

What has that bloody man Logan done now? Thought Pendry. He was determined not to go quietly and if that was the case he would enjoy giving Stuart the martyrdom he was looking for. `Assistant Director we all know that the ARA has failed and is counting the days to its demise. We can't have one disgruntled employee with an axe to grind, disturbing investigations of its successor body. Can we?'

`Indeed but another interpretation is that it might be politically embarrassing for others if the man in question were to be investigated' said the AD. As he had almost point-blank accused him of trying to interfere with an official investigation, Pendry knew he must have something serious to back it up with. `Harry if you please, show Mr Pendry our friends curriculum vitae'. Harry Stanton opened a manila folder and gave a sound and picture show similar to the one he used on Stuart Logan. This time the response was different. Where Logan had been generally revolted by the death and destruction portrayed in the photos, Pendry exhibited a different response. A peculiar heightened interest in the subject matter. Harry had seen it before, the excitement some people got from war porn. There would be no hand wringing sighs of pity from this man. In Harry's experience when you had to kill for a living you valued life. Men like this Pendry just gave orders without thought for the consequences. He knew his boss had seen the same thing and had formed a similar view of Pendry.

`This history lesson is all very well Mr Stanton, but if these things had stood up to a proper investigation at the time the man would not be in the country now. Besides, I don't expect your fellows to appreciate this but there is a real financial crisis coming. Liquidity will dry up and the nation will be grateful to the wealthy individuals who have invested their fortunes here instead of elsewhere.'

`No matter where they made their money?' said Harry.

`We can't afford the moral certainty you fellows had during the Cold War!' Pendry could not help reacting to yet another of these Whitehall types that made it so difficult for the government to achieve progress.

`The Cold War is over Mr Pendry as we both know. Today it's all about the war on terror and the war on drugs. You know the international drugs trade funds the war on terror. The PM has spoken about on several occasions. The most direct example is trade in Afghan heroin. Harry please...' said the AD.

Harry had handed over another photo. ` This is a picture of heroin being removed for onward shipping around the UK. It was taken not twenty miles from this office. Here is a picture taken earlier in the day with that same horse box in the foreground. I believe you recognise the PM's wife in the middle of the scene handing out prizes at the end of a polo match.'

Pendry was dumbstruck. The picture was political dynamite. There would be no coming back from this. No way to distance the PM from this fallout. Pendry knew they had him. He just needed to know their price. `What do you want?' he asked.

`Giles it's in no one's interest to cause political embarrassment' said the AD in the same soft tone Pendry often used when delivering the killer blow. `We would want to give those who might be adversely affected by this ill-considered association the time to disengage themselves discreetly.'

`But the man is an international criminal and likely funder of terrorism' said Stanton playing his part of the double act for Pendry's benefit.

`Quite so Harry. So if we wanted to use him as an asset in the war on terror we would have to be able to indemnify the Service against responsibility for his previous crimes... if they were ever to come to light' the AD rejoined.

`But who could provide such a guarantee Sir?' said Harry.

`I think the ladies husband himself could do that don't you Harry?'

Pendry recognised a negotiating stance he saw one. `Not sure I can do that one but how about the Solicitor General' said Pendry. `It's worked in other cases. Besides, everyone knows what it really means.'

`Yes they do Mr Pendry, that would be acceptable. Two more things. Firstly, only three of us know about this situation at the moment and I expect that number to increase to no more than five. If it does, you will discover how draconian the Official Secrets Act can be.' Pendry nodded. `Secondly, the activities of international criminals here in the UK are not best fought by the good intentions of plod are they? Our new friends at SOCA should not be tempted to let their reach exceed their grasp. We will always happy to advise when that might be the case' said the AD.

`Understood Assistant Director.' Pendry sensed it was time to leave before he was forced into more concessions. `Thank you Assistant Director always a pleasure and you too Mr Stanton. I must be off to another appointment now.' Giles Pendry stopped at the door. `There's just one loose end. Our friend Logan.'

`We will help him come to terms with his disappointment' said Harry.

Giles Pendry left the room miffed that his revenge on Stuart Logan would have to be at arm's length.

`Well that went rather well don't you think Harry?' said the AD. `I don't suppose he's been on the receiving end for a long time.'

`No. He looks the type who is more used to dishing it out' said Harry.

`Serves the bugger right. Smart arsed academics. Give them a bit of power and they think they can mess about for a couple of years and solve problems that have been decades in the making. But what about this fellow Logan is there a chance we could use him?'

`I'm afraid there is a big streak of morality in Stuart Logan and that will be his undoing' said Harry.

`Nothing we can offer him then?'

`Well if we are denying him his swan song at least we can help him keep his word. He's promised to that crook Wheelan back all the property the Agency took from him. Said he wasn't the sort of criminal the ARA was set up to catch.'

`I see what you mean by a streak of morality Harry. Let's use the threat of denying him that opportunity as an inducement for him to go quietly.'

Harry knew it would come down to this and in spite of the obvious operational sense it made he felt slightly uncomfortable. Stuart Logan's morality must be contagious he thought.

15

Kristina nervously checked her face in the mirror again while she waited for his car to arrive. She hoped she had not overdone it. A bit of lipstick, a thicker dab of eye shadow, a tighter top. Not enough to raise a husbands suspicions but a signal that would be understood by somebody else looking for signs she had made the effort for him. She convinced herself again she was just playing a role and her performance was approaching the final act.

Aidan had told her excitedly about what he and Max had discovered at the horse box maker and then of his subsequent meeting with Logan and the man from the Secret Service. He would not tell her what their plans were but he said it would all be over next Saturday and then they and Max would be able to get on with the rest of their lives.

She asked how Max was involved but all Aidan would say was that Lucky was the solution to his problems as well. She had a strop at Aidan for not trusting her and he said he did not know how they planned to do it but if Logan didn't act by the deadline of next Saturday, he would give the evidence they found to the normal police. When she asked him why, Aidan said he was tired of the way Lucky looked at her and of her having to pretend to be interested in his advances.

She thought she had been on top of it all but her husband had obviously been more perceptive than she thought. So here she was just a couple of days later having first got Aidan out of the house on an errand, getting ready to play the tart for a man who had made his intentions perfectly clear the last time they met. But this time she would not be on her own. There would be part of a double act to entertain Lucky. She'd hoped she could trust Petor to play his part and not to let his rage get the better of him after all these years.

She had often imagined making the call to Petor where she told him that she had found the man who killed his father and had taken revenge on behalf of both of them. She's thought the act would have taken place in an anonymous hotel where she would lure Lucky with the promise of giving him what he had wanted for so long.

She'd seen herself stabbing him through the heart as he dozed after making love to her. She had even kidded herself that she could do that and go back to her life with Aiden as if nothing happened. But after Lucky's assault on her at Hannah's birthday party, when he trapped her powerfully against the kitchen counter and locked her mouth against his with one hand while his other roamed crudely between her thighs, she knew she would not have the strength to match her determination. Besides her plan required her and Lucky to be able to get away together unobserved. But he always had at least one of his bodyguards with him and something seemed to have happened recently that had made him more jumpy. Everyone who had seen Lucky in the last few days said he looked preoccupied and not his usual full of life character, although Kristina knew that part of him was an act. Aidan's timetable meant she would have to act before the authorities did and she knew she did not have the nerve. She would have to give the honour of taking revenge to Petor. Perhaps it was right after all that the son should avenge the father. When she contacted him two days before he was amazed she had found the man who terrorised them the night his father disappeared almost thirty years ago. He was angry that she had waited almost six months to tell him about it. Kristina apologised but said she would tell him no more unless he was prepared to follow her instructions on where and when Lucky would be dealt with. He accepted begrudgingly and flew immediately to London hoping to change her mind when they met face-to-face.

In the bedsit in Shepherd's Bush where Kristina stashed him Petor heard the full story of her family's troubles with the ARA over the last five years and the deal they had been offered to wipe the slate clean if their information could convict Lucky. Petor shook his head wryly. `I thought the English is all about fair play. They're just like the Russians.' Kristina said all officials were like that all over the world, but she thought she could trust the man who promised to let them have their property back. `When this man gives your fortune back, then I kill Ludovic Luchenko, understand?' Kristina agreed and said he would not have to wait long as they needed to act quickly.

Peter had joined the Estonian army as a young man when his mother's death had left him an orphan. He served five years before getting a job in what he called private security. On the rare occasions he met Kristina when they were both back in Estonia he told her where he'd been. It was not a pleasant tour; Iraq, Chechnya, Afghanistan. It was clear he was earning his living as a soldier of fortune, but she didn't ask directly and he did not admit it. Then just before Kristina said she was going to settle in the UK, Petor came home for good. He said he was tired of what he was doing and had made enough money to buy a small farm. For the last five years he'd lived happily on his land with his wife and two small children. For their sake Kristina regretted having to involve him in her plans. Petor reassured her misgivings and said it was his right to finish what she had started. He would play the part of gardener/ handyman to get close to Lucky and then he would act when the time was right. Now sitting on Kristina's sofa in his old woolen jumper and dungarees he looked the part.

They heard the toot of a horn and Kristina saw Lucky's Range Rover at their gates. Her nerve suddenly deserted her. Petor stood up and took his cousin's hands and used her pet name. `Don't worry Krista we can do this. Go now and let him in.'

Lucky was accompanied by Timor and both men got out of the car. When Lucky saw her subtle signals of attraction as she greeted him with a smile, the way she pushed her hair behind her ear and smoothed her top down. Lucky told Timor to wait in the car. He was pleased she was prepared to carry through what she'd promised him. He strode towards the house to claim his prize. `Is Aidan here?' he asked as he reached the door.

`He had to go out' said Kristina.

Lucky's eyes widened. As soon as the front door closed behind them Lucky grabbed Kristina toward him and kissed her roughly. `I thought you didn't want to do it here. What made you change your mind?' he asked not caring about her answer. She managed to put a hand between his chest and hers.

`Lucky we're not alone. There's someone here to see you.

`Who? He said. Angry at the sudden change of events.

She called him and Petor came out to join them in the hall. `Petor is my gardener, you said you wanted someone to help with yours.' Lucky was annoyed as he clearly thought he was on a promise and this man was getting in the way. ` Petor is a countryman of mine. He helped me with everything you see in the garden but now he is finished and needs to find new work.'

Lucky's annoyance subsided as he studied the man. He must have been about two metres tall and stocky, but lean not fat. He had big farmers hands and intelligent eyes and a face that looked like it had seen a lot of life in his thirty something years.

`Are you a good gardener Petor?' said Lucky.

`I think I am, I did all of this' said Petor spreading his hands towards the view of the garden from the orangery. Kristina had to suppress a frown as he claimed responsibility for all her hard work.

`What else can you do Petor?'

`I can fix things Mr Luchenko, mechanical and electrical' said Petor.

Lucky did not doubt that but he noticed a certain look about Petor. One he had seen in the faces of many of his customers. Have you been in the army Petor?'

Petor to his credit was bashful rather than boastful. `Yes many bad places, Iraq, Chechnya, Afghanistan.'

Lucky smiled. With the problems he was having elsewhere recently it would be useful to have another man around who could handle himself. `Okay Petor, you come to the house later. The man in the car will give you the address' said Lucky indicating to Petor that he should make himself scarce. Peter could see Kristina's apprehension at the prospect of being alone with Lucky.

`I need to finish my work here first. I will come after lunch'. Petor strutted away towards the kitchen before Lucky could argue.

Kristina could see Lucky was weighing up whether to try it on again when a noise from outside made his mind up for him. Another horn sounded at the gates. `That's Aidan back. He's taking me out to lunch' said Kristina.

Lucky realised that the outfit was not for him. ` I see' he said pointedly. He walked to the front door and then turned back. `Soon Kristina, I promise you soon.' Whatever endearment he meant was submerged under a layer of menace. Lucky strode towards his car as Aidan got out of his. `Lucky I didn't know you were visiting us today?' said Aidan. Lucky grunted something in response.

`Lucky is stealing our beloved gardener Petor' said Kristina brightly from the doorway. Lucky begrudgingly returned the wave Kristina and Aidan gave him from the front door as his car exited their gates. `Who's Petor?' said Aidan under a fixed smile.

`I'll tell you later' said Kristina.

`Why are you all dressed up?' said Aidan.

Kristina realised her subterfuge had not been so subtle after all. `Because you are taking me to lunch after which I'm taking you to bed'. Aidan was delighted at his good fortune. He took his wife in his arms and kissed her and Kristina responded wholeheartedly.

In the end it had not been difficult for Petor to make himself useful to Lucky. In one day he'd dug up the ugly rose bushes which Lucky had complained about several times without any of his men taking the hint to volunteer. He also started tidying up the trees. On the third morning Petor was cleaning weeds from the drive when one of Lucky's men came out and reversed the Mercedes E-class out of the triple garage. `Nice car' said Petor.

`Don't make it dirty said the bodyguard looking at Petor's soiled hands. Peter waited until the man returned to the house before removing his thin rubber gloves and opening the driver's door. He opened the bonnet catch and then looked at the marvel of modern German engineering with hardly any user serviceable parts. He found the distributor and quickly swapped to leads to give an ignition problem before covering his handiwork. He was working on the flowerbeds at the edge of the drive when Lucky and the guard now dressed in a chauffeur's uniform emerged from the house and got into the car. After a couple of failed starts Petor wandered over. Lucky was admonishing the driver for not checking the car was okay. `It started earlier' the driver pleaded in defence.

`Can I help?' said Petor. He lifted up his dirty hands and then peeled off his rubber gloves to show that underneath they were clean.

`I don't want be late, you better get the other car' said Lucky and the chauffeur headed back towards the house to get the keys to the Range Rover. Petor took the opportunity to open the bonnet. He switched the leads back and waited until a chauffeur returned. `I'll just give it one go' said Petor as he leaned into the car and started it. He smiled and the chauffeur glared at him. Lucky looked up from his papers pleased with the result. `Where do you live now?'

`In a bed sit in Shepherds Bush' Petor replied.

`You can move in here for a while. Take the flat above the garage. It will be good to have a man, who knows how to fix things' said Lucky. Gregor was insulted by his bosses slight and was further annoyed when Lucky told him to go with Petor to collect his things when he had finished driving him. Petor watched them leave knowing his opportunity to put his hands around Lucky's neck and squeeze the last breath from him would come soon. What he had not anticipated was having to kill someone else beforehand.

On the Sunday morning Petor was woken by a convoy of vehicles pulling into the driveway at around 6 am. From an assortment of BMW's, Mercedes and Range Rovers exited a collection of men. A few had briefcases and laptops but the majority carried their working tools under their jackets according to the tell-tale bulge of holsters under armpits. Petor knew this was some sort of council of war as Lucky had been hurrying to and fro the last couple of days clearly concerned with some crisis. Petor dressed quickly and went round to the back of the house where one of the maids was already up and preparing coffee and pastries for the twenty odd people who filled the old dining room, which was the biggest room in the mansion. Petor went downstairs to the old cold larder. Next door was the cellar which contained a boiler for the central heating system. He'd been sent down there the day before to fix an airlock in the radiator system. In the end he had to attach an electric car tyre pump to push the water around the system before all the blockages cleared with a number of comical burps and splutters. The whole house had thanked him for the warmth that now spread evenly through the place. In the course of his maintenance Petor observed that the basement floor was the full width of the house. He could move from room to room through small gaps in the basement walls. Petor found the floor below the dining room just-in-time to hear a full-blown argument raging upstairs.

`But they offered you fair terms Lucky' said an unknown voice.

`To be chased out of my own fucking town! Do you realise the fight I had to get established in St Petersburg? I even had to bring my stuff in through Tallinn in the beginning because that bastard controlled the docks. Now he wants to offer me terms' Lucky raged.

It was quiet for a moment and then another more reasoned voice said, `Lucky we all grow out of our roots at some time. Where do you want to be this time next year, squabbling with some old country crooks over the loss of a piece of St Petersburg, or here at the top table with your hand on the Prime Minister's wife's knee?' Everyone laughed and the atmosphere sounded more relaxed. `Lucky think what you are risking, you are so near to being legitimate over here. You are almost removed from the drug transportation business. The hotel cleans your money and we have no girls over here. Added to which you are the only fucking Russian the British like. Those other bastards steal their football clubs and their businesses. You take their polo sport and make it popular. Give it back to the people. You think you can get that popular in Russia? There is only one man who can be popular in Russia and he's too big to take on.'

`Okay okay, I hear you all. Maybe I was wrong to kick the shit out of that man Voxov sent a couple of weeks ago. I should just break his legs not whole body. But to pay me back by burning down my restaurant! I loved that that fucking place.' Lucky was not going to be stoic about his loss.

`Lucky you know we're all behind you. We can go to war with Voxov or we can let things cool down and then make him pay a big fucking bill if he wants to buy you out of St Petersburg' said the voice of reason.

Lucky thought for a moment. `Okay we get out of St Petersburg now instead of next year. That bastard Putin will tax everybody out anyway. Let Voxov pay it all and he can see how he likes it. Alexi you go to St Petersburg and tell Voxov that I'm pretty fucking angry and thinking of how to pay him back. Let him shit his pants for a week and then we will talk about the price.' There were murmurs of agreement all round. Lucky concluded the first order of business. `Good that's settled. Now we eat breakfast and then we talk about how things are going over here. I'm thinking of buying a super yacht, everyone else has a super yacht and I not even have a fucking dingy.' Everybody laughed.

`I talked to one of Abramovich's men at the polo match' said a plummy English voice. `I said how come your boss needs so many ships? He said they are not all his. One is made for Putin. Its tax so his boss can operate in Russia without difficulties.'

There was much swearing in Russian and the discussion descended into an argument about how the country was being ruined and how it might be time for a new revolution. Petor listened to the rest of the meeting hoping to could remember all the names and places they mentioned when he reported to Kristina that evening. The most important thing as far as he was concerned was that Lucky was in a feud with an old country nemesis called Voxov and that might be their way to get to him and not have anyone question his death.

Given that Petor and Gregor had taken an instant dislike to each other it should not have been any surprise that things turned out the way they did. When Lucky sent Petor over to the workshop where the Russian team were doing the electrical fit out of the horse trailers with instructions to sort out problems with the faulty wiring looms; Gregor felt his nose was put out of joint. He ran the workshop and the boss should have asked him to ask Petor. Except Lucky knew that he would not. This interloper was usurping Gregor's position and would need to be taught a lesson. When Petor returned in the afternoon having solved the problem, Lucky's praise stuck in Gregor's throat. He would be going to the workshop that night to fill the dummy batteries with blocks of heroin before sealing them. A job best done without prying eyes. After that he would turn his attention towards getting rid of Petor.

Meantime Petor suspected from what he had been told by Kristina that there were drugs on the premises and this was where they got inserted into the horse trailers for shipment. When Gregor left in the evening to go and fill the batteries, Petor followed him but he had to cover the six mile journey on a bicycle. When he eventually arrived the workshop was in darkness but for the paneled office in the corner which he'd had no reason to enter earlier in the day. Petor let himself into the workshop entrance and crept in the darkness between the part completed trailer bodies until he was up against the partition wall of the office. He risked looking around the corner and through windows and saw what he had suspected. Gregor was at the desk filling the storage battery cases with bricks of cling film wrapped brown blocks. Petor's first bizarre thought was that it was chocolate and then his Afghan memories kicked in and he recognised the heroin. There were four batteries filled just waiting for their end plates to be glued on. The open safe contained enough bricks of the drug to fill another four batteries. This would be enough clear evidence to get the government people off Kristina's back.

It may have been thinking of her that tempted fate. In his haste to catch up with Gregor, Petor had forgotten to put his phone on silent and it now rang loudly in his pocket echoing across the empty workshop. The office door was immediately flung open almost blinding Petor with the strong light. Instinct more than anything caused him to roll back and avoid the slashing arc of the knife in Gregor's hand. He surged forward as Petor stumbled back losing his footing. `You! I knew you were trouble. You're a cop' snarled Gregor.

`I'm no cop' said Petor desperately trying to buy himself some thinking time before Gregor slashed at him again

`No matter I'll kill you anyway' said Gregor pragmatically.

`I'm worth more to you alive' said Petor, pushing over a large oxyacetylene tank as he back pedaled from Gregor. The tank landed with a clang. Both men looked first at each other and then at the bottle waiting for the explosion that did not come. Gregor jumped over the bottle and slashed at Petor again.

`Lucky will want to know what my boss knows' said Petor desperately avoiding the slashing blade.

`Who is your boss?' said Gregor.

`Voxov!' said Petor.

The moment of surprise allowed Petor to unhook a rivet gun from its holder and aim it at Gregor. Gregor grabbed for the barrel to push it away from his face. Petor fired twice and rivets pierced Gregor's palm drawing an agonising scream from him. Petor launched himself at Gregor grabbing his knife hand at the wrist trying to twist it free. Both men demonstrated their combat training as they grappled for advantage, their free hand punching at ribs and kidneys while their legs sought to sweep the other one's from under him. Gregor knew his injury would decide the outcome the longer the fight went on. He needed to end it quickly. He rolled forward taking Petor over him and emerged on top of Petor legs scissoring his waist slowly crushing his ribs. Gregor had the momentum and dipped the knife towards Petor's chest ignoring the pain and blood from his wound as he used his injured hand to add force. Petor's grip on Gregor's knife hand was slipping with the sweat of exertion and blood and Gregor saw the end in sight. But he had not counted on Petor's tremendous upper body strength, honed from a punishing morning routine of sit ups. Petor rose from the waist and managed to turn the knife away from him before head-butting Gregor in the nose. Blood splurged and cartilage cracked and Gregor fell back. Peter grabbed the knife hand in both of his and snapped Gregor's wrist before driving the blade between the man's ribs and into his heart. There was a moments surprise as Gregor realised what had happened then he slumped back and began the shallow breathing that would end his life.

Petor sat in breathless silence watching the man die. He bore him no malice. Just as he bore no malice to the dozen or so other men he killed in stupid wars that changed nothing. He did not know how long he'd been sitting there before ringing brought him back to reality. It was his phone. He retrieved the handset from where he dropped it and looked at the newly cracked screen. It was Kristina again. Now he had time to take the call that had almost cost him his life.

`Petor are you all right?'

`I've killed in him Kristina' said Petor.

`You've killed Lucky you said you would wait.'

`No, it's someone else.'

Kristina listened while Petor explained what had happened. `I'm sorry I put you in danger Petor' said Kristina `It's all my fault.'

`No it's not. I got sloppy after all these years.'

`Are you sure no one heard you or saw you leave the house?' said Kristina.

`I'm sure of that'

`Good Petor, then we can still make this work. We need to make Gregor disappear and in a couple of days we can tip Lucky off that it was the work of this Voxov. He will not think to look elsewhere.'

`Your right Kristina' said Petor glad that she was thinking clearly.

`I want you to put Gregor in the boot of his car along with some of the drugs and your bicycle. Then close up the place. We will both drive to Gatwick Airport and I can drive you home afterwards.

Petor arrived back at the house at 2am having been dropped at a quiet entrance to the estate by Kristina. Gregor and the BMW would be spending the next two weeks in the long stay car park at Gatwick. By the time his body was discovered it would all be over, or it would be too late.

16

Max stood across the road from the betting shop in Kilburn waiting for his pulse to settle. There were two reasons for his concern. First he was worried if he really could pull of his plan to convince the Connolly brothers to raid Lucky after the polo match on Saturday. The second concern was the small Mars bar sized brick in his pocket, an essential prop for the act he was about to play. It was also enough to get him a long sentence for possession with intent to supply if he were unfortunate enough to be stopped and searched.

When Aidan handed him the cling film wrapped block of brown heroin powder and told him how it came to be in this position, Max shared his scepticism of the tale

Kristina had given him. This Petor the gardener was apparently someone Kristina had arranged to get an inside line on what Lucky was doing without drawing suspicion. Aidan blew his top at Kristina for doing this without discussing it with him first. She told him he was not a good enough liar to keep a straight face if Lucky was suspicions so it was better that he didn't know. He said he was glad his wife was such an accomplished liar. At this she broke down and said she just wanted to make sure it was all over as soon as possible. Max tried to calm her down. When her tears had subsided, Kristina told them how Petor came to be in possession of the heroin. His story was that Gregor and the BMW he'd been driving were missing. No one thought anything was wrong until Lucky received a call that sent him into a rage. Petor was tasked to drive Lucky to the non-descript factory unit where he had sorted out an electrical wiring problem with the horse boxes the day before. Lucky went through the doors shouting at all and sundry but it stopped when they noticed Petor on the doorstep. Lucky told him to get out and wait in the car. As he mooched around waiting for Lucky to come back. Petor noticed two packages lying in the long grass at the edge of the tarmac car park. Whoever had robbed Lucky last night must have dropped them in the dark in their haste to get away. Petor pocketed them before anyone could see. Eventually Lucky returned to the car in a foul mood and told Petor he would be the reserve driver from now on. Petor asked if this was until Gregor came back and Lucky said if Gregor came back it would be a while before he could drive again. It seemed that suspicion of the robbery was on Gregor although the motive was not clear. Kristina had received a call and rushed off to meet Petor at lunchtime. She returned in the afternoon with the two bricks and her tale of how she got them.

Whatever the truth of how Kristina had come by the two bricks they were a windfall for Aidan and Max. They agreed there was no time to loose. Max checked his watch. It was nearly 5 pm. At that very moment Max knew Aidan was meeting with Stuart Logan giving him this incontrovertible evidence of Lucky's illegal activities. Logan could not fail to organise the raid now but Max knew he would have to be even more convincing to get his side to come to the party. As there is nothing more conspicuous than a man trying to act inconspicuous Max knew it was time to stop loitering across the road and make his move. As he entered the betting shop he noticed the odds on Saturday's football matches and he thought they were all better than his chances of success. This time his trip down the corridor to the back office was in the company of a young man whose dress and demeanour suggested he was an associate of Connolly junior.

`I didn't expect to see you so back so soon Quinn' said Connolly senior sat behind the desk.

`Must've been the power of my persuasion' said his younger brother. `You've come to pay us in full have you Quinn?'

`You won't get a penny more from me, because I don't have it. I won't have it by Saturday either' said Max.

`He's got some fucking balls' said Patrick Connolly.

`Or a death wish' said his older brother.

`Perhaps you'd like to watch while we collect your debts in full from your family. The daughter is a bit too young for me. I prefer them to be at least teenagers, but the mother is all right from what I hear' said Connolly junior.

As Max failed to react to their provocation both brothers fell silent and looked at him. `I said I wasn't going to pay you. I didn't say you weren't going to get paid' said Max.

`Stop talking in riddles man before I lose my patience' said James Connolly.

`I thought you might be able to make use of this' said Max taking the heroin brick from his pocket and throwing it on the desk. The brothers looked at each other and then at Max.

`Is it real? Patrick Connolly said to his brother.

`We'll get Quinn here to open it up so we can have a look' said James.

Max knew the only prints and DNA on the cling film would be his own. The older Connolly took a letter opener out of the desk and dug into the block before sniffing the point. He cut off a piece and dropped it into an envelope which he gave to his brother. `Take this to those Indians down in Cricklewood. The ones we used before.'

`I'm not a fucking delivery boy. Besides Mr Quinn here has a story to finish before I go anywhere' said Patrick Connolly. It was clear to Max that the age difference between the brothers had been a source of animosity all their lives.

`I've got an older brother, who knows what's best for me too' said Max empathising with the younger Connelly and getting a scowl in return.

`Patrick's right, you do have a story to tell Quinn. It had better be a good one' said James Connolly.

Max looked from one to the other. It was now or never. 'I've been working for this rich Russian for a couple of weeks. Billionaire type lives on the St Jude's estate in Surrey. I've been filming his polo team, training sessions and matches. It's a nice gig but it's not going to earn me the money I need to get you's off my back.'

`What's he into this Russian?' said Connolly senior.

`Big-time gangster in St Petersburg back in the day, but apparently clean since he's been over here. Property investment is his thing now and he's a patron of the arts. He's on speaking terms with the Prime Minister's wife apparently' said Max.

`Very nice, I'm sure' said James Connolly. `So where does this come in?' he said pointing to the block of drugs.

`He's got a drugs distribution business, something to do with the horsey world, I'm not sure how it operates. But I have a man on the inside' said Max.

`Will you feckin' listen to him, he's got a man on the inside?' said Patrick Connolly completely sceptical. `He's talkin' bollix.'

Max knew if they did not believe the next bit the game was over for him. `There's this guy who brings all the kids gear to the polo training sessions. They use folding bikes, don't you know. Anyway he got talking.'

`What just like that' said James Connolley?

Off course not. I noticed him sitting in the van with a bottle of vodka while the training was going on. It's a couple of hours in the cold so I can't blame him. One night he's really overdone it. Everyone's gone home except for him and me and he hasn't put the bikes back in the van yet. I open the door and he almost falls out dead drunk. I prop him up and load up his van. He begs me to drive the van back because his boss will have his balls if he fucks up again. He tells me he will never get out of his debt to Lucky if he doesn't work for him. And if he doesn't pay back what he owes Lucky will take his debts in other ways.'

`Sounds like my kind of businessman' said James Connolly with a grin.

`Exactly. We are in the same boat. I told him of my predicament with you's. By this time I've got him home he discovers a second wind and he's back on the vodka. I open half a bottle of Paddy I use to keep the wind out and we sit there matching each other nip for nip.'

`Very touching scene' said Patrick Connolly impatient for Max to get the point.

Max ignored him. `That's when he tells me that he's tired of taking all the risk for such a small reward. He does not want to spend the rest of his days in an English jail. He misses his wife and family, he wants to get back to Minsk. Whether it was the drink or the loneliness or just having a shoulder to cry on I don't know, but he tells me that he's a delivery man for Lucky and with one load we could be millionaires, but he doesn't know how to get stuff out. I'm still not sure how much of this is true so I told him I know some people who could shift the product fast but we would have to show them a sample to prove we're serious. Then he starts to sober and doesn't want to talk about it anymore.'

`When did this happen?' asked James Connolly.

`About four days ago. I didn't see him for a couple of days but when I did I asked him if he remembered our conversation. He says yes and I'm asking if he is still up for it, he says yes but he's scared because something is up. I told him we just need to know where and when the next delivery will be made. No one needs to get hurt. He will get his cut and he'll be able to get home when the fuss dies down. I thought he'd bottled it, but yesterday he gave me that and says that it's on for this weekend. He will only know where a couple of hours before but he will get a message to me. So there you have it'. Max finished knowing that it left more questions unanswered, but it would sound fishy if he tried to embellish the story any further. What they said next would confirm if they were interested.

`How big is this load likely to be?' asked Patrick.

`About forty bricks like this. You can work out the value' said Max noticing the younger man's eyes widen.

`How many men are there?' asked his more cautious older brother.

That depends on how this load is split. At least two per car. Sometimes two and sometimes four cars' said Max.

`So probably eight armed men to deal with if we want to grab it all in one go' said James starting to cool to the idea.

`I didn't say it would be easy. Making real money never is. Ain't that true Patrick?' said Max

The younger Connolly's mind was too fixed on the prize to recognise that Max was playing him.

`The numbers aren't a problem' said Patrick. `There's guys at home we could call who are itching for a payday.

Business is slack since peace broke out. For fuck's sake Jimmy isn't that why we came here?'

`We can talk about that later' said the older brother not wanting Max to know more about their plans than absolutely necessary. `What you want from this Quinn?'

`I want you to cancel my debt. I walk away and we never see each other again.

`And your homesick Russian?'

`He's not greedy, his family can live well on fifty grand back in Minsk.

`Okay Quinn tell the Russian he has a deal' said James Connolly.

`I have to give him something on account as a sign of good faith. After all he has come up with the goods.'

Connolly senior looked Max in the eye and opened a draw and pulled out a wad of used twenty pound notes and started counting. `Here's five grand. We'll add that to your debts for the moment and I promise you if there is any fuck up on this we will take your eyelids first so you have to watch what happens to your wife and daughter.'

Max swallowed involuntarily. He did not doubt the sincerity of James Connelly's threat. `I have everything to lose and nothing to gain from crossing you' he said. He got up to leave. `I'll be in touch about Saturday, but I'd be ready to move any time after tomorrow if I were you. This is not a bus service they are running.'

The two Connolly brothers waited until they could hear the door to the betting shop close behind Max. They looked at each other and the brick on the table. `What you make of that Patrick?

`I say we go for it. Get a few of the boys over and we can have a party. Fucking Russians, we need to teach these foreign crooks a lesson. Think they can come over here and do this do they?'

James Connolly looked at his younger brother, who was oblivious to the irony of his statement. It was too good a windfall to pass up and Quinn was genuinely scared of what they would do if he crossed them. But he was not convinced that he heard the whole truth. Perhaps Quinn just had one of those faces. James Connolly made his decision. `Patrick now will you take that down to the Indians to check. I need to make a few calls'.

Max realised he'd been holding his breath all the way from the betting shop and into the pub a couple of minutes away. He downed a Bushmills in one and felt its heat unlock the tightness in his chest. He'd done it. They would be there on Saturday. Now he would have to hope that they were all picked up by the police. He would have to phone Siobhan as soon as it was over and get her to leave the house without asking any questions. He could not risk alerting her beforehand; they knew where she lived and were bound to be informed if she changed her habits. Suddenly the twenty to one odds the bookmakers offered on his team beating Manchester United on Saturday looked like a good bet in comparison to what he had just set in motion.

17

Tito and Hannah emerged from the darkness of the underground into the noise and crowds of Leicester Square. As young people they naturally preferred the hustle and bustle of the capital to the orderly quietness of the St Jude's estate. This was their secret escape. Hannah from her overprotective mother and stepfather and Tito from the influence of his uncle. They were so similar. They both loved the violin and music and as the offspring of first-generation immigrants whose male parents were not their blood relatives; they both squirmed under their attempts to direct their lives. They both had friends whose real parents did not take so much interest in their lives and they joked that Aidan and Lucky were over compensating for their loss.

Tito met Hannah when she went for interview at the Guildhall School of Music and Drama where Tito was already in his first year. Tito was showing a group of prospective students around and as soon as they laid eyes on each other the attraction was mutual. When they discovered by chance that they were practically neighbours, although Tito lived with his mother in Chiswick rather than at his uncle's mansion on St Jude's Estate and furthermore that Hannah was a player in his uncle's polo team, their relationship seemed preordained. After an initial awkwardness when Hannah had tried to hide their relationship from her stepfather with the subterfuge of a decoy boyfriend, both families had eventually welcomed it. In spite of all Aidan's concerns about the sort of boy Tito was, it was Hannah who moved their relationship forward by asking Tito to take her virginity and end their mutual longing. Later lying in bed together after that first time Tito said he had incontrovertible proof that God existed because his prayers had been answered.

This was the second time they had snuck into town to busk for the tourists. Hannah had left the house carrying her violin openly, having told her parents she was going to practice for the end of term recital at school. Tito was a gifted but lazy student and his mother would not believe he'd give up a Saturday morning in bed for extra study. So he hid his violin in a sports bag and said he was going to the gym. This was their first time busking in the West End. Their earlier attempt had taken them to South Bank and that grey concrete graffiti covered complex beloved by skateboarders. When Hannah asked why here Tito said that if they weren't any good, it wouldn't matter because no one was listening anyway. They attracted mild curiosity as they went through some popular classics. In the middle of a movement from Vivaldi's Four Seasons Tito suddenly stopped and said `Your call is important to us. Please continue to hold.' Tourists and skateboarders alike laughed and cheered them on and when they moved onto their versions of pop tunes the coins started to drop into their open violin cases. `Smells like Teen Spirit' got an encore and they finished with a rendition of `Come on Eileen' with audience participation before the police arrived and told them to move on as the crowd were blocking the route to the National Theatre. They were both psyched up by the excitement of performing for an audience and Tito picked up Hannah and spun her around.

`What are we going to do with the money?' She asked looking at the pile of pound coins and the odd fiver in their cases. They walked into town and entered Fortnum and Masons. The dormant frowned slightly at their jeans and carefully scruffy look but the violin cases and the way Tito enquired where the restaurant was betrayed obvious good breeding. It was clear the young man was trying to impress his girlfriend and there was no point in being surly. `As you are not wearing a suit today sir you may prefer luncheon in The Gallery or The Parlour if the lady has a sweet tooth for ice cream.' Tito gave him a wink in thanks for not embarrassing him and they spent the next two hours gorging themselves on pretty sandwiches and ice cream. On the way out Tito asked the doorman to call them a cab and ostentatiously gave the man a tenner in thanks. When the cab moved off Tito told driver to stop before the meter got to eight quid because that was all he had left.

Emboldened by that first foray they decided to try the West End next, where students from the other London music schools also practised on the busking circuit. They were seen off from Leicester Square itself by the licensed buskers and pavement artists but they found themselves a good spot at the corner of Orange Street, where they hoped they might pick up passing traffic to the National Portrait Gallery. A more intellectual crowd than those queueing outside the Odeon cinema for the latest instalment of the `Fast and Furious' franchise. After a slow start while they try to gauge the interests of the passing crowd, they struck gold with a violin version of `Dueling banjo's'. It earned them yeehaw's from a tour group of Americans and the praise of one old gal for their fine fiddle playing. Their takings included a good few dollar notes and yen to go with the odd fiver. Tito noticed a couple of thirty-something bloke's take an interest in their earnings so he removed the folding money from his violin case and put it in his pocket. By mid-afternoon they had been playing for three hours and they decided they'd had enough. They packed up and Tito searched his bag to find something to store all the change in. They headed towards Soho having built up an appetite for Chinese food. In the fading afternoon light they did not notice they'd picked up a tail of the two Turkish looking men. The young couple had just strolled into the comparative quiet of St Anne's church yard to drink their Starbucks coffee when the two men appeared. Hannah noticed there were only four of them in the place and the two men were between them and the only exit. Tito could see the worry on her face.

`We don't want to hurt you we just want your money' said one of the men in a foreign accent.

`We're students we don't have any money' said Hannah trying to bluff their way out of it.

`We saw you play. You make a lot of money' said the other one. `Hand it over or we will make you' he threatened.

Hannah looked over at Tito and was surprised by his expression. He did not seem to be as frightened as she was. He seemed to be weighing the two men up. The second man then produced a knife.

`Oh my god Tito. Just give him the money!' screamed Hanna.

`Okay, don't hurt us, it's in here' said a frightened sounding Tito as he bent down to open his sports bag. The knife man moved forward as Tito searched in the bag and when he was close enough Tito swung his hand out of the bag and something white flashed in his hand before it struck the knife man in the face. The sports sock containing pound coins was a heavy and effective cosh. The knife man screamed as blood spurted from his broken nose. He held up his hands instinctively and his knife hand took the full force of Tito's second blow causing him to drop the blade. The second man was shocked at how quickly they had become the victims and was lead footed as Tito turned and kicked him in the balls. He fell forward on his knees retching, his hands automatically going to his aching groin and was unable to defend himself from the final swing of the bloody sock which hit him in the face and then burst showering coins over the grave stones.

Both men lay wounded and defenceless as Tito's heavy biker boots lashed into their heads and backs. He was lost in an orgy of violence. Hannah's voice came to him from a long way away.

`Tito stop it, you'll kill him!'

He let her drag his arm and was aware of her struggling with her violin case and his bag as she tried to pull him out of the church yard where a small crowd drawn by Hannah's scream were blocking the exit. They were almost out before the police car pulled up and the two officers told them to stand still.

`They are the victims. Me and my wife saw it all.' Hannah looked up and recognised a couple from the group of American tourists they had entertained earlier. `Those men were trying to mug them but the boy gave them a whooping' said the elderly Texan woman.

The policeman looked at the two teenagers. The girl was of average build and the boy although tall was skinny. He looked more like a male model than a vigilante, but nevertheless they would have to take both of them in given the state of the two men lying on the ground.

`Come with me' said the officer.

`But we've done nothing wrong, they tried to mug us. We were defending ourselves' said Hannah, fear now giving way to anger.

`Be that as it may for whatever reason a serious assault has taken place and those two will need to go to A&E before we can charge them.

`Where are you taking us?' asked Hannah as they were both bundled into the back seat of the patrol car.

`You need to give us a statement and then we'll have to see if either of these two want to press charges for assault' said his WPC partner.

Hannah and Tito looked at each other in astonishment.

Aidan and Kristina and Lucky and Tito's mother Vera arrived at West End Central police station behind Regent Street within moments of each other. After being reassured by the desk sergeant that their children were okay and it was the muggers and not their intended victims who had been taken to hospital Kristina broke down in tears and Aidan comforted her. The other couple's reaction was quite different. Vera sat shaking her head in sorrow while Lucky could not contain his pride. `They try to mug him and Tito fucked them up good. Those sons of bitches will know not to mess with him next time.'

`Mr Luchenko these men have been violently assaulted. They have the right to press charges' the desk sergeant said.

`You've got to be joking' said Aidan not believing what he was hearing.

`You fair play English are mad. I will have a word with them... sort the whole thing out' said Lucky.

They were kept waiting two hours while the injured muggers were brought back to the police station so they could be questioned. The two bandaged men were led in handcuffs to the Desk Sargent to book them in. He gave Lucky the nod and Lucky winked in return. Although it was subtly done Aiden had caught it from the corner of his eye and knew the copper would be getting a little present for his cooperation.

`Armenian's' spat Lucky catching sight of the two men fully. He said something to them in Russian and if the blood could have drained from their swollen faces it would have. The rapid torrent of words from both men was obviously some sort of apology but Lucky was having none of it. The two men looked really frightened and Aidan knew they would bring no charges against Tito and Hannah. The two men were led away and Lucky said to the desk sergeant `No problem now officer, we go home yes?'

`It's not that simple sir. Even if they don't want to press charges the police still can.'

`What you mean you have no evidence?' said Lucky aggressively.

`But we do sir' said the desk sergeant. `It's obvious that the kids were the intended victims but the evidence shows so much more. Please come into the interview room now.'

Aidan, Kristina, Lucky, and Vera were led to a grim office with four chairs, a table and a tape machine for recording interviews. They grey walls were dirty and the threadbare carpet was sticky. It was a room everyone recognised from a scene in every TV cop drama. This room boasted the addition of a flat screen TV on the wall. They sat in silence as the depressing atmosphere of the place provided little incentive to speak. A couple of minutes later a harassed looking man in a poorly fitting suit entered the room. `I'm DC Marston. I've interviewed your children and we will be letting them go in a moment. But first I want to show you this.' He switched on the TV and picked up an old fashioned phone on the wall and said to the person at the other end to play the tape. Black-and-white footage of the churchyard appeared on the screen. `This place is a popular spot for drug deals and it's where vagrants go to sleep off their drinking. So that camera is set up to deter them. Regulars to the area know to avoid this place' said Marston. `We did not expect to capture a scene like this in the middle of the afternoon.' The silent CCTV film showed Tito and Hannah entering the churchyard with their violin cases over their shoulders and coffees in hand. Not long after the two muggers enter. The knife appears and they can see Hannah scream silently and then there followed what Aidan could only describe as a choreography of violence. Tito swinging the cosh surprised the knife man and then him spinning round to viciously kick the second one in the balls. Aidan winced involuntarily as the second man doubled up. They watched in shock as Tito's feet lashed into the two prone men again and again until Hannah dragged him off. Vera was crying and Kristina had her hand to her mouth but Lucky, Aidan noted has a gleam in his eye and was nodding his head in appreciation of a job well done.

`That boy has some serious anger issues. He needs to control his temper before it controls him. I've seen it before, he could go either way' said DC Marston.

`I will do what I can' said his mother sounding defeated. Lucky said nothing and Aidan and Kristina just looked at each other.

When their children were released both parties said their farewells in the foyer of the police station. The young couple with hugs and promises to talk to each other tomorrow. One of Lucky's men was waiting with a Mercedes parked on double yellow lines and Aidan declined his offer of a lift, preferring to get his family away from his company for the evening.

Over a quiet pizza Hannah relived her ordeal after gentle coaxing from her mother. `We're just so glad you're both safe and off course we're upset you felt you had to sneak off to go busking. I know you're not small kids but you're not as streetwise as you think' said Kristina.

`Well she isn't, I don't know about him' said Aidan earning himself a look from Kristina which said he was not being helpful. `Well you saw the CCTV Kristina. He was like a madman.' Aidan was torn between wanting to support Hannah and wanting to say I told you so about his disapproval of Tito.

`He was like a different person all the time he was doing those terrible thing to those men. He was so calm.

And his eyes had this look. I don't know how to describe it' said Hannah.

Kristina knew the look her daughter was talking about. It was the look she had seen on Lucky's face as he kicked her aunt's body all those years ago. `He needs help Hannah' she said sympathetically.

`I know he does. He says he is going to try and I will be there with him. I won't give up on him mum. I won't' said Hannah looking defiantly at both parents.

Aidan looked from his step daughter to his wife and did not know what to say.

Vera slept in the back seat of the Mercedes. Her relief that her son was not being arrested and charged with assault had given way to exhaustion after a few minutes. Even though she was asleep she still held her son's hand in a grip of iron. Tito was unwinding. The adrenaline and endorphins of earlier had given way to fatigue. In the front seat Lucky turned around and recognised what was happening to the boy. `Not so good when you come down is it? Some people take drugs but it's not the same.' Tito just nodded. `You should have seen my boy Timor' Lucky said to the driver. `He was fucking brilliant, smashing one in the face and the other in the balls. They fell like fucking bricks.'

`Chips of the old block as the English say' said Timor continuing their long running competition to prove who understood English better.

`Your mother. She don't like this but it's in your blood. You cannot deny it' said Lucky. Tito just shrugged his shoulders. `What you want to do Tito, play the fiddle all your life? Don't you want to have a nice house like mine, good car like this, take Hannah to fancy restaurants? You need a proper job.'

`What would I do if I worked for you Uncle Lucky' said Tito.

`How do you think I make my money?' Said Lucky.

`Do you really want to know?' said Tito.

`You're a smart boy. What do you think?' said Lucky.

`I think you make it illegally. You supply things that people are not supposed to have' said Tito.

`He is a smart boy' said Lucky to Timor. `In this country a criminal is a bad thing, but in Russia a career criminal is a noble profession. To be a *Vory* is an honourable job, not everyone can be this. It is special, not cheap like politician or businessman.' Timor made disparaging sounds to signal his agreement. `In this country, my business is almost legal... almost. I cannot do more. I need the next generation to make it legitimate ... Be one of them on the inside, not a stinking foreigner like me. You can do this for our family Tito. And if you still want to play the fiddle I hire the fucking Albert Hall and we can invite all family and friends' said Lucky. Timor started laughing and Tito could not help joining in.

Their laughter woke Vera. She was pleased to see her son looking more like his normal self. `What's so funny?' she asked.

`Nothing moma. Uncle Lucky made a music joke. He wants me to join him on the fiddle' said Tito. The lack of response to his pun told him they still had more work to do on their English euphemisms.

18

Tito looked out of the window of their living room on the quiet Chiswick side street. He could feel his mother's stare in the back of his head.

`Give it a rest, will you mum. It's another day, it's time to move on.'

`I'm your mother Tito, not one of your smart mouth student friends. Don't talk to me like that. You cracked a man's skull and broke another one's arm and you don't seem bothered' said Vera.

`They were a couple of muggers. Honestly mum would you be happier if me and Hannah had been stabbed up? I'm the victim here or I could have been.'

`That's just it Tito. You don't act like a victim. No shock, no tears. Just that look on your face.'

`What look is that moma?'

`That arrogance just like your uncle. A sneer that says nothing can touch you' said Vera.

`Well maybe that's what I need. I can't stay tied to your apron strings for the rest of my life. Maybe it's time to move out and get a proper job and the place of my own!'

`What job are you going to? You are interested in music and nothing else. How are you going to buy your penthouse; from what you earn playing on street corners? Is that what we came to this country for?'

`What did we come to this country for mum?'

`To get you away from Lucky. But he came here after us and he's turned your head' said Vera.

`What is it you have against your brother? He took us from that one bedroom, shit hole in Stoke Newington and gave us this house in Chiswick. Why are you so ungrateful?'

`Why do you think he did that? He does nothing without his reasons.'

`So then tell me mum. You obviously know all the answers' said Tito.

Vera looked at her son. She had provoked this conversation but now she did not want to go through with it because it would change everything. Tito's look still demanded an answer. `Lucky can't have children. He thought it was his wife's fault and he got rid of her. Since then he's been with so many woman and still nothing. Meantime she has had four children with a new man, a good man. Lucky wants an heir to his empire. He wants you Tito. And he always gets what he wants. Your father God rest his soul, tried to tell Lucky where to go and he... he'

`He what mum?'

`He had him killed! Your father could not drink two vodka's without falling asleep. People used to laugh at him in bars and at parties. So when he was killed crossing the road with a bottle of vodka in him I knew that was not possible. He had marks on his neck like he'd been held, while the drink was poured down his throat, but there was no investigation because Lucky had the police in his pocket.' She broke down in tears, the secret she carried the past fourteen years, and the thing she swore she'd never reveal was out. She felt both relieved and exhausted that she no longer needed to shoulder the burden.

Tito looked at his mother sat with her head in her hands on the sofa. He wanted to say she was a liar and make her take back the words, but in his heart he knew it was true. He always felt that Lucky's interest in him came partly from guilt and now he knew why. His memories of his father were hazy. The few well-thumbed photos of him with his dad ended when Tito was five. Birthdays, days at the beach, Christmas. Tito did not know whether the memories of everything else were real events or some fantasy he'd created to fill in the gaps. He put his hands on his mother's shoulders. `I'm sorry moma, I'm so sorry.' His words were as much for himself as in sympathy for her losing her husband.

`I can't stop you if you want to go and work for him Tito; but I'm not going to come and see you in prison or on a slab because that's where you'll end up. Lucky is lucky and people around him are not.'

`I know I'm like Lucky mum. I know I would enjoy the things he does. Maybe it's in our blood, maybe that's our weakness. But with music I escape from those feelings' said Tito.

`Then you need to escape from here son, if you're going to have any hope of living your own life' said Vera.

`I won't go without Hannah. We need each other.'

`You are so young, both of you. You can both ...'

`Don't say that mum. Why does everyone say that to young people?'

`Then you need to speak to her and her parents. Maybe you can study abroad together at a conservatoire in Austria or somewhere.'

`Okay mum. I'll talk to Hannah. We'll work something out.'

Tito sat nervously folding and unfolding a serviette as he waited for Kristina to arrive. He looked at the faces of the mid-morning shoppers who'd stopped in the coffee shop for a breather. I wonder if any of them are going to be asking a mother for permission to take her daughter away for their own selfish reasons. Kristina had always been his ally and he knew Aidan only tolerated him to keep the peace with Hannah. After the mugging he could imagine Aidan saying I told you so to the two of them.

Kristina arrived and joined him at the table. Her brief smile of greeting quickly gave way to a frown. She looked tired and her striking looks were not on display today. `Thank you for coming Kristina, are you okay, you look tired?'

`I have a lot on my mind Tito. What is it that you wanted to say to me that you couldn't in front of Hannah or Aidan?'

`I wanted to talk to you without the distraction of Hannah's fussing and Aidan's anger getting in the way.'

`Okay that's sensible' said Kristina knowing that the unnatural calm at home could be broken at any moment.

`I have to go away Kristina. If I don't get away from Lucky I will end up like him. There is too much of him in my blood to resist. Plus he can be a very persuasive man and if he does not get his own way other people will suffer.'

`What are you talking about Tito?' said Kristina fearing what he was going to say.

Tito leaned in. `My mother told me something about Uncle Lucky. I could not believe it at first but then I realised it's true. I've always known it was true. Lucky...Lucky...' his voice broke with emotion.

`Calm down Tito, calm down and tell me' said Kristina gently. She put her hand on his arm to comfort him.

`She said he had my father murdered because Lucky could not have children and he wanted me as heir to his business. Can you believe that?'

Kristina looked at his worried face. Her instincts had been right that the boy was not the same as his Uncle. He had to be saved. She grabbed his hands. `I can believe that completely Tito. Underneath that facade your uncle is violent and dangerous and people who get in his way get hurt.'

Tito was relieved Kristina believed him. `I would go away on my own if I knew that would keep Hannah safe, but he knows he could get to me through her. Besides even if I go somewhere on my own there is no guarantee that Hannah would not try to follow me. You know how headstrong your daughter is.'

`Yes, she has all her mother's faults' said Kristina with a smile.

`That's why I want to take her with me. Somewhere where we will be safe together. I'm not trying to be selfish I hope you understand.'

She looked at the young man whose hunched body betrayed his desperation for her to believe him. `If I thought that would keep you both safe then I would let her go with you. I would not be happy but I would understand. But the only way for everyone to be safe is for Lucky to go away. Would you care if that happened Tito?'

`The man had my father killed. That doesn't earn my affection' said Tito bitterly.

Kristina looked at the old-fashioned day/date clock on the wall. It was Monday, only five days to go before Stuart Logan sprung his trap at the end of the last polo match of the season. Then Lucky would be out of all of their lives. She could not give anything away just yet. `Thank you for coming to see me first Tito. If you need to go away I will allow Hannah to go with you. But please wait. It's the last match of the season on Saturday and she would be disappointed to miss it. Don't say anything to her yet. The three of us will sit here this time next week and discuss how we are going to do it.'

`Thank you Kristina, thank you.' The relief flooded across Tito's face and he leaned across the table and gave Kristina a hug.

`I need to go now Tito. If you're worried we'll speak on the phone. But please don't say anything to anyone else.'

`No Kristina. I won't, I promise.

As Kristina drove home she thought how what had started with a knock on their door six years ago had ended up engulfing everyone and everything she cared about. She now wished she had gone with Aidan when he handed over the sample of drugs to Stuart Logan. But she knew Logan and the other man, the one with the scar would ask questions about how she got it and that would have put Petor at risk. Especially if the body of the dead man was found. They had not had time to clear up properly and there might be evidence that could be traced back to them. It nagged at her why they had to wait until Saturday to lift Lucky now they knew where he kept his drugs. Instinct told her something was not right, so at the roundabout at the end of the High Street Kristina turned left and headed for Weybridge Station instead of going home.

An hour later, Kristina sat in another coffee bar. This one was across the road from the ARA offices as Stuart had instructed her not to come in. `Mrs Whelan is everything all right? I was not expecting to see you again before matters were concluded. Thanks to your evidence we're almost there' said Logan.

`That's just it. You have what Aidan gave you and you know where it came from. So what are you waiting for?' said Kristina.

`Mrs Whelan we have to wait until the weekend for operational reasons' said Logan.

`What bullshit is that? Don't lie to me Mr Logan.'

She had picked the table in the corner so they could not be over heard, but all the same when she raised her voice people turned to look at them. Stuart waited for the heads to turn back before he leaned over and said, `Your husband thought it better that you did not know. He did not want to worry you anymore.'

`About what' said Kristina?

`His friend Max Quinn has got himself into difficulty with ,people he owes money to. They threatened his wife and daughter if he does not pay up. The plan is to tempt them to the rendezvous with Lucky where the police can apprehend everyone.' Stuart immediately regretted telling her.

Kristina sat back in shock. She had no idea that Max was in such dire straits and she knew Aidan could not fail to help his childhood friend. She thought for a moment. All that extra confusion might actually work in her favour. Petor could take Lucky while the police were busy dealing with the two gangs. `I see Mr Logan. Thank you for being honest with me. How long will Lucky go to prison for' she added to keep up the pretence.

`It's not that simple, Mrs Whelan. I will restore your property to you. You have my word on that' said Stuart evasively.

`What are you not telling me?' said Kristina.

`The man we are talking about is too well-known. Many important people will be embarrassed by public criminal proceedings against him. He will be confronted with the evidence and given the opportunity to make restitution quietly and in return for this he will act as an informant against others like him.' The words sounded no better to Stuart hearing himself say them.

`And keep politicians out of the newspapers' said Kristina.

`You have it exactly Mrs Whelan. It has been taken out of my hands.'

`Then we have both been lied to Mr Logan.'

`Yes Kristina. We have.'

`You said some time ago my husband was not the sort of criminal your agency was set up to catch. But do you see what happens when you go after these big fish? They swallow you up.'

Stuart could say nothing. Everything he had worked for would go up in flames.

`I'm so sorry Mrs Whelan. I am sorry for both of us' said Stuart.

On the journey home Kristina seethed. They had been betrayed twice. First when Aidan had agreed to settle with the ARA after Kristina had put pressure on him to do so; only to have them come back for more after the deal was done. This time they were allowing Lucky Luchenko to escape justice. Any misgivings she'd had about involving Petor in her scheme to take the man's life had evaporated. The two of them were the only people who could get justice for what Luchenko had done and they would have to act before Saturday. But what could she do in so short a time that would guarantee everyone, including Max's family would be safe? By the time she got back to Weybridge Station an idea had taken hold. For it to work everybody had to believe what they were seeing was true. It would involve her doing a horrible thing and she wondered if the people she loved would ever trust her again.

19

Hannah and Tito sat at the table in the posh restaurant. The food was very good but they didn't have much appetite.

`Your mum will be disappointed if we don't eat Hannah. This is also her treat for us.'

`I know Tito. She'd been brilliant since the mugging but she's become overprotective. I mean driving us to the restaurant and booking a cab to take us home after, it's too much' said Hannah.

`She just cares, it's very sweet. I know Aidan would not let you out of the house to be with me if it was up to him' said Tito.

`He's just being overprotective in his own way. He may be my step dad but I've never felt anything less than complete love from him. He makes no difference between me and Eva and she is his own flesh and blood' said Hannah.

`Then we should be happy. You look beautiful in that dress and I'm wearing a suit and I'm not even in the dock or at the altar.'

`You shouldn't joke about that' said Hannah.

`Which one the dock or the altar?'

`The dock off course.'

`That's okay, for a moment you had me scared' said Tito.

`Don't be afraid. There's no chance of me dragging you to the altar' said Hannah.

`Really? I might not fight so hard' said Tito.

`Shut up and eat the food my mum paid for' said Hannah suddenly embarrassed and noticing a flip in her stomach.

They were back to their old selves by the end of the meal and things were complete when a man in a suit appeared at their table carrying a wine cooler. `Compliments of the lady who made your booking' he said pouring from the open bottle into two glasses.

`This is really good champagne' said Hannah who drained the glass a little too quickly.

`We must get your mum some flowers tomorrow to say thank you' said Tito, downing his glass and refilling for both of them. By the time they phoned the pre-booked cab they were both worse for wear, having finished the bottle of champagne and a couple of brandies afterwards. Tito steadied Hannah's arm as she walked awkwardly on her high heels towards the curb and the waiting car. He was looking forward to them spending the night together, but he realised he was as far gone as she was and they might have to wait until the morning to consummate their passion. He did not seem to be able to do his seat belt up and the driver had to help them both. `We're not usually like this' said Hannah and she had a fit of the giggles that Tito found himself joining in with. When the driver stopped the car in a quiet road saying he was going to investigate a banging noise from the back neither of them were paying attention as they slumped drowsily in their seats. All Hannah remembered after was a sudden rush of cold air as the door was opened and then a hand covered her face and it went dark.

Tito's shouting woke Hannah. She tried to look at him but the harsh white light made it impossible to keep her eyes open. `Do you know who my Uncle is? He will have you fucking killed when he finds out what you've done' shouted Tito in Russian.

A voice replied in Russian. `We know exactly who Mr Luchenko is and we have taken you to get his attention. If you co-operate you will not be harmed.'

Hannah tried to raise her hand to shield her eyes and found her arms were taped to the sides of an old office chair. She looked at Tito and saw his hands and feet bound in a similar way. The man stepped in front of the lights and shielded from its harsh light Hannah noticed he wore a blue boiler suit with incongruously black polished shoes. His gloved hand held a piece of paper and when he said read this, Hannah noticed he was wearing a balaclava with only the eyes showing. As he stepped back she saw the silhouette of someone else in the room. A red light came on and she realised they were being filmed. `Read please' the man prompted and Hannah read the words on the paper. Then she added, `Mum, dad we are okay.' Then to the masked kidnapper `Let us go please.'

Tito could not help himself. `If my Uncle does not kill you, I will do it myself' he threatened. The bright industrial light went out and the only lamination came from an old metal Anglepoise lamp shining dimly in the corner. He could see they were in a sparse, windowless room.

`There is food and water and a bucket to use' said the kidnapper. `There are blankets and a bed to lie on. You should try and get some sleep. No one will hear you and no one will come. Cooperate and you will be free in twenty-four hours.' The kidnapper's accomplice similarly dressed stepped forward and used a pair of scissors to cut the binding tape on Hannah's wrist. This was done carefully and gently and Hannah noticed how small this person's hands were. The second kidnapper then removed Hannah's necklace, deftly opening the clasp.

`No that's a present from my mum' Hannah said.

`We need to give them proof that we have you. You will get it back afterwards' said the first kidnapper.

The accomplice dropped the scissors into Hannah's lap and stepped back. The first one said `Remember you will not be harmed, it is Luchenko who must answer for his crimes.'

Both kidnappers made their way to the door and the second one paused and turned to look at her before closing it. In that brief moment Hannah realised that the second person was a woman and she was certain it was someone she knew. The kidnappers made their way upstairs from the old bank vault, locking various doors along their way. The vacant building had been bought by a developer who was waiting for planning permission to turn it into a coffee bar and the offices above into flats. The kidnappers quietly locked the street door and went over to their car. Inside they removed their disguises and drove in silence for a while. Any casual observer would think they were a couple who'd been out for the evening and were now enduring the uncomfortable silence after an argument. As they pulled up at the traffic lights the woman looked at the necklace in her hands and broke down in tears. The man put a consoling hand on her shoulder. `It will be over soon. Like you said they had to be believable and for that they had to believe it themselves.'

`I know' she said weakly `I know.'

`Jesus, what time is it?' said Aidan.

`Nearly nine o'clock' said Kristina, sitting by the bed already dressed.

`Why didn't you wake me up love?' said Aidan.

`Well after all that whiskey you had last night, I thought you needed a rest.'

`It was not the drink that did me in. It was you. What got into you?' said Aidan.

`Well Tito and Hannah went out to dinner and Eva was on a sleep over so I thought you might enjoy a little grown up time' said Kristina.

`I'm not complaining love far from it. I'm sorry I went spark out afterwards, but I'm ready for the second half now' said Aidan reaching for his wife as she slipped away from his grasp.

`Well I've got no time for that now. I've got to pick up Eva. I'll be back soon.' She kissed him on the lips and avoided his groping arms. Aidan slumped back on the bed and heard Kristina go downstairs and search her bag for keys before shouting `I'm off.' The front door opened but it did not close. The next thing Aidan heard was Kristina screaming. He stumbled down the stairs to find her shaking on the doorstep.

`What's wrong Kristina?' He took a package from her shaky hands. A typed sticker on the envelope just read Mr and Mrs Whelan no address. It was hand-delivered.

`It was on the drive. Someone must have put it through the gates' said Kristina.

Aidan shook out the contents of the open package. There was the necklace Hannah had been wearing last night. A typed note also came out of the package. All it said was `*If you want to see them again.*' It contained an e-mail address and password.

`They've been kidnapped' said Kristina and she burst into tears and hugged Aidan's chest.

`Oh my god' said Aidan. It was only his need to support his collapsing wife that prevented his own legs from giving way.

Aidan and Kristina sat staring at the screen of his office computer. There was a single e-mail message in the drafts folder. It said

The boy and girl are safe and will not be hurt if you follow our instructions. Do not go to the police. Show this message and video to Ludovic Luchenko and await instructions via this account. Create your own draft message to say you understand.

Aidan looked at Kristina. She seemed numb with shock. `It's Lucky they want, they won't harm the kids' he said, trying to reassure her with confidence he did not feel. Kristina just nodded. `What's in the attachment?'
Aidan clicked on the media clip and they saw Hannah and Tito tied to office chairs against the bare brick wall. The harsh white light added to their already frightened expressions. `Oh my God!' said Kristina. Hannah started reading from the card.

Ludovic Luchenko. This proves you are not beyond my reach. I sent a messenger to you and you beat the man half to death. I am not an animal like you, but you must make restitution to the man's family and for the damage you have caused me. The price is two million euros. One million in cash, small bills. The other half is the same value in heroin. Put it in one of your horse trailers and await instructions. Do this properly and then we will discuss the price for your St Petersburg's interests and you can stay in England with the rest of your kind.
Voxov.

The video ended with Hannah's plea and Tito's threat to the kidnappers. Kristina and Aidan sat in silence before Aidan said `We've got to go to the police. I can get Logan and that Stanton bloke to sort this out.'

`You think we can still trust them Aidan? They want to use Luchenko not throw him in jail' said Kristina.

`How do you know that?' said Aidan.

Kristina could not give away that she has been to see Stuart Logan behind his back. `I don't. But that's how they work isn't it? They went from Victor Garcia to you and from you to Lucky. Who do you think he'll be able to catch for them?'

Aidan looked at his wife and could see the sense in what she was saying. He had been so focused on the end for him and Max he could not see what might happen after that. `Okay, Kristina, what do you suggest?'

`This is Russian business. Let them settle in their way' said Kristina.

`But can we trust this Voxov character. We don't even know who he is?'

`If he really wanted to hurt them he would have sent us more than just the necklace' said Kristina.

Aidan shuddered. She was right.

He changed his mind several times before finally making the call. `Lucky it's Aidan. Tito and Hannah are missing.'

`What you mean missing?' Lucky boomed into the phone.

`They've been kidnapped but it's you they want. We received a package and an email with instructions. A man called Voxov is behind it.' Aidan could hear a roar like a wounded animal and then a stream of swearing and instructions in Russian. A breathless Lucky came back on the phone.

`What has this bastard said?' demanded Lucky.

`He sent me the necklace Hannah was wearing last night and an e-mail message. It's all in there, I can forward it to you' said Aidan.

`No, no traces. Give me the account details and stay where you are.'

Fifteen minutes later Timor was at Aidan's door. `Come with me please 'he demanded.

`I have got to get Eva' Kristina objected.

`You can pick her up on the way. Come now please, Mr Luchenko wants this contained until we have them back safely.' Timor was not going to take no for an answer. When they arrived at Lucky's house the door was opened by a man Aidan had not seen before. Under his jacket the holster of a gun was clearly visible.

`Who are you?' asked Aidan.

`I am a cousin of Mr Luchenko. I'm here to help sort out this business. Don't worry, we will get your daughter back safe.'

In the living room Lucky was holding forth to three other cousins. `That fucking bastard son of an Albanian whore. He thinks he can come from St Petersburg and do this to me, here where I live? When this is over I'm going to pull the trigger on him myself.' He turned to see Aidan, Kristina and Eva standing behind him. He threw his hands out. `Don't worry your daughter and Tito will be safe. This man has been my enemy for many years. When I came to England, I thought I would leave behind my... what is the phrase... my chequered pasts. But Voxov won't let me and now we have to settle this for good. This will be a big surprise for him.'

`I like surprises. Are we going to have a party? Why is Hannah in trouble?' said Eva. Kristina had told her that Hannah was in trouble for sneaking out to go busking again. `I'm a good girl mum. I'm never going to play the violin.'

`Come with me to the toilet sweetheart' said Kristina to distract the child. `You put on yesterday's clothes again and there are clean ones in your rucksack for today.' One of the cousins asked Kristina for her phone. `Yours too Mr Wheelan in case they try and contact you directly.' Their phones were put on the table and Kristina took her child by her hand and led her to the toilet. She had not anticipated this and she hoped against hope that she would find what she needed in the child's bag. As she searched in the bag for clean tights and pants for her daughter Kristina could feel the outline of the old phone in the zipped pouch. She pocketed it while Eva was on the toilet. `Now you change into your to clean clothes out there while mummy has a pee.' In a few moments she closed the door and sent Logan a text.

Voxov has kidnapped Hannah and Tito and he wants to exchange them for Luchenko tonight at the polo ground. Please help us.
Kristina.

She switched off the phone and wrapped it in the sandwich bag that had contained Eva's flannel and toothbrush. Then she lifted the lid off the cistern and dropped the bag into the water. When they got back to the living room Lucky's mobiles were also on the desk.

`Is it a game?' said Eva.

`I think so' said Kristina trying to make light of the situation.

`I want to play' said the child rummaging in her rucksack before Kristina could stop her.

`What's the matter darling?' Kristina whispered in her ear.

Eva whispered back. 'Don't be angry mum, but I've lost the phone you gave me to call you if I got scared in the night'.

Kristina hugged her daughter fiercely. `Don't worry darling. Lucky has enough phones for his silly game.'

The thumping in his head was competing with the thumping on the front door. Max looked at his bedside clock. It was almost 10 am but it felt like five minutes since he'd slumped into his pit. The banging stopped but now he could hear his phone ringing from wherever he dropped his jacket the night before. `Feck off its Saturday' he said, pulling the duvet over his head. Now he wished he had not had so much to drink the night before but he had bumped into some guys in the pub he had not seen for nearly ten years and the craic had been good. He even remembered phoning Aidan at one point to invite him down but he had declined saying he was just about to get into the bath with Kristina and a bottle of champagne. Max remembered offering to swap places so she would not be disappointed. Aidan had ended the call with some very specific advice for Max.

The drink alone would have been enough but the late night curry afterwards in a restaurant willing to accept the trade of four piss heads should have told him something about the quality of the meal and how he would feel next morning. His stomach grumbled menacingly. It would not be a day for company or for straying too far from the toilet. That was okay because his plans that day were for no more than surviving the next few hours. A heavy bang on his door changed that. Someone had let the insistent caller in the front door and they had made for his bedsit.

Timor growled from the other side of the door. `Max Quinn open this door now or I will kick it in.'

`Okay, okay I hear you' said Max trying to clear his head and work out what the panic was about.

Max let Timor in and the minder took a quick disparaging glance around the living room and at the dishevelled state of Max standing in his underpants. Timor sniffed the air.

`You shit yourself Max?'

Max tried to look behind him like a dog chasing his own tail. `Not yet apparently.'

`You need to come right now Max. There is a big problem, everyone is at Mr Luchenko's house' said Timor.

`Okay Timor just give me fifteen minutes for a shit and a shower.'

`No you come now Max and give me your phone.'

The look on Timor's face said he would not take no for an answer.

The collection of phones on Lucky's table increased when Max was ordered to give his up. He looked around the anxious faces of the Wheelan family as they sat on one of Lucky's expensive sofas.

`What's wrong? Timor strong armed me here this morning but he won't say anything' said Max.

`Hannah and Tito have been kidnapped by someone with a grudge against Lucky. They send us a message and we're waiting for their ransom demands' said Aidan.

`What the fuck' said Max scarcely believing what he was hearing? The sharp looking cousin who had asked for all their phones studied Max and concluded that his reaction to the kidnapping was genuine.

`The kidnapper's message talks about money and drugs. Mr Luchenko does not have anything to do with drugs. Do you know what they are talking about?' he asked looking at Max, Aidan and Kristina.

She answered for all three of them. `Do we look like we know about drugs? We've had the authorities investigating us for five years. Do you really think we could deal drugs right under their eyes?'

`What about you Mr Quinn?' said the cousin.

`Gambling has been my vice for all the good it's done me. Poker, roulette and horses yes but never drugs.'

`Let's talk about horses shall we?' said Lucky who had also been studying their reactions to the questions. `My horse box business was robbed a few days ago. You two were seen there asking questions. Why can't you come to me?' said Lucky.

Aidan wondered who could have seen them. `Actually it's a bit embarrassing' he said. We went to Barton's to see if we could order one of your special horse trailers for Hannah. When she goes to university she might have to train elsewhere. I'm getting back on my feet now. I can't impose on your generosity anymore. I asked Mr Barton not to say anything to you. Is he okay? I hope no one was injured in the robbery.'

`It was a different site that was robbed' said the cousin.

`Well we don't even know where that is. Mr Barton just said that the trailers went to another site for their final fit out' said Max.

Lucky and the cousin looked at each other and it seemed that their answers confirmed what they had already been told. To defuse the situation Kristina turned away and started talking to Eva.

Lucky seemed to mull all this over for a while and then a pronounced `Okay, it's good to get that cleared up. That bastard Voxov...oh sorry child, he seems to know too much about my business affairs and I want to know where this is coming from.'

`Has anything else gone missing?' asked Kristina.

`Gregor is missing three days now' said the cousin.

They all fell silent until Lucky said `I have men looking for Voxov's people. He will send demands soon and then we will meet him. Now we wait. Timor get their housekeeper to bring us all coffee and juice for the little girl.'

A text message came to Aidan, Kristina and Lucky's phones at the same time. It just said to check the e-mail. A new draft message was in the folder. It said that the hostages had been split up and were being held in different locations. A rendezvous at 8 pm at the building site for the new St Jude's polo team clubhouse was proposed.

The ransom would be checked then they would be given the address where one of the hostages was held. When Voxov's men had made good their escape they would be given the address of the other hostage. They also stipulated that it should be Kristina who handed over the ransom.

`He is a cunning bastard. He wants to do this at my own clubhouse to rub my nose in it' said Lucky. `It will be slow and painful for him in the end.'

`Please don't do anything to jeopardise things' said Kristina.

`Don't worry, I will deal with this. I have done this before' said Lucky.

The rest of the day passed slowly as they waited for the hours of darkness. Lucky was in and out of the dining room many times while Max and the Whelan family were under virtual house arrest. Kristina could see Max's mood darken. This kidnap would probably make Lucky change plans for Saturday and thereby ruin Max's chances of getting the Irish gang off his back. She could not face the thought of Siobhan and her daughter being victims of this whole mess. In the afternoon she managed to attract Max's attention where they would not be overheard. `You need to make a call, don't you Max?' she said. Max looked at her wide-eyed. `In the cistern of the downstairs toilet you will find a phone. Tell them to wait for the arrow.' She spilt her tea on his foot before he could jump in to say anything. `Oh silly me look at the mess I've made' said Kristina.

The distraction gave Max time to process this information. He thought they'd all been victims of this random event but he realised that the only one who really knew what was going on was Kristina. He nodded his understanding to her and then flicked his eyes towards Aidan. Kristina shook her head slightly, letting him know that Aidan was not aware of what was happening. He gave her a wink and Kristina saw the despair in Max's face had been replaced with hope. While waiting for his opportunity to go to the toilet, Max could only marvel at how Kristina seemed to be able to sing nursery rhymes with Eva and Aidan to calm the pair of them while tension raged all around.

In the toilet Max found the hidden phone and his relief moved his aching bowels which had been clenched ever since he had arrived at Lucky's. The horrible curry was finally taking its leave and it was not going quietly. He had to phone the bookies office number and explain in a horse whisperer that he needed to speak to James Connolly urgently. The agony of the wait went to his guts.

`Hang on a minute' said Max.

`Jesus Quinn what's that noise? Are you on the shitter? I'm glad I can't smell that' said James Connolly.

`Listen its happening tonight, 8 pm at the polo field on the St Jude's Estate in Surrey. Its private property so you will have to blag your way in. Wait for the arrow' said Max.

`Wait for the what?' said Connolly.

`Wait for the feckin' arrow' said Max cutting the call. There was a loud bang on the door and an angry Russian accent demanded that Max open it. His long absence had aroused suspicion. `Won't be a moment just finishing up the paperwork' Max joked as he fumbled with the phone but managed to switch it off and put it back in its hiding place. `Hang on, hang on, I'm done' he said flushing noisily to cover the sound of the cistern lid being replaced. He opened the toilet door and his interrogator eyed him suspiciously for a second before he was caught by a hefty waft which caused him to gag.

`What do you think I've been doing in here all this time?' said Max. `I'd leave it for a while if I were you, a week should be enough.' He laughed at the man's disgusted face and he knew no one would be searching that toilet in a hurry.

20

You were right sir somethings up, the target is on the move. He took a call from Surrey CID and then said he would call them back. He must have used a phone we are not aware of.' Harry Stanton smiled at his phone. So Stuart Logan had taken his words about Moscow rules to heart. `Okay you stay on him and report to me but only on my mobile. This operation might be going hot.'

`Okay sir' said the surprised surveillance operative, wondering what he had done to deserve all this shit falling on his shift.

Harry paced his office for a few moments before he made another call. `Sir it looks like our suspicions were right. I've had eyes on our colleagues since we told him we were taking the target ourselves. He seems to have gone off piste and Surrey CID are involved. It looks like it's going to go hot ... I agree the target is too valuable to lose now. I suggest I lead a team of three and we try and extract him from whatever is going down. If the mad Mick's have been tipped off it could all get very silly ... Yes Sir I agree, it is the Home Counties not Helmund Provence. We will be discreet. What about the couple, our informers? ...No sir, I understand. If it can be avoided we will try. But as you say, bad things happen to good people every day.'

Half an hour later Harry had changed into black clothes similar to those used by police tactical teams. He finished briefing his team of three. `I don't know exactly what we are going into but our mission is to avoid contact with friendlies and hostiles alike and to extract the target. We expect the hostiles to include Luchenko's own men, whoever he is selling his drugs to, perhaps also a man called Voxov and some Irish cowboys who are planning to gate crash the party. It could get very messy.'

`Any friendlies we should help sir?' asked Simms, a young recruit from Harry's old regiment.

`Yes a couple, the Wheelan's. They are our informers and their daughter plays for the target's polo team.' Harry pointed to the white board at pictures of Aidan, Kristina and Hannah next to those of Lucky and his entourage. `There is also likely to be an unknown number of Surrey CID and their armed response team, although at the moment were trying to get them out of the picture.'

`Jesus what a carry on' said another member of the team.

`Exactly, it's going to be amateur hour out there. So we must be efficient and inconspicuous and focused on our target. He is the priority' said Harry.

`Yes sir' said all three in unison. There was nothing else to be said, but they could all feel that surge of adrenaline. Whether it was jumping out of a snatch Land Rover in Belfast or and APC in Iraq or as in tonight's exercise from a luxury Range Rover Sport in leafy Surrey, it was all the same.

`Gentleman it is time to visit the armory. Tonight will be wearing Russian weapons. It will be less confusing for the Scene of Crime Officers if all the munitions are the same' Harry grinned.

`Let's go hunt bear' said Simms as they filed out of the briefing room.

EARLIER THAT DAY.

Stuart Logan knew he would never have a day like this again. After receiving Kristina Whelan's desperate text he thought of how he might contact her in spite of her pleas not to. The number she had called from was not answering and he did not want to risk trying their mobiles if they were being monitored. Posing as a delivery courier he phoned the house and got the housekeeper who told him that she could not get Mr or Mrs Wheelan to sign for a package later as the whole family had gone out with one of Mr Lucky's men.

Stewart then called Harry Stanton. `Harry I'm just tying up our end of the Luchenko files and I came across another name you might want to follow-up.'

`Who is it Stuart?' said Harry.

`Does the name Voxov ring any bells?' said Stuart.

`We don't have much in our system.' Harry Stanton looked at his database and saw the briefest of details confirming that Voxov and Luchenko were in the same gang during their youth in St Petersburg. All other enquiries were supposed to be directed to the liaison at MI6. `Looks like they were young punks together. No mention of them still being associated.'

`Okay Harry. Just thought you should know. I'll be glad when we can wrap this up.'

`Me too. I'll be in touch about Saturday to make sure you have a ringside seat. It's the least I can do considering.'

`Okay Harry, thanks.'

Both men put down their phones knowing that the other was lying. Stuart phoned his own old contact in Surrey Trading Standards. He'd come across Roger May when an ARA investigation had unearthed a huge supply of knock off DVDs. He'd handed that aspect over to May's people who managed to grab wholesalers as well as the poor bastard illegals who were press-ganged into selling these things in pub car parks.

`Hello Stuart. If you're going to offer me the latest `*Pirates of the Caribbean*' I've already got it' said May laughing.

`Actually Roger I want a favour. I need an inconspicuous way to make contact with your Chief Constable and also the head of your armed response unit' said Stuart.

`I see' said May knowing that it would not be a typical job.

Three hours later Stuart sat in a nondescript cafe in Guildford hunched in a quiet conversation with a stocky man with cropped grey hair and alert brown eyes. `That's quite a story Mr Logan' he said.

`I'm not a lunatic or a fantasist Mr Bradley. I hope Roger May convinced you of that or we would not be sitting here' said Stuart.

`That's true, but even so...'

`Listen you must have come across the security services before. They play by different rules. If need be they will settle for taking their assets and leaving you to deal with the rest. In this case a possible dead kidnap victim and a gunfight amidst the mansions of the St Jude's estate. I don't think your Chief Constable will give much thought to national security issues if leafy Surrey becomes a war zone for Russian gangsters' said Stuart.

Bradley mulled this over. `Stay here while I make a call.' He left the cafe and got into the unmarked car waiting outside. A few minutes later he was back and the sceptical look with which he first greeted Stuart was replaced by a serious frown. `The Chief Constable has been in contact with the spooks, who are of course not saying anything, but Harry Stanton cannot be contacted at the moment for operational reasons. Discrete enquiries at the betting shop have also revealed that the Connolly Brothers left earlier in the day to go fishing with a group of men. No one knows anything about this Voxov character.'

`Oh my God is going to happen' said Stewart.

`You're coming with me now. I need you to brief my men on everything you know about these people.'

As Bradley's driver sped through the traffic on the A3 Stuart sat back and thought of Hannah Wheelan and her boyfriend being held prisoner in fear for their lives and he wondered how it had all come to this.

Harry Stanton and his companion stopped outside the Bishop of Lambeth's residence near the roundabout where Lambeth Bridge Road split in three directions. It was a popular rendezvous for MI5 and MI6 agents who needed to have a brief chat off the record before shuffling back to their offices a few minutes' walk away. `So you're quite sure this Voxov is not in England Alex?' said Harry.

`I put in a call after we spoke. He was spotted in St Petersburg this morning. The feud with your man has made him concerned about travelling' said Alex.

`Well someone wants him to think that Voxov is over here, taking the fight to him on his home turf' said Harry.

`We are not aware of that. Looks like someone is trying to make mischief between them. Who would profit from that?' said Alex.

Harry thought about who else might benefit. Only one idea came to mind but it was so preposterous he dismissed it immediately. `Okay Alex, thanks for that. I'll let you know if the local goes global.'

`And vice versa' said Alex. 'We're still on for golf at the end of the month aren't we?'

Both men turned to walk back to their offices and not the first time Harry mused at how they had managed to grab the prettiest side of the river. He knew something was up and he hoped the surveillance he had ordered on Stuart Logan would give him the jump. If it was going to end today Harry had to go through his options before putting in a call to the old man.

In the office of a closed up garage in Cricklewood, James Connolly tried to blank out the background noise from the workshop as he listened to his caller. `You said he wanted to talk to me or Patrick about a special bet but he wouldn't leave a name or number?' James Connolly did not like what he heard. Of course it could be legitimate. People often came and put on a big bet for a race they knew was fixed. Bookies would take a hit but not before they laid of it off with other bookmakers and made a tidy profit themselves. It was a good ruse but it could not be used too frequently for fear of drawing unwanted attention. `Keep me posted if any more strangers come into the shop today' said James before killing the call. The door to the office opened and in walked a wiry middle aged man. James Gilligan or `Gilly' as he was commonly known was a dyed in the wool Republican who had not taken peace well. His commitment to the cause had never waned but he despaired of some of those who joined the struggle towards the end. They did not seem to share the same ideals as his generation. They were interested in the income from drug smuggling and protection rackets for its own sake not as a source of funding for a more noble cause. But things being what they were he had to work and for a man of his skills the opportunities were limited in the peacetime economy. He had taken a few jobs from the older Connolly brother before but he had misgivings about working with Patrick who he considered to be a loose cannon. `My men are not happy. You need to come out here and cool your boy and his playmates down' said Gilly.

James Connolly came out into the workshop where two distinct camps had formed. Gilly and the three other men, old hands like himself were sitting quietly playing cards. They knew the importance of calm before a dangerous mission. In contrast Patrick Connolly and his posse of four similar youths in tracksuits and baseball caps were ostentatiously cleaning handguns to a soundtrack of hip-hop music. `What do you think this is Patrick, some fucking computer game? Turn that shit off and come over here we need to talk. There's been a development 'said James Connolly. Patrick stung by his brother's rebuke took his time in joining the combined group at the workbench. `Someone has been asking around the betting shop for us. It could be nothing but we have to be sure that we're the only ones giving out the surprises tonight.'

`I don't like the sound of this' said one of Gilly's colleagues.

`We're not scared are we boys?' said Patrick Connolly to his fan club.

James Connolly looked at Gilly and both of them could see they were going to have problems. `Patrick I want your lads to go in and snatch the gear. Gilly's men will provide covering fire on the ground if it gets messy. Gilly will be the sharpshooter to keep the Russians pinned down while you all get away' said James Connolly.

`So we're the feckin' bullet catchers are we?' said one of Patrick's crew.

`I thought you lot weren't afraid' said Gilly.

`Just make sure you shoot straight old man. I don't want us to be hit by friendly fire' said Patrick Connolly.

21

The mock Victorian street lamps had come on in the roads of the St Jude's estate. The pools of light were sufficient to illuminate the well maintained roads but not enough to pollute the bedrooms of the well-heeled residents. But up in the woodlands surrounding the polo grounds it was pitch black and the clear sky had brought a chill to the air.

`Okay, I understand Sir. Of course, if we can't achieve our mission we will leave the rest of it to the locals' said Harry Stanton finishing his call. The other men in the Range Rover searched his face for an explanation. `Surrey police are aware of our interest and the AD has had to deny any mission. We can't show our hand. If we can't get the target out we are to leave it to the locals.'

Harry could sense the disappointment in his squad who were keyed up for action.

`Let's make sure it does not come to that sir?'

`Yes Simms let's do that' said Harry. ` We better get out of the car. I know it's dark but four men is a car will attract attention.'

`But if we stand outside and look in the windows, people will just think we're dogging' cracked one of the team. They all laughed, grateful for the stupid banter to take the edge of their nerves. As they dispersed Harry shivered. Not with fear but from the chill in the air from the rapidly falling temperature. They made their way carefully through the woodland and stopped in the trees just before the grass of the polo field took over.

Harry's team took up their positions observing the dark shape of the polo club construction site. Ten minutes later Harry heard in his ear piece `Black Range Rover approaching pulling a horse trailer. Interior light is on and only female driver is visible.'

`Okay everybody, radio silence until it goes off' said Harry. He looked through his night vision goggles wondering who else apart from his team was observing the scene one hundred meters away. The woman got out of the car and opened all the doors. The interior light showed the car was empty. Next she went over to one of the lighting rigs on the construction site and threw some switches. The whole area was suddenly bathed in stark white light from two towers. Harry could not hear a generator and realised that the lights must be battery powered. Harry removed his goggles and when he is eyesight had adjusted he recognised the woman was Kristina Wheelan. A thickening fog was rising off the grass as the earth gave up its heat to the cold night air. He had to squint to see what she was doing as Kristina was reached up to open the ramp on the back of the horse trailer. The floodlights caught her shapely silhouette in a white cashmere sweater and tight jeans. She emerged from the horse trailer with two cases and then she unhooked the trailer from her car. Standing under a pool of light she opened first one case and then the other and both appeared to be full of money. Her voice was both scared and angry as it rang across the silent polo grounds.

`We have done everything as you've instructed. Your million euros is here and the rest of it is in the back. Now tell us where Hannah and Tito are, I'm begging you.' Kristina Wheeler looked around her but no one could be seen on the empty polo field or in the woods opposite. Harry processed this new information. Hannah Wheelan and Luchenko's nephew had been kidnapped and her mother was paying off a ransom. Who had taken them the Irish, this mysterious man Voxov?' Kristina's voice broke through his thoughts. `Please tell me where my daughter is.' She sounded at her wits end and he felt more than a little sympathy if her family were to end up casualties of this operation. Kristina paced nervously at the edge of the arcs of light. She scanned around the polo field looking for signs of life but the thickening fog obscured visibility to all but a few feet in any direction. `Please for god's sake don't do this. Tell me where my daughter is!'

Harry felt the tension in his chest and breathed slowly. When were they going to make their move? It was almost a minute later when he caught a glimpse of light on something as it entered the arc of the floodlights and embedded itself into the skin of the horse trailer. It was an arrow. Harry glanced around but could not work out its trajectory. Whoever had fired it was a good shot as it had covered at least a hundred and fifty metres to reach its target. Kristina Wheelan jumped in fright at the noise of the arrow piercing the metal sheet. She had to reach high to grab it. As she wrestled it free her cashmere jumper rose exposing her bare midriff. Finally she freed the arrow and rotated it. There must have been a message written on the shaft. She looked towards the dark woodland and shouted thank you to the unknown archer, before getting back in her car and doing a U-turn around the back of the construction site and heading back towards the entrance of the polo field.

The two cases stood in the glare of the spotlights just in front of the horse trailer. The thickening mist had now risen to five feet and covered the polo field like a blanket. What would have been a suicidal dash for the cash half an hour earlier was now possible. The mist would now provide cover for anyone traversing the polo ground in a low crouch. The kill zone was now restricted to the arcs of the flood lights which penetrated no more than a few metres in front of the building site. Harry knew that at any moment a figure could dash out of the mist and make a grab for the cases and then proceedings would start for real. He flicked the safety off his AK-47 machine gun and tried to calm his breathing.

James Connolly watched Kristina Wheelan from the woodland about a hundred metres south of where Harry Stanton was hidden. He did not realise the size of a polo pitch never having seen the game before. It seemed crazy to contemplate running across such a large expanse of open ground to retrieve the cases and whatever else awaited them in the trailer. He had worked out that this was not the normal drugs exchange that Quinn had tipped them off about. This was a ransom payoff. And if there really was one million euros in those two cases it would be a nice nights pay. The gods seemed to be smiling on them again as the mist on the field was now a fog thick enough to hide your hand a yard from your face. `Patrick the angels are with us tonight' he said to his younger brother who was keen for the off. He gave him a kiss on the top of his head before sending him out across the field.

Patrick's team kept low to the ground and having been persuaded to exchange their lurid tracksuits for more sober boiler suits they were now almost invisible in the thick mist. Patrick emerged from the mist first about fifteen feet from the horse trailer. He and his crew were scanning the area around the horse box and behind them with their weapons ready for anyone who may have followed them through the mist. One was armed with a pump action shotgun. The others with machine pistols with wire stocks. Patrick turned back towards where James was hidden holding one of the bags of cash. `It's real Jimmy it's...' He did not get to finish the sentence because another shape glinted in the light and Patrick Connolly was pinned to the side of the horse trailer with an arrow sticking out from just below his Adams apple. His hand felt the entry point in disbelief. It was in that dip between the collar bones where the old nuns at school had said that an angel had touched Jesus. Wonder gave way to pain and he screamed in agony. `Jimmy help me!' His plea was answered from inside the horse trailer with machine gun fire that made his body jump spasmodically as bullets punctured the thin wall against which Patrick was pinned. His companions' unloaded shots into the horse trailer but two were cut down by gunmen firing from the building site. They must have sneaked through the mist from the other side of the club house.

James Connolly came through the mist with two of Gilly's men. His was shouting to his brother. A gunman in a flak jacket and helmet rolled out of the horse trailer and shot one of Gilly's men before James Connolly shot him in the face.

Machine gun fire now broke out from the construction site and was answered by unseen figures in the mist. Angry voices shouted. Some with Irish accents, the others in Russian.

A voice shouted from the shell of the polo club house. `Voxov. You think you can come here and do this to me? I fucking kill you myself.' It was Luchenko.

`That's out target' said Harry breaking radio silence. `We need to get down there and take him.' Harry's three colleagues confirmed and they slid out of the woods and into the misty field keeping to a low crouching run.

One of the Irish gunmen shouted `We have the money let's get out of here.' They started backing towards the mist from where they had come. James Connolly noted that they were Gilly's men. He looked back at his brother pinned to the horse trailer like some macabre butterfly in a specimen box. Patrick was dead.

`For feck's sake we need to get out of here Jimmy.' It was the last living member of Patrick's crew.

`Help me take Patrick home. I'm not leaving him here' said James Connolly.

The man thought of running for a moment but then he turned and put Patrick's arm over his shoulder while James tried to pull the arrow from his brother's throat.

`Hurry up Jimmy we...' He got no further because a high powered snipers bullet had splattered his brains on the side of the horse trailer. James Connolly turned in the direction the shot had come from. It could only have been Gilly. Now his men had their money for the cause there was no point in leaving witnesses who could lead the police to them. He saw the muzzle flare from Gilly's second shot then it went dark.

A shout went up. `Armed police put down your weapons'. Everyone stopped and turned towards the line of armed police in helmets and flak jackets making their way towards the two group's combatants. It looked to Harry like the action was over then something happened to change the outcome completely. The floodlights were being extinguished by machine gun fire from the retreating Irishmen. Harry heard the report of a high velocity rifle and a scream from the police lines. The field was plunged into darkness as the floodlights were extinguished. The Russians and Irish took their cue and jointly turned their guns on the remaining light which came from torches attached to the police weapons. They were also making an attractive target for the sniper. A second policeman went down from a shot followed quickly by another. The remaining force would be hard pressed to ward off a combined attack from the Russian and Irish gunmen. `Get our man quick' shouted Harry into his throat like as he sped across the field in darkness. His Makarov pistol barked twice, once catching an Irish gunmen with a moneybag in the chest and then wounding a Russian in the thigh. Harry was about twenty metres from the horse trailer when he heard an engine roaring through the mist. The lights were off but he caught the briefest glimpse as door courtesy lights illuminated the interior. `Quickly Lucky get in!' shouted the driver. It was Kristina Wheelan, she had comeback for Luchenko who dived into the passenger seat before she roared back into the mist. Harry had always suspected there was something between Wheelan's wife and the Luchenko. Why else would she risk everything to rescue him while her daughter was still in danger? Harry saw the brake lights go on briefly and then the car sped off again. `The targets gone, the Wheelan woman has taken him. Let's get out of here' said Harry.

`Sir the police are taking heavy casualties from that sniper. They won't be able to hold it together' said Simms.

`That's not our problem' said Harry. A flare went up and what he saw changed Harry's mind. Against the red lit tableau of the gun battle Harry saw the figure crouched in the tree was a man he had given up hope of ever seeing in this lifetime. `Gilly stop' he shouted. The face moved from the rifle sight and looked at Harry in mutual recognition. His surprise snapshot missed Harry by inches and Harry rolled down into the mist before the Gilly could get another one off. `We're going after that sniper and I want him alive' said Harry.

`Yes sir' said Simms.

`Sir, Jarvis is hit. I'm taking him out' said another member of Harry's squad.

`Okay, Hendry, you do that. Get him to the rendezvous point' said Harry. His squad was now down to the two of them but that should be enough. He set off in the direction where he had spotted the sniper and came across the rope he'd used to make his quick exit from the tree. In his ear Harry could hear that Simms had found the man's trail and was relaying directions to him. Harry set off after them fingering the scar on his face and thinking that it was time to pay back the man who was responsible for his Irish souvenir.

It was nearly seventeen years ago when Harry last saw the man he was now pursuing. That time Harry had been a platoon commander in the second Land Rover on a night patrol in Armagh. The first car had been caught by a massive roadside bomb which flipped the burning vehicle ten feet in the air before it came to rest just in front of his car. There was a moment of shock and disbelief from the driver and his passenger before machine gun fire raked their windscreen ending their interest in events. In the back of the Land Rover high velocity rounds punctured the metal skin and one soldier who had not done up his flak jacket regretted his mistake for the brief remainder of his life. Another man was hit in the thigh. `We're sitting ducks here' said Harry. `I'm going out there. You return firing when you see their position. If I go down don't come out until you know where they are.' Harry burst through the double doors and started running towards the hedge where he would have hidden if it was his ambush. A single rifle shot took his leg out from under him and he fell face forward on the ground. He heard the whoosh and felt the heat of the blast as a rocket propelled grenade entered the back of the Land Rover and killed the rest of his squad. A few moments later he heard voices and looked up to see two men illuminated by the light of the burning Land Rover.

`Is that all of them then?' asked the man with the rifle.

`Just that one left' said his companion holding the discharged grenade launcher. The rifleman aimed at Harry and discovered with a hollow click that his magazine was empty. `Looks like it's your lucky day pal' said the man Harry had misheard being called Billy. The beating blades of a helicopter turned the gunmen's thoughts to escape and Harry slipped into unconsciousness as the helicopter searchlight bathed the scene of carnage.

This night Harry could also hear a helicopter in the distance, but it would not be bothering with him. Its work was back at the main scene of action almost a quarter of a mile away. He heard the report of warning rounds and Simms commanding the gunmen to get down from the fence or he would shoot him where he hung. Harry turned left and it brought him to a small clearing next to a chain link fence. About ten feet up was the exhausted Gilly hanging from the fence while Simms pointed his shouldered AK-47 at the man's head. Gilly climbed down slowly as instructed and turned to face Harry who also pointed his gun at him. `Looks like it's your lucky day Gilly' said Harry having waited years to deliver the line.

`Okay, you've got me. I won't give you any trouble' said Gilly.

`Oh no you don't. I'm not having some mealy mouthed politician give you your freedom as a sign of goodwill because they're scared it might upset is upset the peace process' said Harry.

`So what are you going to do? Kill me here in cold blood' said Gilly.

`Well we are fighting a war on terror' said Simms indicating he was happy however Harry played it.

`I see' said Gilly. `You know that night seventeen years ago when my gun jammed. The man I was with offered me his and I refused because I thought you deserved to cheat death that night.'

Harry dropped his gun and stripped of his flak jacket. `Give him your knife Simms.'

`Sir!' said Simms.

`Give him your fucking knife and we'll finishing this here!' said Harry.

`He wants to give me the chance to cheat death' said Gilly with a smile.

Simms stood back and threw his knife at the feet of the Irishman then turned on his torch to allow both men to see each other better. They circled each other on the edge of the ring of light. They crept side on to present the smallest possible target. Gilly taunted Harry. `Come on then. You've waited seventeen years for this why the delay now?' Harry darted forward but Gilly neatly side-stepped and his own slash nearly caught Harry in the face. `Almost gave you another souvenir to match the one you've got' mocked Gilly as he patted his own cheek. Gilly slashed and Harry caught his wrist in his free hand and then twisted trying to bring his own knife up into Gilly's ribs but the jab of a bony elbow into his bicep caused Harry's nerves to freeze in his arm and he dropped his knife. Both men struggled to get a grip on the single weapon and Gilly had the upper hand turning the blades towards Harry's chest.

`Sir!' said Simms, taking aim at Gilly.

`Stand down' grunted Harry as he managed to throw Gilly. His knife fell from his hand as he hit the chain link fence. Harry recovered his own knife and advanced on the unarmed Gilly to end his life. Gilly rolled and sprung out of a crouch surprising Harry. In mid-air Gilly's head exploded and his body dropped to the ground.

Harry panted and glared angrily at Simms. `What did you do that for? I had him.'

`With respect sir you fucking didn't. Look at his hand.' His torch fell on Gilly's hand confirming an eight inch stiletto blade Harry had not seen at all. `He pulled it from his boot as he came out of the crouch.'

Harry knew he would be dead if it were not for Simms.

`Thank you. I'm getting too old for all this' said Harry. When Simms said nothing Harry said `I'm not looking for confirmation you know.'

`Of course not sir. But I think we should be making a move. It's gone quiet out there and my shot is bound to attract attention.'

`Yes it will. Let's get out of here' said Harry

.

22

Lucky Luchenko looked out of the rear window of the Range Rover at the gunfight raging behind him. Where was Voxov and who were these fucking Irishmen? He did not believe Voxov would sub contract the job and miss out on the pleasure of seeing him pay. More importantly how did the police find out? His men who survived knew they would be looked after if they kept quiet, but only if Lucky got away. He had to go when he did. He could not believe Kristina had come back for him.

`You've got some balls Kristina. You risk your life to come back and save me' said Lucky.

`Yes, I came back to get you' said Kristina.

`We go and rescue the kids now. Then after we work together and we get the people who did it. We fuck them up good.' Lucky often had dreams of finding a woman who could be a partner his enterprises as well as his bed and Kristina had all the qualifications. She was wasted on that husband and his petty schemes. She had to see that. He looked at her determined profile as she sped through the dark with the lights off and he wanted her even more. Kristina stopped the car in a small secluded area of woodland. It had a reputation as a place for courting couples, but tonight the sound of gunfire and a police helicopter had kept lovers in doors.

`Lucky I need to ask you something' said Kristina turning towards him with a nervous smile in spite of the drama of the last half-hour. She leaned closer. `I want you to close your eyes and remember something.' She was so close to him, the smell of her lingering perfume and a musky mixture of sweat and fear coming from her skin were intoxicating.

`Yes Kristina' he breathed. His eyes closed and he felt the heat of her close to his skin.

`You remember when you were a young man you used to do business in Tallinn at the docks. But one night the shipment got lost and someone had to be punished.' Lucky's eyes opened in surprise. `You came to our house and questioned a woman, beat and kicked her and before you left you kissed a frightened little girl.'

`That was you Kristina?' said Lucky looking into her face and finally realising why he always thought he knew her from the first moment he saw her at a polo match.

`Yes Lucky, that was me.' Kristina leaned forward and kissed him gently on the lips. In his confusion Lucky did not notice the nylon rope which had dropped down across his neck. Then it was too late. It snapped tight across his windpipe holding him against the head rest. Lucky's hands scrambled fruitlessly at the rope before trying to reach behind him to hit his assailant. But Petor just leaned back in his seat with his foot on the back of the head rest and pulled the rope tighter. He had been hiding in the back of the car since Kristina had collected him in the midst of the confusion of the gunfight. His bow and arrows had been enough to start what they needed. Petor could feel the life starting to flow out of Lucky Luchenko. Kristina grabbed Lucky's now limp hands and fastened them in a plastic ties and then did the same with his feet. Petor released the tourniquet on his neck easing Lucky's bruised and crushed windpipe. Life remained in his body but not for long.

Petor leaned forward so Lucky could see him through watery eyes. `You remember me? I was the boy with Kristina. The woman you were kicking was my mother and the man you had killed was my father.'

In the final moments before he died Lucky saw the truth. The kidnap by Voxov had been a ruse. Everything had been organised to bring him to this place and this moment so these two children could extract their revenge. The last image he saw was the calm, almost serene smile on Kristina's beautiful face as his life left his body.

23

It was nearly 2am before Kristina and Peter arrived at the disused bank where they had imprisoned Hannah and Tito.

`I can't do this again Petor' said Kristina.

`You must be strong Kristina is nearly over. If they are going to be safe they must never know' said Petor.

`Off course you're right. I hope they will come quietly. They were drugged and afraid the first time. Now they'll be prepared and I can't see Hannah cooperating, there's too much of her mother in her' said Kristina.

`The boy too. His manhood has been challenged. He will want to protect her' said Petor.

`I don't want to hurt them' said Kristina.

`Let's find our things and get changed. I have something from Lucky that can help' said Petor.

They stood in their balaclava masks and boiler suits at the top of the stairs leading down to the old bank vault. `Are you sure it won't hurt them?' Kristina asked again.

`I'll throw it in the far corner. He will be by the door if he is going to do anything. While they are confused, you must cuff them, you understand?'

`Yes' said Kristina not believing how it could be in her daughter's interest, but too tired to argue anymore. Petor banged on the door. `We are coming in. The ransom has been paid. We are here to release you. Do not make any problems.'

`Okay, we won't' said Hannah and in those few words Kristina could detect both fear and determination in her voice.

`I'm going to open the door now' said Petor. He opened it a couple of inches and threw something in. He was too quick for Tito who was standing next to the door with the broken arm of a chair ready to bring it down on Petor's head. They could see the bright lights of the thunderflash under the door and a moment later the noise of the explosion. They pushed the door open and found the teenagers collapsed on the floor eyes shut, hands over their ears. Kristina could not help herself.

`My poor baby' she said.

`Shut up' said Petor and he put a bag over Tito's head urging Kristina to do the same to Hannah. Reluctantly she copied him and they cuffed their captives and got them onto their feet and steered them up the stairs and out to where their car was parked. They bundled them into the backseat of the Range Rover and drove off. They did not want to risk driving too long with hooded captives in the back as the distant noise of ambulances and police cars reminded them that they were only a few miles from the crime scene.

Petor pulled up at a crossroads. `Can you hear me in the back? I'm sorry we had to do that, but we told you not to try anything stupid.'

`You bastard, when my mum and dad find you they'll kill you' spat Hannah. Tito expressed similar sentiments in Russian. In the front Petor and Kristina smiled. If they were angry, they were on the mend.

`Listen we're going to take you out now. We will give you food and water and take the handcuffs off. There is a village down the road and you can phone the police for help from there' said Petor.

By the time Hannah and Tito had removed their handcuffs and hoods the sound of the car had disappeared. They were at a crossroads and they had no idea which direction the car had taken. Even though it was still dark they blinked. The after-effects of the thunder flash were still playing on their retinas. As promised there were two brown bags containing water and a sandwich and standing neatly next to them were Hannah's high-heeled party shoes that she last remembered wearing as she staggered from the restaurant. She looked at the three items in a row and smiled. It reminded her of how her mum arranged her shoes and schoolbag the night before so they would find things quickly in the morning.

Petor dropped Kristina at another phone box almost ten miles away. `We've done it Kristina. Don't worry they will be okay. They are young. They will forget soon.'

`I hope so Petor. I hope so. No parent should ever have to do that to their child' said Kristina.

`Try not to think about it too much. It was the only option we had. If we had left it to the authorities we would never have got our revenge. You must make your phone call now and I must get rid of him' said Petor nodding towards the boot of the Range Rover.

`Take care Petor. You must leave immediately. Go home to your wife and family and live in peace. I will come and see you when it is safe.' Kristina hugged her cousin and watched the tail lights disappear before trudging to the phone box. There was just one more lie to tell then it would be over.

Petor knew he would have to improvise as dawn would be breaking soon. He'd left Kristina at a phone box where she could contact the police with a tale of how Lucky had dumped her and made off. Petor turned the car towards Hampshire, keen to put as much distance between him and the crime scene as possible. He kept to B roads and it was down one of these he stumbled upon the pig farm. He switched off his lights and coasted up the pens which were some distance from the accommodation which thankfully was still in darkness.

Petor opened the boot of the Range Rover and pulled out the tarp containing the body of Lucky Luchenko. It had been a last minute theft from the bank building site that now proved to be a godsend. Petor pulled the shroud like a sled across the damp grass to the side of the pig pens. It took him a few moments to find what he was looking for in the pens but he knew every farm building would have one. He returned to the corpse carrying a shovel, last used to shift pig shit if the smell of it was anything to go by. Petor dragged the body to the kerb and lay the head in the gutter. It took several hefty blows but eventually he was able to separate the head and hands from the body. He put his grizzly pieces on the tarpaulin while he went in search of a bucket to sluice down the bloody path. It took three trips to the water butt before all the traces of blood were gone and Petor was sweating with the effort. If the farmer was anything like him he would be up soon and dogs would be scrambling to get out of the door to do their business.

Petor dragged the tarpaulin to the far end of the pens where the pigs were already grubbing around in anticipation of their morning feed. The smell of the blood probably told them that today's meal would be a bit different. He stripped the body and manhandled the headless corpse over the gate into the pen. While he wrapped Lucky's remains in the tarp the pigs nervously circled the offering. For a moment Petor thought his plan would not work and then one of the braver animals broke from the group and came over to nibble at the bloody stump of a wrist. Seeing no response from the body the others rushed forward and soon there was a feeding frenzy. Petor watched as the flesh containing the tattoo of the Madonna and child was stripped from Lucky's back by hungry mouths. The sound of bone crunching confirmed to Petor that nothing would be left. Satisfied, he left the pigs to their breakfast.

Petor drove to Portsmouth where the tarp containing Lucky's remains were buried at sea. The Range Rover met a fiery end by a set of disused garages on a rough council estate in Fratton.

24

A fine pair we are, trussed up here and literally holding the baby while Kristina is out there trying to save our daughter' said Aidan.

The cousin who has asked all the questions finally had enough of his anxious pacing and had tied up Aidan, Max and Eva. It had been remarkably easy to do in the end. He pulled out the gun that had been making an uncomfortable bulge in his suit. `So now you know it is a fucking gun and I'll blow her head off first if you don't sit down.' Eva had annoyed the nervous gunman all afternoon with questions about where her mum and Lucky had gone. He had made the mistake of saying it was a surprise and had endured two hours of questions as she tried to guess what it was.

Aidan knew things were not going well when Lucky had refused to let him and Max come to the ransom handover with him and Kristina. The cousin had been tasked to guard them. The man still remained unconvinced by their answers to the questions about their snooping around at Barton's. `You two are not right. You have a smell. My nose is never wrong' he said.

`Sorry that's me. It's the curry from last night' Max said trying to make a joke of it.

As the hours wore on the guard must have sensed Max and Aidan were trying to hatch a plan to escape. So whether as a precaution against that or to shut Eva up the three of them were now tied to chairs with the elaborate gilt curtain ropes. Although Eva was the only one with a gag in her mouth. She had earned that for telling him that his gun was pretend because it was too long. He told her to shut the fuck up or he would show her how a silencer worked. She told him he would go to hell for swearing and that had earned her the gag.

An hour later Max tried to reason with him again. `Look she's quiet now. Do we really have to do this? Lucky will not be happy you have treated us so badly.'

`When Mr Luchenko comes back and all is well I apologise and we all have a drink and joke about it. If not...' he opened his jacket and showed them the gun. The timing could not be worse for at that moment they heard the sound of gunfire coming from the polo field a mile away.

Eva tried to shout from behind her gag. `It's just fireworks Eva. No need to get upset' said Max.

`Yes fireworks. That's the surprise you could not tell her about isn't it?' said Aidan trying to calm the gun man as well as his daughter.

The gunman looked at the three of them and Max and Aidan could see what he was contemplating. `If you do this you will never be safe. The police will always be after you' said Max.

`And if you are wrong you will have to answer to Mr Luchenko as well. How is he going to explain three dead bodies in his living room when the police arrive?' said Max.

The man seemed to way things up. `Leave us and go and see what is going on. Save yourself if it has all gone wrong.' Aidan's appeal to his self-preservation instinct worked and the gunman headed towards the locked door. `Ungag my daughter first please.'

`You will have to listen to her for your punishment' said the gunman as he untied her gag then ran for the door. He almost got out before he was hit by a stream of Irish swearing from Eva. No word was spared from the six year olds vocabulary. She had memorised all of her father's bad language despite Aidan's attempts to kerb his tongue in front of his daughter.

Max and Aidan looked at each other in astonishment. `I blame the mothers' said Aidan sheepishly.

The gunfire continued. `Oh my god Max. I hope Kristina and Hannah are not anywhere near that. I don't know what I would do if...' Aidan suddenly remembered Max's own predicament. The safety of his own wife and child were now at risk from this change of plans. `Max we have to warn Siobhan now... the Connolley's...'

`It might not be as bad as you think' said Max. `I managed to get a call through to the Connelly's. Kristina has a phone hidden in the cistern. She knew I needed to make a call today. She knows more about the kidnapping than she is letting on.'

Aidan did not know what to make of his wife's actions. She'd got this gardener Petor into Lucky's house without first telling him. But the man had come up with the drugs evidence which would bring everything to an end. Except now with this kidnap how would that change things? Was this some elaborate hoax that she had got Hannah and Tito to go along with? But the two of them looked genuinely terrified on the video they weren't acting. Unless... the idea was too horrifying to contemplate.

Max could see his friend was stunned by his disclosure. `Aidan, don't judge Kristina too harshly. I'm sure she had a good reason for what she did and why she could not confide in us. Don't make her into something she is not. She loves you.'

`She was always afraid that people would judge her for being something she was not. Then she thought it would be easier to let people think what they liked because they would not believe the truth anyway. Like how we met.'

`You said you met in a nightclub?' said Max.

`It was what people would believe. Glamorous Eastern European woman with a young child looking for a wealthy western meal ticket. Isn't that the cliché? And I've got form, especially after the way Andria turned into such a money grabbing snob' said Aidan.

`Don't do this Aidan' said Max.

`How did you meet mummy?' said Eva.

`It was funny actually' said Aidan and Max was glad to see his friend's face brighten at the memory.

`I was refurbishing this office block. First one I'd ever done. It was the one I'd bought with the money I'd raised from the syndicate that included Victor Garcia, the crook who brought me to the attention of the ARA in the first place. Anyway I was there that day helping the guys to knock out partition walls and one of the blokes says sandwich woman is here. I looked out of the window and I saw Kristina getting off her tricycle with a little trailer behind. She had this little catering business with this other woman. They made sandwiches and sold them to office workers. They delivered by bicycle straight to the desk. A good idea for those who were too busy or lazy to go out of the officer at lunch time.

Anyway she was trying to chain it to the railings except they were all covered with boarding now. She was about to give up and go on when I opened the window and shouted that I would bring the blokes down. She looked up and smiled and that was it. I was gone. I don't know what, but it was the most beautiful face in the world. My reaction was obvious to all the other blokes and they started to take the pi... mickey. I was the last one in the sandwich queue and she said everything was gone. My face must have looked like a slapped ar... well anyway. Then she pulls out this baguette and says she's saved the best for last.'

`That's nice dad' said Eva.

Aidan looked sheepish and Max grinned at him. Aidan continued.

`Well she promised to come back the next day only this time the guys are winding me up. `We don't want sandwiches today. We're going to the chip shop.' I said I would buy them the sandwiches and they had me. The day after they made me a bet `Ask her out and if she says yes we will pay for our own sandwiches.'

`What did you do Aidan?' aid Max.

`I bottled it and had eight hairy arsed builders eating lunch at my expense again and laughing at me' said Aidan.

`So how did you ask mummy to be your girlfriend?' said Eva.

`That was an accident sweetheart. I was always the last in the queue for sandwiches so I could talk to your mum without the other blokes hanging around. I knew she must have liked me because she was not in a hurry to get away. I would work myself up to the point where I would ask her out but then I'd get nervous and stop. I was pretending to be one of the builders and the guys had all joked about the horrible man who was their boss and I had to go along with it because I could not admit I was pretending to be a builder.'

`That wasn't going to last was it?' said Max.

`No. It came to Friday and I'd been at a meeting with the bank all suited and booted and by the time I arrived back at the site Kristina was already serving the blokes. I walked right past without her recognising me. I ran into the site office to change into my builders clothes and I am stood there in my underpants when the door opens and Kristina is there with the foreman laughing behind her. He walks off and I tell her to come in and she says only if I put some clothes on. So I put my suit back on and confess that I am the Managing Director not a labourer. She asked me why I tried to pretend and I said I didn't want her to see me as just some dick in suit. Truth be told I guess part of it was as a protection against meeting another gold digger like Andria. She asked me if there were any more lies and I admitted that I was buying lunch for everybody because I did not have the courage to ask her out.'

`What did she say to that?' asked Max.

`She said she had known men who had tried to impress her by dressing up and spending money on an impressive meal for her but never one who tried to do it by dressing down and buying lunch for his friends. She came over and kissed me and asked me if I would go out with her' said Aidan.

`Ahhh, a happy ending daddy' said Eva.

`It gets better than that pumpkin. Mummy took my hand and a small megaphone on my desk and we went into the main building where the men were working. It was very noisy with drills and banging. She shouted into the microphone `Attention deceitful workers. I have asked Aidan Wheelan to go out with me so from tomorrow you pay for your own sandwiches.'

`That's a lovely story Aidan' said Max.

`Yes mate. The truth can be beautiful' said Aidan.

`Listen daddy there are fireworks outside' said Eva.
The sky had a red glow and the thumping sound of rockets being launched transformed itself into the beating rotors of the police helicopter. Max and Aidan looked at each other. They did not think there was any cause for celebration.

Twenty minutes later they heard the sound of cars outside Lucky's gates and then crunching metal. Something was being used to force them open. The house shook as they smashed in Lucky's front door and then moments later the door of the living room. Three armed policemen burst in and pointed guns at them. `Put your hands in the air where I can see them' shouted the first policeman taking control of the situation.

`Our hands are tied to the feckin' chairs' said Max.

`Yes the feckin' chairs' said Eva, trying to get away with swearing for a second time.

`Can you identify these people?' said the officer over his shoulder.

Aidan looked back to see Stuart Logan enter the room. `This man is Aidan Whelan and that one is Max Quinn. They have been our inside contacts on this operation. The little girl with a potty mouth is Aidan's daughter Eva Wheelan.'

Eva's embarrassment now knew no end and she did what any six year old girl would in the circumstances and started crying. `I want my mum she wailed.'

Aidan looked at Stuart. `Your mum will be home soon Eva. We sent a car to pick her up. She is fine. Your sister and her boyfriend are coming back as well. They are okay too' said Stuart Logan.

`Oh thank god' said Aidan. Whatever Kristina had done had worked.

`We heard all the fireworks' said Max nodding towards Eva

`Well Mr Luchenko and your mum had to leave after the fireworks started and then Mr Luchenko dropped your mum down the road and drove off' said Stuart Logan.

`He is very rude man' said Eva.

`Yes Eva when we find him we are going to teach him some manners' said Logan.

`Is anyone else missing?' said Max.

`I think there is a betting shop in Kilburn that will be looking for new owners' said Logan.

`Thank god' said Max sagging with relief.

`Your wife is a remarkable woman Mr Wheelan. Our friend on the Embankment was going to spoil Saturday's party and keep all the presents for himself. Kristina managed to make sure everyone got what they deserved.'

Epilogue

Harry Stanton winced as he eased himself into the visitors chair in the Assistant Director's office. His chest was heavily strapped to protect the cracked ribs he'd sustained during his fight with Gilly three days before.

`Still bloody sore I suppose. When we wrap this up I'll sign you off on sick leave' said the Assistant Director.

`Thank you sir' was all that Harry could muster. For the past three days he'd been fully immersed in the investigation to understand what had really gone on at what the Red Top press had already dubbed `The Surrey Shootout'. Thankfully the police had been able to control access to the gated community in the aftermath of the fire fight, which had claimed eight lives. Due to the number of celebrities, sportsmen and well-to-do types who lived on the Estate, the press were having a field day speculating on what had happened. TV crews had been kept out but an enterprising radio journalist had been able to get an interview with a media tycoon who was a resident. It was perhaps more than a coincidence that the station concerned, was also owned by the media mogul. The man had not had any real facts but in the absence of other sources, his speculations and the story of how the journalist got to scoop were replayed endlessly by other media outlets desperate to fan the flames of the story. Two days later it was going head-to-head on the front pages with the collapse of Lehman Brothers.

The door opened and the Director General of MI5 walked in. `Don't get up Stanton' said the DG as Harry struggled to his feet. `We'll deal with you afterwards. First there something we all need to see. Charles please turn the TV onto BBC News'.

Harry sat back down wondering what it was that was delaying in the end of his career. He looked at the DG and his boss but their faces did not seem to be set in bollocking mode. Besides if they were going to give him the boot the interview would have been conducted in the DG's office. The TV news reporter broke into his thoughts.

'We are now taking you live to Surrey police headquarters, where the Chief Constable is about to make a statement concerning what has been described in the press as The Surrey Shootout.'

The picture changed to a crowded press briefing room inside Surrey police station. A policeman in full dress uniform sipped from a glass of water as he prepared to address the press. The Chief Constable was normally a confident performer on TV but this incident was headline news and having to deal with MI5 had added to his irritation although he was grateful to them for saving his men from further injury. He gave a nervous tug at the front of his jacket before launching in. He hoped it would play out as the spooks had assured him it would.

'Ladies and gentlemen. Thank you for your patience in the aftermath of what happened three days ago. We have had to conclude our investigations and I can now give you the events of last Thursday night and thereby end the wilder speculation that has appeared in the press over the last few days. On the evening of Thursday last, officers from Surrey CID armed response unit, acting on information received from the Assets Recovery Agency and with tactical support from the security services, intercepted a kidnap and ransom operation against a resident of the St Jude's Estate. The kidnap was perpetrated by dissident Irish Republican elements. The targets of the kidnap were a young man

Tito Miasnikov, nephew of the Russian billionaire Ludovic Luchenko a resident of St Jude's Estate. Also kidnapped, was his girlfriend Hannah Wheelan another resident and a member of Mr Luchenko's polo team. The couple were released unharmed the following day. Mr Luchenko agreed to pay a ransom for both children but during the handover something went wrong and gunfire broke out between the kidnappers and Mr Luchenko's security staff. It was the only the intervention of my officers that limited fatalities to the three kidnappers. There is a lesson here that private individuals no matter what their resources should not try to deal with desperate criminals. That is the job of the police. We remain concerned for the safety of Mr Luchenko who has not has not been seen since the incident and we urge him or anyone who knows of his whereabouts to contact us urgently. That is all I can tell you at the moment.'

A flurry of questions were answered unhelpfully by the Chief Constable and then a question from a reporter who had been Googling on his laptop changed the slant of the enquiries. Stuart Logan could not confirm or deny Ludovic Luchenko was involved in his Agency's investigation of the Wheelan's. As more journalists uncovered pictures of the Wheelan's they could see there was a better story here and questions turned to the welfare of young couple. The DG smiled. `That's it. They're on the right scent now. You can switch off Charles.' Harry looked at the two of them. `When you have lemons you make lemonade Stanton' said the Director. `Wheelan is a good-looking rogue with a beautiful wife and attractive daughter. The press just needed to discover the real story for themselves.'

`And what about Luchenko Sir?' said Harry.

`Well between them your two Irish chancers and a benefits agency investigator have come up trumps. Now we will take his empire apart, slowly and quietly although not so quiet that his contemporaries might fail to understand that we won't tolerate their illegal actions on these shores' said the DG.

`You mean send them a warning that while they can spend the proceeds of their crimes here, they can't undertake the actions that generate that income in the UK' said Stanton.

`Stop digging, Harry' said the DG. `While, you have been otherwise occupied over the past few days the world has been going through a banking crisis. Lehman's has folded and others might still go belly up. Lending will dry up and international trade will grind to a halt making the world more unstable. We can't purge all those dodgy Non Doms. The government is too indebted to them.'

`So we're not going to panic the herd and have the other oligarchs take flight with their money like Pendry feared.'

`No Stanton' said the DG. `But to use your metaphor were going to corral them and keep them playing by our rules. In fact your friend Logan will become a part of that effort.'

`How is that Sir?' said Harry.

`In a few days' time, the ARA will be wound up and he will be offered a job at the Home Office running a team to keep an eye on the financial dealings of our oligarchs friends. He will become the go to guy for intelligence on these people. When word gets around that the man who did for Luchenko is on the case, it will help the others to play nicely.'

`That will please Captain Ahab. He needs a whale to hunt' said Harry.

`Speaking of intelligence, I'd like to get that man Quinn in front of our boffins when he comes back from Ireland. The information he got from that helicopter spotting our own surveillance equipment was embarrassing 'said the AD.

`Good idea Charles. He'll be looking for new clients now that Luchenko has disappeared. Anymore on that situation Stanton?'

`No Sir.' said Harry in frustration. `The last person known to have seen him was Kristina Wheelan. I've questioned her several times in the last two days but she sticks to her story. You know I suspected she was having an affair with Luchenko but now I believe the relationship was something different. She was keen to gain his confidence even when her husband had his own misgivings about her dealing with the man. What her motives were, we will never know.'

`Remind me again what she said about her role in the events of that day' said the DG.

`She said that the kidnappers had contacted her instead of Luchenko directly to make sure he could not keep things quiet and to use her as an intermediary in the exchange' said Harry.

`But why did she go back to him when the gunfire started? She had the details of where her daughter was being held' said the AD.

She knew something had gone wrong, if Luchenko was killed she would have no way of starting another negotiation for the release of her daughter and Luchenko's nephew. Turns out she was right to go back because the address she was given turned out to be false' said Harry. `But both young people were released unharmed anyway. Very strange.'

`It looks like the kidnappers might have nothing to do with the people who were trying to collect the ransom' said the DG.

`Neither could we find a link between the Irish tearaways nor this Voxov, Luchenko's nemesis since they fell out with each other about the St Petersburg drugs business over a decade ago' said the AD.

`Mrs Wheelan still maintains she has no knowledge of Luchenko's whereabouts' said Harry. `Her story is that she got him out of the firefight and he made her drive to a house she had never seen before and from there he made some calls. Then she asked him to call the police but he pulled the phone from the wall. Heavily armed he drove her into the countryside and stopped at a small village where he let her call the police from a phone box. When the police dispatcher confirmed who she was she told Mrs Wheelan that her daughter and the boyfriend had been released unharmed. She told Luchenko this and he told her to look after them and that he must go and finish it now. He drove off leaving her by the side of the road.'

The DG pondered Harry's report for a few moments. He shared Harry's dissatisfaction with the story but like him could not come up with an alternative scenario. `It seems that Kristina Wheelan will remain a beautiful enigma. What about this gardener, the Wheelan's inside man who gave Kristina Wheelan the drugs?'

`I'm afraid he's a conundrum as well. Aidan Wheelan claims never to have met him and all his wife will say is that this Petor was some down on his luck Estonian she met while taking some old clothes to a charity shop. She offered to help find him a job. She told Luchenko he was her gardener when he insisted on knowing who looked after hers. She did not want to admit she did it herself as it would have resulted in a request from Luchenko. Aidan

Wheelan was happy to go along with his wife's' subterfuge as it kept her away from Luchenko's advances' said Harry.

`Now he's disappeared along with Luchenko?' said the AD.

`It may be a coincidence. The man may just be an illegal keeping his head down. Although when Kristina Wheelan last spoke him he said he had been promoted to driver after Gregor disappeared?' said Harry. `I would not bet against him and Luchenko turning up in St Petersburg soon.'

`And what about this Gregor then Stanton?' said the DG becoming frustrated at the number of loose ends in this affair.

`No news yet I'm afraid. He's been missing since the night the drugs were stolen from the horse trailer workshop. Luchenko suspected him of working for Voxov. I'm sure he will surface soon. Or at least his body will.'

The three men sat in silence as Harry waited to learn his fate. Like his superiors he found the whole state of affairs unsatisfactory. They were the ones who were usually making the smokescreen to cover reality and they had done as good a job as possible, but they all knew someone had beaten them to it and they might never know the truth of what happened that night.

The DG broke the silence. `These Russians they are never what they seem. Now what about this other man

Gilly? The one Simms had to dispatch. Are you sure it was the same man, the sniper from Armagh?'

Harry was happy to be able to end on a positive note. `Absolutely sir, he admitted it. Besides that was one face I was never going to forget.'

The DG looked Harry in the eye. `Good I don't like loose ends, it's not good for the regiment is it?' The DG was a veteran of the Falklands War who had seen action with the Parachute Regiment years before Harry had his Northern Ireland posting.

`Yes, the good of the regiment Sir' said Harry returning his smile. He knew he had escaped a bollocking... for to-day anyway.

In the Wheelan household the police statement was watched with a similar sense of incredulity. They had turned Lucky into some sort of noble hero who had van-ished mysteriously. Lies upon more lies. In the days since the release of Hannah and Tito the Wheelan's had not left their home. They were joined by Tito and his mother could not face the prospect of Lucky turning up in Chiswick. Eva Wheelan had become very clingy, not allowing her mother to go anywhere without her.

Suddenly in the aftermath of the news conference all their mobile phone started ringing. It had not taken the press long to track them down after having been pointed in their direction by the Chief Constable, keen not to field any more enquiries about Ludovic Luchenko.

`That will be the newspapers' what lies should we tell them Kristina?' Kristina looked at her husband. She had been evasive in the last couple of days about what had really happened. She wanted to see what was going to be said publicly before she volunteered anything. Now she couldn't avoid it any longer.

`Put all your phones on the table and switch them off' she said echoing Lucky from a few days earlier. `I'll tell you the truth, but it must not leave this room. She waited for the phones to be put on the coffee table. She was grateful that Eva had fallen asleep on the sofa. So just the expectant eyes of Aidan, Hannah, Tito and his mother waited for her answers.

`I first met Ludovic Luchenko when I was six years old' Kristina began. She told them of the night her uncle disappeared and the shock of discovering years later that Luchenko was the man they were investigating and he was also the uncle of her daughter's boyfriend. `All our lives, all of them were wrapped in the hands of that evil man' said Kristina, her voice breaking. Tito's mother started crying her tears triggered by knowing that someone else had suffered from what he did. `Tito your uncle was a bad man who dealt in drugs and misery and I feared you would be drawn into that life and I would lose my daughter to it as well. Then you came to me after the mugging and asked for my help. I could not tell you that it would all be over on Saturday when the police were supposed to catch him dealing drugs after the final polo match. But then you were both taken and I feared the worst' Kristina was shaking.

Aidan was desperate to comfort his wife but he had to know the rest of it. `And you knew nothing more about the kidnapping than you've already told us?' he asked.

`They contacted me because they did not want Lucky to keep a lid on it' said Kristina.

`Why didn't they turn up to collect their money at the polo ground?' said Aidan.

`But they did. They were the ones who sent the arrow. But then these stupid Irish guys started shooting and Lucky's men shot back and it all got out of hand' said Kristina.

`Oh god mum' said Hannah jumping up to hug her mother. `You didn't say anything about this.'

`It's over now Hannah. Besides it would not have been so dangerous if I had not had to warn Max so he could get the Irish guys to go there. They were going to hurt Siobhan and Annie. What did you want me to do Aidan?' said Kristina.

Aidan was torn between forcing more out of Kristina and being grateful that his friend's family were now out of danger because of what she had done. `Did you phone the police as well?'

`I spoke to Stuart Logan he day before the kidnap and he told me the security services with were planning to arrest Lucky quietly. They wanted to use him like they had used us' said Kristina.

`Bastards the lot of them' said Aidan.

`I got a text to Stuart Logan after we found out where they wanted the ransom delivered. I said that if he really want to help us he had to do it now. It was him who contacted the Surrey police' said Kristina. Now Aidan stood up to comfort his wife. `No Aidan. You have to know the whole truth' she said moving away from him. ` Petor was hiding in the boot of the Range Rover when I dropped off the ransom at the polo field. When we heard the gunfire, he insisted we went back to get Lucky, because if he was killed there would be no need for the kidnappers to keep Hannah and Tito alive. When we stopped at the house where Lucky made his calls Petor hid in the back of the car. We then drove off and Lucky stopped at a phone box to allow me to contact the police. We found out you were both safe and that's when Petor took his chance. He slipped one of those plastic tie things around Lucky's neck and secured him to the head rest. His face had turned blue by the time Petor had secured his hands and feet in the same way. I help Petor to put Lucky in the boot of the car after Petor cut his neck free. He was coughing and choking but he was still alive. Petor said to me. `Thank you from my father' and he drove away leaving me on the side of the road. I think Petor made Lucky pay for the death of his father thirty years ago.' Kristina slumped into a chair unburdened.

`Good and for the death of my father too' said Tito. `I wish I could've been there'.

Aidan and Hannah hugged Kristina, while Tito consoled his mother. Eva woke from her slumbers on the sofa and looked around.

`Why is everyone crying?' she said.

That evening there was an impromptu dinner party at the Wheelan's. Tito and Hannah announced they were getting engaged and both sets of parents were too weary to argue with them as they sat around the table.

`Help me put this on mum I want to wear it.' Hannah handed Kristina the necklace she had been wearing the night they had been kidnapped. Kristina leaned over and fastened it around her daughter's neck. Hannah leaned back to her mother's ear and whispered `You are the only one who now knows how to open that clasp. Even with gloves on.'

The End.

Authors note

As ever most novels are a mixture of fact and fiction. Readers may be interested in where my story departs from reality.

The story is inspired by the experiences of a good friend who fell afoul of the ARA. There were no Russians involved in his case. When it was finally over after six years he said it could have been any worse. I said off course it could. I wrote the book to prove it and he agreed.

The **Assets Recovery Agency** (ARA) was a non-ministerial government department in the United Kingdom. It was established under the Proceeds of Crime Act 2002(POCA) to reduce crime by confiscating the proceeds of any crime. It was granted a new power of civil recovery through the High Court, and could also take over the powers of the HM Revenue and Customs (HMRC) to levy tax without identifying a source for taxed income.

The ARA became operational in February 2003, but it failed to meet its targets for the confiscation of criminal funds. It was announced in January 2007 that it would be merged with the **Serious Organised Crime Agency** (SOCA), which was established in 2006. Provisions to achieve this were contained in the Serious Crime Act 2007. There were also proposals for other law enforcement agencies, such as HMRC, to be given similar powers of civil recovery at the same time. On 1 March 2008, the transfer of the Director and staff of the Assets Recovery Agency, its property, rights and liabilities to SOCA and the National Policing Improvement Agency started in anticipation of the Agency's abolition. The agency ceased to exist on 1 April 2008.

The **St Jude's Estate** is a location on the outskirts of London although its real name is different. It has been popular for generations with those who have achieved success in business, sport and entertainment. An Act of Parliament controls building on the estate limiting the number of dwellings per plot but not their size, so many hotel sized properties have sprung up recent years. St Jude's does not have a polo field but other sports are catered for.

London billionaires accounted for almost ten per cent of the world's total in 2014 according to The Daily Telegraph London has been a popular second home and sometimes first home for wealth Russian's ever since the fall of the Berlin Wall.

Quadcopters have been flying since the 1920's although piloted versions did not appear until the 1950's and the remote controlled drones or Unmanned Aerial Vehicles (UAV's) are really a product of advances in a number of technologies in the last ten years which allowed the creation of small, light, easy to fly vehicles able to record digital video and follow GPS routes. Commercial models were just starting to appear at the time this book was set.

Irish people still live in Kilburn.

About Sam Flint

Sam Flint is a pen name I use for my crime thrillers. I also use the name SM Flint for my adult romances. I have a funny real name which no one gets right so I thought this would be easier to publish books under this one. I've had earlier careers in IT in the public and private sectors as well as working in public relations, marketing and as an economist.

I enjoy motorcycling and walking the dog, both of which were unlikely at one point. I read a lot and of course like to write. You can see more at samflint.uk where you can also sign up for my newsletter to get details of reader special offers. My blog also talks about my writing journey. (www.samflint.uk)

Acknowledgments

When I started writing I had the hubris to believe it was a solitary occupation reliant just on the author's skill. I came to this pious state of mind having become jaded from selling things I'd lost interest in to people I did not care about.

It was not long before I discovered the errors of my ways and I am very grateful for the help and support I have had in getting *Nothing but the Truth* completed. Special thanks go to John and Ken and Yvonne for advice on various drafts and to Tony for cover design. I must also thank all the other self-published authors whose websites and blogs have been a source of advice and inspiration.

Off course any faults and errors remain mine alone.

My new book Lives Taken

If you enjoyed *Nothing but the Truth* you may be interested to read an extract from my second crime thriller *Lives Taken* which will be published shortly.

Lives Taken is a race between rescue and revenge. Time is against Ben Prime as he attempts to prevent his abducted children from becoming the next victims of a suspected paedophile who also happens to be their grandfather. During his mission Ben finds himself at the centre of an international cigarette smuggling network run by an alliance of criminals and corrupt police.

As Ben's six year old son is a witness who can link his uncle, a serving policeman to the murder of a key player in the network; Ben knows that his legal battle to recover his kids is only buying time. He embarks on a frantic search for evidence that will guarantee his family's safety.

Without this even if he wins in court the network will kill them all to keep their secrets safe.

When Ben discovers his best friend Carsten was the cause of events that led to his children's abduction both men become locked in a race to find Ben's father-in-law. Can Ben Prime evade the efforts of corrupt police long enough to discover the whereabouts of his children from the man Carsten has vowed to kill? Can Carsten control his lust to avenge the tragic death of his wife's brother long enough to help Ben?

In *Lives Taken* the first victim is innocence.

Extract from Lives Taken

Ben Prime felt his headache was eternal punishment for a misspent life. Pneumatic drills thudded in a black void. `Welcome to hell' Ben thought with that part of his head not already given over to experiencing pain. Eventually he drifted towards the light and back to corporeal form which was at odds with popular accounts of near death experiences. His dry mouth and aching back fought with the drilling in his head to confirm Ben was still in the land of the living. A monster hangover not eternal damnation would be the price for his excesses the night before. He would be fragile today but he would recover and in time would only remember the good things about his fortieth birthday party.

The bright Spanish sunshine on his eyelids was still too much to brave so he groped for the bottle of mineral water he kept by the side of the bed to combat the dehydration of the warm Mediterranean night. The bottle was not there but something unexpected was. It took a few moments for his hands to confirm it was the bedside table from the spare room. Memories of the night before started to return. Images of him climbing the stairs with Louise's assistance and his wife throwing him on the bed in the spare room. He thought he was being banished for his drunkenness and their argument earlier in the day but when she pulled his trousers down `I want to give you your present without waking the kids' , Ben was surprised, both by her enthusiasm and his ability to still perform given the state he was in. In truth his wife had done all the work, riding him to the finish after which sleep claimed him quickly. He would have to remember to thank her for the understanding and the sex, both of which had been in short supply recently. There had been too many false starts for Ben to hope that this might signal a new beginning with Louise, but if this was detente then he would be cordial. Perhaps his headache would be the only price for last night's enjoyment.

Ben tried to open his eyes but the merest hint of light on his retinas again set of pounding in his head like it was going to explode. Instead he stood up shakily, eyes closed and felt his way back to his bedroom. He had the fleeting image of a zombie in a B-movie he had worked on and wondered if his state would count as method acting. In the bedroom the heat and the brightness of the sun reflecting off the white walls told Ben it was later than he thought. He remembered the reason for his mission and retrieved the bottle of water and glugged several mouthfuls. An urge to get going propelled him into the wet room where the cool of the marble on the floor and walls seemed to calm his head. He turned the thermostat lever to cold and took a few deep breaths in preparation for an icy blast. The shock of hot rain falling from the oversized shower head forced Ben's eyes open and he reached for the lever to prevent himself from being scalded. It was still on cold. He realised what had happened at the same time as the standing water finally cleared the pipes and a fresh cold blast took him unawares. After two minutes under the jets Ben was awake and feeling metaphorically cleansed even thought it would take his body the rest of the day to purge the alcohol from his system. Why had he mixed his drinks last night? He had been fine sipping beer all day and had moved onto whiskey and soda with plenty of ice as the evening drew in. He was drunk but not enough to warrant the way he was feeling now. It has all got worse after he finished the glass of white wine Louise had given him for a birthday toast. Perhaps his resistance was disappearing with age.

Ben surveyed the damage in the bathroom mirror before pronouncing `You look like shit man'. Today he felt every one on his forty years. He examined his face in a way he had studiously avoided for many years. The drink had an odd effect on it. The skin around his eyes was drawn tight and he did not want to count the number of laughter lines. He squinted into the mirror `face like a wanking Jap' he heard in his head, recalling his father's pronouncement that his mother should stop squinting and get a pair of glasses if she wanted to watch the telly. Ben plucked the loose skin on his cheeks and noticed it did not spring back. That's it, no more drink he vowed. The prospect of being greeted by his dad with a cheery `Hello bollock chops' was more of a deterrent than the do gooder advice of his doctor. When Ben chanced a smile in the mirror the lop sided grin which had given him inexplicable success with woman refused to oblige. Instead it gave him a faintly constipated look. He decided to quit while he was behind and get dressed. He found a tee shirt and pair of beach shorts in a drawer and put them on. It was time to re-join the land of the living.

Now the pain in his head had receded Ben became more aware of the quietness. It was after 10 am and Louise could not have kept the kids quiet if they were in the house. Was it another concession from Louise, a temporary ceasefire in the latest round of hostilities? He would make sure he acknowledged her generosity. A nice lunch at that place up the coast he discovered when he first came to Spain. Louise liked it there. He hoped she would not see his thanks as an opening to talk about private schools again. When was it that their marriage turned into a series of negotiations?

Ben opened the shutters and went out onto the balcony but the glare of the sun on the sand made him retreat and grab his sunglasses from the bedside table. He returned to the window and scoured the beach. There were a few people out but no sign of Louise and the kids. Two boys pushing bikes came down the access road at the side of his house and he recognized Michael's friends. “No Senor Prime we have not seen Mikey” was their reply. Louise could have taken the kids shopping but it was unlikely. Like Ben she was a fan of a lazy Sunday. It was one of the things they still had in common. An uneasy feeling crept through Ben. He could not suppress his anxiety as he moved through the house calling all their names. Michael's room was empty. The footballers of Manchester United and Barcelona smiled vacantly from the walls. Clothes hung out of a chest of drawers and on the floor like the room had been ransacked. Ben stepped on a jumper with something hard underneath, it was Michael's beloved Nintendo. He would not go anywhere without it...if he had a choice, came the worrying echo in Ben's mind. Tracy's room was similarly dishevelled. The neat row of Chapsticks which she used to pretend applying lipstick in front of a mirror were knocked over. Ben checked Louise’s closet. Her getaway bag was missing and so too was her big case. It hit him all at once like a wave of nausea. Louise had left in the middle of the night and had taken the kids with her. This was not a spur of the moment petulant exit like others in the past; this one had been planned. She had deliberately seduced him in the spare room so she could move around their bedroom afterwards without fear of him waking.

Ben gripped at the tightness in his chest. It had been nearly three years since she had last gone off with the kids to stay with one of her friends. The kids themselves had put an end to their participation in these trips and Louise had seen the sense in that. Since then she went by herself but her departure was always preceded by a tantrum of some sort; that was her point. It could take two days of shouting and slamming doors before she finally blew and departed. Ben had got used to her shouting, but what really scared him and the kids was her violence. He would not have believed a woman could hit herself so hard if he had not seen it with his own eyes. Afterwards she tried to hide her bruised arms and legs with make-up but Ben noticed the accusing looks from strangers as they glanced from her to him. Her temper got worse, first attacking him and then accidentally hurting the kids as she lashed out in a blind rage. Many times Ben had tried to talk her into seeking professional help but her sense of shame would not let her. Now they all lived in dread of one of her episodes; their safety valve was to let her go before she exploded then wait for her to return in a calmer state.

Their marriage was hanging by a thread but as much as Louise might hate him now, she would never take their kids back to England to her family. She would never put them at risk of the abuse she had suffered. Would she? Ben phoned a few of her friends on the pretext of Louise having said she was going to visit them. They could hear the concern in his voice and agreed to let him know if Louise got in touch. He knew they would all be on the phone to each other to swap this latest piece of gossip but it did not matter to him as long as they tracked her down. Ben breathed a sigh of relief when he found the kids passports were still in his secret hiding place. Louise would get in contact when she thought he had suffered enough or when the kids had nagged her once too often about wanting to speak to dad. He hoped she would come to her senses without anyone getting hurt.

As the tension ebbed out of him Ben's stomach heaved. He just made it to the kitchen sink where he threw up violently. The realisation came as a shock. This was not just a hangover he'd been poisoned; drugged to sleep through events he was not supposed to see. It struck him that Louise's departure had been very carefully planned, although hastily executed judging by the randomness of the things she had taken. She had gone too far this time. `I'll report her to the police maybe that will bring her to her senses.' Ben put his head under the kitchen tap to clear it. It was a few moments before he realised there was a knock at the door. The knocking grew more insistent.

An angry command was issued, first in Spanish and then English. "This is the Guardia Seville; open the door Senor Prime or we will break it down."

`Oh my god, something awful has happened to Louise and the kids and the police think I'm to blame' Ben panicked. He opened the door just as the officer was giving instructions to his assault team.

There were two cars and four officers on his doorstep. The scene drew stares from their neighbours in the close. Many of them had suddenly developed the need to tend their front gardens. "Have you found my wife and children, are they okay?" Ben blurted out before the officer could speak.

The policeman looked puzzled. "Your family has gone?"

"Yes, isn't that why you're here?" said Ben.

"No Senor, we will deal with that afterward. We are here to search for drugs."

Ben was stunned. "I have no drugs. This is a mistake officer." Then he remembered. "Listen, I can explain. It was my birthday yesterday, we had a party. Most of the neighbours came but it did go on until quite late. Someone was annoyed by the noise and is making their point by getting you out here today. Okay, someone might have smoked a joint last night but it was no more than that."

The officer asked Ben to sit on the sofa. The policeman put on white rubber gloves and a handler with a sniffer dog entered the room. "Officer let me speak to Colonel Sanchez, he knows me. He knows I would not get involved with drugs." Ben had come across Colonel Sanchez two years before when he was involved in a dispute with a Spanish company who had not paid him for some filming work he had done. It looked as if the police were going to side with the local against the foreigner in the dispute and Ben went to see the officer to find out what could be done. He noticed all the football trophies and pictures in the display cupboard and discovered that sadly Colonel Sanchez had no videos of his team's performance. Three weeks later Ben presented the Colonel with edited footage of their semi-final and cup final exploits which heavily featured the Colonel's heroics in goal. Ben's problem with the Spanish company was resolved soon after and Ben suffered no more hassles from other companies. Sanchez knew him, he would sort this out.

"Colonel Sanchez has been promoted and has moved to Bilbao. We have a new commander" said the officer taking glee in letting Ben know he had no friends left at court.

Ben watched as they searched his house. The dog and handler were doing random sweeps but the other officers seemed to be looking in specific places. It dawned on him that they had been tipped off where to search. This raid had been planned in advance and was designed to keep Ben here. Just like whatever had been put in his drink the night before was meant to keep him out of the picture until Louise had gone. This could not be just her doing something else was going on here. Eventually the handler and dog came back both shaking their heads. The other officers also appeared. The tall one said he had found nothing but the fat one slipped up and gave the game away. Ben pounced and turned to the officer in charge. “He said it's not here but the others said they found nothing. You've been told where to look.” The officer was surprised at the quality of Ben's Spanish; much better than the typical Brit's, who had moved to the Costa. “You were told where to look for drugs by someone who wants me out of the way. Officer my wife and young children have been abducted and if you don't take this seriously you will find yourself in a world of trouble you're not paid to take.”

The policeman looked at Ben and sized up the situation. He had done what he had been asked. Someone obviously wanted to make trouble for this foreigner and if that involved kidnap then the man was right, it was above his pay grade. He made his decision. “Okay Senor Prime, tell me what happened to your family.”

Order your copy to read the rest of Ben Prime's story

Your bit

Join the mailing list for exclusive free content and offers on forthcoming titles.
http://samflint.uk

Think you can do better?
Have you ever watched the exciting opening sequence of a film only to be disappointed by what followed? Here is your chance to prevent that happening with my new novella *The Box*. The exciting opening chapter involves a car chase and things blowing up, but what should happen next and what's in the box? That's all up to you. The story will develop based on reader feedback. When you join my mailing list you will receive the first chapter of *The Box* I look forward to receiving your suggestions on what should happen next.

Best wishes

Sam.

50889760R00202

Made in the USA
Charleston, SC
10 January 2016